STIGER

STIGER

Tales of the Seventh: Part One

MARC ALAN EDELHEIT

Tales of the Seventh, Part One: Stiger

First Edition

I wish to thank my agents, Andrea Hurst and Sean Fletcher, for their invaluable support and assistance. I would also like to thank my beta readers who suffered through several early drafts. My betas: Barrett McKinney, Jon Cockes, Norman Stiteler, Nicolas Weiss, Stephan Kobert, Matthew Ashley, Melinda Vallem, Jon Quast, Donavan Laskey, Paul Klebaur, Russ Wert, James Doak, David Cheever, Bruce Haeven, Erin Penny, Jonas Ortega Rodriguez, April Faas, Rodney Gigone, and Brett Smith. I would also like to take a moment to thank my loving wife who sacrificed many an evening to allow me to work on my writing.

Editing Assistance by: Hannah Streetman, Audrey Mackaman

Cover Art by Piero Mng (Gianpiero Mangialardi)

Cover Formatting by Telemachus Press

Stiger, Tales of the Seventh is a prequel novel. Make sure you pick up the series that started it all!

Excerpt from Thelius's Histories, The Mal'Zeelan Empire, Volume 3, Book 2.

The Mal'Zeelan Imperial Legion

Pre-Emperor Midisian Reformation

The imperial legion was a formation that numbered, when at full strength, five thousand five hundred to six thousand men. The legion was composed of heavy infantry recruited exclusively from the citizens of the empire. Slaves and non-citizens were prohibited from serving. The legion was divided into ten cohorts of 480 men, with First Cohort an over-strength unit numbering around a thousand. A legion usually included a mix of engineers, surgeons, and various support staff. Legions were always accompanied by allied auxiliary formations, ranging from cavalry to various forms of light infantry. The Imperial Legion was commanded by a legate (general).

The basic unit of the legion was the century, numbering eighty men in strength. There were six centuries in a cohort. A centurion (basic officer) commanded the century. The centurion was supported by an optio (equivalent of a corporal) who handled minor administrative duties. Both had to be capable of reading and performing basic math.

Note: Very rarely were legions ever maintained at full strength. This was due primarily to the following reasons:

retirement, death, disability, budget shortages (graft), and the slow stream of replacements.

The most famous legion was the Thirteenth, commanded by Legate ...

Post-Emperor Midisian Reformation

Emperor Midiuses's reforms were focused on streamlining the legions and cutting cost through the elimination of at least half of the officer corps per legion, amongst other changes.

The basic unit of the legion became the company, numbering around two hundred men in strength. There were ten twenty-man files per company. A captain commanded the company. The captain was supported by a lieutenant, two sergeants, and a corporal per file.

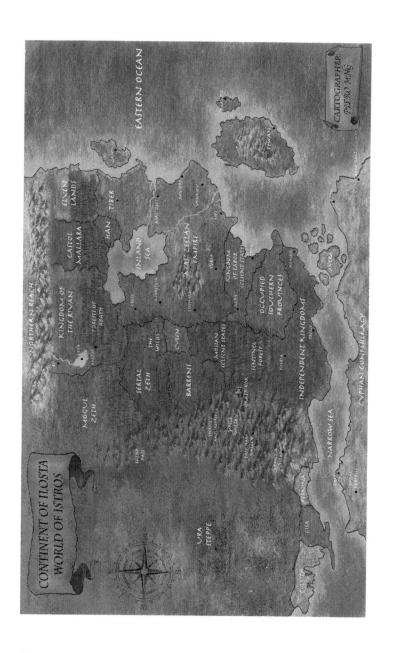

CONTINENT OF ILOSTA
WORLD OF ISTROS

CARTOGRAPHER:
PIERO MING

EASTERN OCEAN

NORTHERN REACH

ELVEN LANDS

CAPITOL MALLARA

HAN TIBER

KINGDOM OF THE RIVAN

FOREST OF ABATH

INLAND SEA

MOGUL ZEETH

SERIAL ZEETH

THE WILDS

CYREN

SAMI-ZEELAN EMPIRE

BARRENS

RADIAN (CLUSTERED)

KINGDOM OF LABOR (CLUSTERED)

SENTINEL FOREST

OCCUPIED SOUTHERN PROVINCES

URA STEPPE

INDEPENDENT KINGDOMS

NARROW SEA

CYPHAN CONFEDERACY

To my fans who have made the Chronicles of an Imperial Legionary Officer series so successful!

This one is for you.

ONE

"Ah, yes ... the young Lieutenant Stiger. How can I help you?"

"Captain Bruta." Stiger offered a salute.

Bruta ignored the salute, turning back to his drink and companion. Corporal Varus, who had been following Stiger, stopped a few steps behind him. Stiger sensed the corporal was bored and longed to be somewhere else—really anywhere else—than with him, a junior lieutenant. Seven levels, Stiger thought, I want to be anywhere but here at this supply depot.

Bruta looked up from the roughly cut wooden table he sat at with another officer and simply gazed at Stiger, an irritated expression on his pox-marked face. Both officers before Stiger were wearing their service tunics, which did not carry rank insignias or the trappings of office. The two had been sharing a drink. The other officer scowled at Stiger's presence before taking another pull from his cup.

A merchant had set up shop inside the rapidly growing supply depot, which sprawled around them. The merchant had clearly just arrived. He had yet to pitch his canopy to provide some shade from the early summer sun, but had managed to set out several rough tables and a few rickety-looking stools, at which several patrons were enjoying cheap, watered-down wine or ale.

Two slaves were busy digging holes for what Stiger presumed would be the canopy's support posts. The rolled-up canopy lay next to the merchant's heavy wagon loaded with wooden casks, amphorae, and crates. A third slave was slowly unloading the wagon.

Behind Bruta and his drinking companion, Stiger could see several auxiliaries on sentry duty slowly walking the walls, on the lookout for any approaching trouble—particularly the Rivan, with whom the empire was currently at war. Inside the depot, several crude wooden buildings, including a headquarters and barracks, had been raised with a number of other structures in partial states of construction. The growing, fortified compound gave the impression the empire expected to be here for a long time to come.

Bruta said nothing for several uncomfortable and embarrassing seconds.

"I have been waiting much of the day," Stiger said. "I need..."

"Bruta, tell this pup to go on his way," the other officer said in a bored tone. He then looked up directly at Stiger. "Let us men drink in peace, boy."

Stiger bristled at this, but held his tongue. Not only were both officers senior to him, they were also much older. He had no idea who Bruta's companion was, but the man's age and manner alone told Stiger he was at least a captain. Stiger assumed that he was the prefect commanding the auxiliary cohort that had been stationed at this depot. There was no other reason for a senior officer other than Bruta to be here.

Stiger was still relatively new to serving with the Eagles, and he was unsure of himself. He had only recently arrived to take up his first military appointment as an infantry lieutenant serving in the Third Legion, Seventh Company. Stiger had discovered, to his disappointment, the legion's officer corps had been anything but welcoming. In fact, his fellow officers had been outright discourteous to the point of rudeness.

"Lieutenant," Bruta said, looking up with a scowl, "can't you see I am having a peaceful drink here with my friend, the prefect?"

"Yes, sir," Stiger conceded. "I can."

"Then why are you still bothering me?"

"I have orders from Captain Cethegus," Stiger said stiffly, "my commanding officer."

"Cethegus." Bruta barked out a laugh. "That fool deserves you Stiger, you know that, don't you? An incompetent fool saddled with a traitor's son. Somehow, I find that fitting."

"Sir," Stiger said, struggling to contain his mounting anger. The accusation, however true, burned. Stiger glanced over at Varus, ashamed the corporal had heard the outright insult. Varus glanced quickly away. Perhaps Stiger should have left him with the rest of the escort like he had with Corporal Durus. He looked back to Bruta. "All I want is for my wagons to be loaded with the requisitioned supplies and then to be on my way."

Bruta took a pull from his drink. He sucked in a deep breath that turned into a heavy sigh. For a moment the supply officer said nothing and then turned his gaze slowly back up to Stiger.

"You and every other company from the Third wants something from me," Bruta said heavily. A fly buzzed around his drink. The captain shooed it away with a hand.

"My supply train is the only one present," Stiger said, becoming exasperated. He gestured with a helpless feeling over to the neatly organized stacks and piles of supplies just a few yards off. A number of slaves lounged about, doing no work under the hot midday sun. "Your slaves are doing nothing."

"Even slaves occasionally need rest," Bruta said with a barely concealed chuckle and smirk directed at the prefect.

"They are slaves," Stiger said, the helpless feeling growing more acute. He knew damn well the supply officer was toying with him, intentionally dragging his feet. It had been the same act each time Stiger had come to fetch supplies for his company.

"That is an exceptionally keen observation," Bruta's companion said sarcastically.

"I am expected back this evening," Stiger said, trying another approach. "If we do not get the wagons loaded soon, I will be unable to follow my orders."

"That's your problem." Bruta laughed openly, sparing Stiger a broad smile with a number of broken teeth. The man's nose had been shattered many times and was mashed off to the side slightly. Combined with the pox scars, Captain Bruta was one devastatingly ugly man. "My slaves need the rest."

"Then we shall load the wagon ourselves," Stiger said. "That way your slaves can get the rest they so well deserve."

"You will do nothing of the kind," Bruta barked. "I won't have your thieving men go near my supplies. No telling what they would take. No, lieutenant, your men touch nothing."

Stiger was silent a moment as he considered the situation. Being treated abominably due to his name was something to which he had become accustomed in recent years. Stiger had no friends or patrons in Third Legion. As such, he worked himself harder than anyone else, determined to let his actions speak for him. In essence, Stiger was struggling forward to make a name for himself, apart from the disgrace his father had inflicted upon the family.

Until this moment, Stiger had bit his tongue and taken whatever abuse had been thrown his way. Disgraced or not, his family was still powerful. Somehow they had managed to hold on to their senatorial seat, one of only a hundred. The man before him, an officer from a relatively minor house, was intentionally disrespecting him. It was an affront not only to his, but also his family's, honor. What little there was left.

Stiger knew he would be justified in challenging Bruta to a duel. However, he also understood such a challenge was impossible. General Secra, commander of the Third Legion, had prohibited all such contests of honor. It had been made clear that any officer issuing a challenge or participating in a duel would be harshly punished. Unfortunately, General Secra had recently sickened and died. Yet, even in death, the order stood, and Stiger was bound to obey.

The legion was waiting on its new temporary commander, General Treim, who was due to arrive any day. The emperor would eventually get around to selecting a permanent commander for the Third, who would in turn be approved by the senate. That would take months. With luck, General Treim would put such useless officers as Captain Bruta in their place. Until then, Stiger was completely helpless and at the mercy of this lazy, incompetent officer.

Prior to Stiger's arrival to take up his appointed posting, the Third had driven a small Rivan army from the frontier back into enemy territory. It had fought several pitched battles along the way. With the death of its general, the Third had been ordered to wait for a replacement. That had been two months ago. Accordingly, the legion had stopped its pursuit and now stood idle. Supply depots like this one had been erected all the way back to the frontier, with the intention of keeping the legion and a number of newly made garrisons supplied.

"Well then." Stiger let out an explosive breath and shifted his stance slightly. "When do you expect your slaves to be sufficiently rested and able to return to work?"

"That's hard to say." Bruta furrowed his brow in an exaggerated appearance of consideration. Bruta's drinking companion chuckled. "Perhaps in a day or two."

Stiger was silent as he thought things through. He was tired of feeling helpless. There was simply nothing he could do to influence the situation to his advantage ... or was there? Stiger's eyes narrowed slightly. Bruta was a bully, inflicting petty cruelty on someone he thought was in an inferior position. Though the supply captain was higher in rank, Stiger could easily turn the tables on him. Bruta could be put in an inferior position. Stiger almost smiled but resisted the temptation. He would play Bruta's game, but change the terms.

"I guess there is nothing more I can reasonably do," Stiger said with a quick glance over at Varus, who was studying the ground at his feet and still looking very much like he desired to be anywhere but here. "You have tied my hands."

"I have, haven't I?" Bruta laughed openly as he took another gulp from his drink. It was a harsh barking laugh that Stiger found doglike, and it grated on his nerves, as did just about everything to do with this man. Bruta was a mockery of what a legionary officer should be.

At that moment, the merchant came around the corner of his wagon and suddenly provided Stiger a welcome interruption. Stiger beckoned for the man to come nearer.

It was hot. Stiger glanced up at the sun and wiped sweat from his brow with the side of his hand as the merchant made his way over.

"How may I help you, sir?" The merchant smiled. Filled with yellowed and rotten teeth, it was not a pleasant smile.

The merchant had been working, and he quickly wiped a hand on his greasy apron. Stiger looked disdainfully on the man, wondering if he had ever heard of such a thing as a bath, or for that matter having his tunic and apron laundered. He stunk of stale wine, ale, and sweat—all made worse by the heat of the day.

"What is your finest bottled wine?"

Stiger feared the response. They were in barbarian territory, hundreds of miles from civilization. There was likely nothing good to be had, and he suspected he would be forced to settle for some inferior vintage that was overly acidic. The thought of it almost made him cringe.

"I have several cases of red from Venney," the merchant said after considering the young officer before him. The merchant had made a quick study of the quality of Stiger's armor and had likely judged him to be of some means, which was why he had suggested such an expensive vintage. "Just came in on a caravan from Cress a few days ago."

"Venney?" Stiger asked him, surprised.

"Indeed, sir."

"How much?" Stiger was pleased that such high quality wine could be had, but also concerned with what he would have to pay.

"For you, young sir..." The merchant thought for a moment. "A half silver talon."

"That's robbery," Stiger scoffed. "I shall pay no more than a quarter."

"I could not accept less than a half," the man countered. "Alas, we are far from civilization, and such a fine vintage is difficult to come by."

"What is your name?" Stiger scratched at an itch on his arm.

"Trex, noble sir." The wine merchant bowed in a show of respect.

"Do you know Arrus the wine merchant?" Stiger asked him with a raised eyebrow. He had a feeling the man knew his competition. It was time to test it.

"I do," Trex said, the smile slipping from his face. It returned a moment later, a little forced. "He is most untrustworthy in his dealings."

"I have no doubt he is as dishonest as you say," Stiger said, and the wine merchant's smile became more genuine at that. "Yet, Arrus has set up shop with the Third's camp followers."

"He did?" Trex looked unhappy at such news.

"A few days ago, he sold me a similar vintage that was quite fine for a quarter talon." Stiger did not mention that the wine he had bought was not from Venney, but a half talon was highway robbery, even this far beyond the frontier. A quarter was high too, but it was to be expected, and Stiger considered it a reasonable price to pay.

The smile disappeared at that. "He did?"

Stiger nodded. "I would much rather do business with someone like you. Arrus is disagreeable, but his prices are better. I am sure you can see the position I am in."

The merchant looked agonized as he considered the possibility of losing business to a competitor and weighed that against potentially getting a better price from another noble of sufficient means at a later date.

"Very well," the merchant conceded and bowed his head. "A quarter then."

Stiger took out his purse and removed a quarter talon from it. He handed it over. "Have the case delivered to my detachment immediately." He paused and gestured with a hand. "We are on the other side of the depot over that way."

"I will, sir. Thank you for your patronage." Trex bowed and turned. He then stopped and looked back. "I hope you will seek me out for future purchases. May I have your name noble, sir?"

"Stiger."

The merchant froze. His eyes widened. Then he rapidly recovered. Trex bowed very respectfully, then bustled around to the other side of his wagon to see to the order. Stiger watched him disappear.

"You should have been a merchant, Stiger," Bruta grunted in amusement.

"Corporal Varus," Stiger snapped, ignoring Bruta and turning to the corporal.

"Sir?" Varus said, clearly surprised that he was being addressed.

"Have the men fall in and the mules hitched up," Stiger ordered. "We will leave as soon as my wine is delivered."

"Yes, sir," Varus saluted. He glanced briefly over at the supply captain and then back to Stiger before he turned to go.

"Leaving us?" Bruta asked, a surprised and mocking expression on his face. "So soon?"

"Yes, sir." Stiger turned back to the supply officer.

"Without your supplies?"

"I will report that I was unable to obtain the supplies the Seventh and the Tenth companies require to continue operations."

Bruta paused mid-drink and turned slowly to look over at the lieutenant. The man's eyes narrowed dangerously.

Stiger continued in a bored tone. "Captain Cethegus might not say anything, sir, but I am quite confident that Captain Lepidus will file a complaint." Stiger shrugged as if it were no concern of his.

Stiger knew the captain of the Tenth would be furious. Unlike Stiger's own captain, Lepidus was a stern, no-nonsense officer. He would either make the trip himself to see Bruta or would indeed put in a complaint. If that happened, command would likely wish to know why the supply captain had denied the properly requisitioned supplies. Stiger did not think it would get that far. He was betting Bruta would not allow it.

"Well then, I believe our business here is concluded. Good day, sir." Stiger snapped a smart salute and turned to Varus.

The corporal had stopped to watch the exchange and was looking on his lieutenant with a funny, almost amused expression.

"Wait," Bruta barked harshly, standing and pushing his stool back with a leg. It toppled over in the dry dirt. "You don't threaten me, you little shit, even if you are a Stiger."

Stiger turned back to Bruta with an innocent look. "I am truly sorry that you think that, sir. I assure you that was not my intention. I make no threats."

Bruta took a step toward him, hands flexing in anger. The man was not wearing his armor. He had on only his service tunic, and unlike many of the legion's frontline officers, he was overweight and going soft. This was likely the result of eating well, a perk of being in the supply branch.

Safe behind the walls of the depot, Bruta was also unarmed. Stiger, on the other hand, wore his segmented armor. He was armed with his short sword and dagger. Despite that, the supply officer towered over him, and Stiger questioned himself for a moment. Then he ground his teeth. The man was a petty bully, and Stiger had tired of his game. He was determined to see this through.

He stepped closer to Bruta, into the man's personal space. Jaw clenched, he was unafraid.

Stiger's father had paid some of the best tutors the empire had to teach his son how to fight. Though fresh to his posting and still unsure of himself, Stiger was in perfect shape. He was confident in his ability to defend himself, both armed and unarmed, especially against a soft supply-type like Bruta. His hand came to rest casually on the pommel of his sword.

"I am a Stiger, and I will report as I have said I would." Stiger allowed some of the anger he was feeling to seep into his tone. "I assure you, sir. I make no threats."

"You little shit," Bruta breathed. Stiger did not back down. He was unsure whether it would shortly come to blows, but he had taken enough grief from men like Bruta. However, beating a senior officer insensible would not advance his career. Stiger was beginning to regret his decision somewhat. Though he had to admit to himself that it felt good to goad this disagreeable man to anger.

Bruta glanced quickly over toward the officer he had been drinking with. The prefect, who outranked both of them, simply looked on but said nothing. Though likely from an influential family, the man's tunic was cut from inferior quality. He was probably of the equestrian class and had more sense than Bruta.

"Very well..." Bruta exhaled when it became clear the other officer would not back him up. He seemed to deflate. Stiger smelled the onion mixed with cheap wine on the man's breath.

The supply officer turned away and shouted for the overseer of the slaves, who had been sleeping nearby in the shade from a pile of stacked crates.

Bruta quivered with anger. "You will have your supplies, you bastard."

"Thank you, sir." Stiger saluted and restrained himself from smiling. He had won. It had been a minor victory, but it felt good nonetheless. He found Varus eying him with a trace of a grin. The corporal wisely said nothing as they made their way back to their wagons. Stiger noticed that the prefect's eyes followed him as he walked off.

"Make sure my wine arrives before we leave," Stiger said to the corporal.

"Yes, sir," Varus replied neutrally.

Two hours past noon, Stiger had his twelve heavy wagons fully loaded. The teamsters, all hired civilian contractors, looked on with bored expressions as Stiger's two files of legionaries formed up. One file, Corporal Varus's, would march to the front of the supply column and the other, Corporal Durus's, to the rear, with a few men floating about the middle.

Sitting astride his horse, Stiger swatted at a fly as he waited impatiently for Corporal Varus, the senior corporal, to get the men organized. It seemed as if things were taking longer than it should. Seven levels, Stiger thought with frustration, everything the army did took longer than it should. The men were moving slowly, and it infuriated him. Stiger stifled the urge to yell at Varus and instead forced himself to project the calm countenance of an officer in control.

In the sweltering heat of the afternoon, Stiger found even that difficult. He was hot, uncomfortable, and cooking in his armor. There was no breeze, only waves of heat that rolled down from above. The sooner they got moving, the sooner he would have some relief.

"All ready, sir," Varus reported finally.

"FOORWAAARD," Stiger hollered without a second's hesitation. "MAAAARCH."

Shields in their canvas coverings, short spears resting on shoulders, and helmets hanging from ties about their necks, the legionaries to the front of the column started moving, armor chinking and jangling. A few moments later, the lead wagon, with a snap of the teamster's whip and a braying of the mules, followed by an ungodly rattle, trundled forward.

"Join your file," Stiger said to Varus, who dutifully saluted and left at a jog. Stiger watched the corporal go and felt relief. He had difficulty tolerating the man's presence. Varus was big, even for a legionary. The corporal was brutish and uncouth. Though he could write and manipulate numbers, a requirement of his rank, he was fairly uneducated. Stiger found Varus dull and boorish company, certainly not fit for a proper conversation. Like the rest of the men, the mere presence of the corporal irritated Stiger immensely.

"Hup, my beauties," the teamster in the second wagon called loudly to his drowsing mules. A crack of the whip followed. "Hup now, hup."

The covered wagon, neatly stacked and piled high with supplies of all sorts, rattled forward, following the first. Stiger watched and waited with barely concealed patience. He hated supply escort duty, but it was what had been assigned to him. He had to see the duty through. There was no avoiding it. After the sixth wagon started rumbling out of the supply depot, he nudged his horse forward and into a walk. A bored-looking auxiliary guarding the gate offered a weak salute, which Stiger sullenly returned.

Stiger pulled his horse off of the dirt road and onto the grass. The supply depot had been constructed alongside the main road going north and into Rivan territory, in a grass-covered prairie that rolled with gentle hills. The depot sat atop one of the larger ones, tall enough that it provided a fairly good field of view in all directions.

To the north, Stiger could see a dark tree line in the distance. This marked the beginning of a small forest through which they would need to pass before the prairie continued for a number of miles farther. Then they would enter another wooded area. The North seemed replete with small forested patches. Stiger let out a slow, unhappy breath. At least the trees would provide some relief from the baking sun.

Stiger's horse whinnied, eager to be off. He patted his mount affectionately. Nomad was a good, solid animal. The horse was a parting gift from his father, and one of the few things that Stiger was grateful for from the old man. His commission in the legions was another gift from his father, who had paid the price to buy his son a lieutenant's commission. Though he could easily have afforded a captaincy, Stiger's father had started out his military service as a lieutenant and felt that was where his son's career should also begin. At first, Stiger had been elated with his rank. Then he arrived to take up his duties with the Third and been assigned to Seventh company.

Almost immediately, his fellow officers made it plain they disdained him for who he was, his father's son. They took every petty opportunity to snub him, acting as if they could barely tolerate his mere presence. Frequently, they played the game of pretending that he did not even exist. Senior officers were worse, demanding more from him duty-wise than other lieutenants. It was all very ungentlemanly and bothered him to distraction. This led Stiger, whenever possible, to actively avoid the company of his peers. The injustice of it pained him greatly.

Stiger's father had once been a great general, one of the more accomplished military leaders the empire had ever put in command of a field army. Stiger's family had been proud, powerful, and above reproach. That had lasted until the elder Stiger had backed the wrong son and the losing side in a civil war over succession to the throne. It had cost the family greatly and seen his father confined to his estate outside of Mal'Zeel, a prisoner in all but name these past five years. As punishment, many of the family estates and lands around the empire had been confiscated, but through some miracle, the family had managed to hang onto their senatorial seat. Stiger's older brother, his father's firstborn, now served in that capacity.

With no lands or titles to inherit, the younger Stiger had turned to the military, as his father once had. But where his father had been accepted and welcomed as a noble from a great house, Ben Stiger was shunned and cut out of camp society.

Stiger gripped the reins tightly with irritation. He found it terribly humiliating. It was so unfair. He was being judged on his father's merit and not his own. He slapped the palm of his hand on his thigh as Nomad continued to walk alongside the tail end of a wagon. All he wanted was to serve and win glory for himself and his house.

Upon joining the Third, Stiger had expected constant action and excitement. There was a war on. Instead, he suffered through boredom and a tedious existence that continually tested and frustrated him. Life in the legion was exceedingly boring, made worse by the attitude of his fellow officers.

Captain Cethegus was the worst. He seemed to resent Stiger even more than the rest. The captain was also a recent appointment. From the moment Stiger had arrived, the captain had not hesitated to let his feelings of disgust be known about having Stiger serve as his second-in-command. Cethegus had handed over to Stiger every shit job there was, including supply train escort duty.

The senior officers of the camp usually rotated the duty amongst the junior officers, but Stiger seemed to get stuck with it more often than not. There was nothing he could do about it, and so Stiger had privately resolved to do his duty to the best of his ability, no matter what injustice was heaped upon him. There would come a time, he vowed, that would see him treated for his ability and the glory he achieved on the battlefield. He would not be treated for who his father was. Each night, before he turned in, Stiger made a point to pray to the High Father, asking for the great god's assistance in sustaining him during this difficult time.

Stiger's mind drifted as they continued up the dry and dusty road that was little more than a track. They passed through the small forest he had seen from a distance, and beyond. The dirt road was nothing like the paved solid roads of the empire. Abandoned farm fields lined both sides of the road. They had become depressingly familiar, and though it had been many weeks, the barren fields still bore evidence of the scorch-and-burn tactics the Rivan army had employed as it pulled back before the might of Third Legion, stopping only long enough to occasionally counter-punch and offer battle.

A small, mean hut just off of the road to his left had been burned, leaving only a charred shell of rounded stakes and blackened foundation stones. What Stiger took to be a modest planting patch had also been scorched by fire. The enemy had burned everything for miles around. They had also driven their own people from their homes and marched them north. Nothing of value had been left behind, only desolation.

Once the war ended, life would return. These burnt and charred fields would be replanted. Before long, the empire would send imperial land agents and speculators. Soon thereafter, settlers would follow. It would only be a matter of time before this land became a new imperial province.

Stiger walked his horse around a large rut in the road. Even this sad track would be converted into an imperial road. As it had in other places, the empire would bring civilization, order, and law to these lands. A rich province filled with villages, towns, and cities would grow from the newfound order. Third Legion led that noble effort, and Stiger was proud to be part of it.

The Rivan were a determined foe, perhaps the most serious the empire had faced in centuries. Upon imperial decree, the legions had crossed the border in retaliation for repeated Rivan raids into the border provinces of the empire. The Third Legion was the empire's vanguard and spear point for the much larger imperial army, aimed at putting this dangerous enemy down. Four additional legions had been gathered. Now that the fighting season had arrived, they would soon follow the Third's advance north.

In the weeks and months ahead, Stiger understood keenly there was bound to be the opportunity to win glory. Thus, he would begin the hard work of wiping the stain from his name. The men of the Seventh, as foul, uncouth, and uneducated as they were, would help him achieve that. In Stiger's eye, they were no different than any other tool at his disposal.

The wagon Stiger was riding next to suddenly ground to a halt. He looked over at the teamster with an unhappy scowl, and then ahead. All of the wagons to the front had also stopped. They had entered another small forest, and the road bent around to the right and out of sight. Stiger could not see the cause. He spurred his horse forward and galloped up to the front. When he rounded the bend, Stiger pulled Nomad to a stop. Several hundred head of cattle were blocking much of the road ahead. Just beyond the cattle was a small river, which the road crossed in a narrow and shallow ford.

Drovers, along with as many as a dozen slaves, were busy beating the herd across the river. They yelled, called, and with long reed switches smacked the behinds and sides of the animals in an effort to move them across. Under the heat of the baking sun, the cattle desired nothing more than to drink when they reached the water's edge and seemed quite immoveable.

Stiger spared an exasperated glance up at the heavens and then down at the corporal, who was striding over. It seemed everything was conspiring to slow him down, which would not go over well with Captain Cethegus.

"Sir," Varus saluted, "cattle for the Third."

"I can see that," Stiger said irritably. "Do you suppose we can move them aside?"

"I don't think so, sir," Varus replied with a wary look at his lieutenant, almost as if he expected Stiger to give such an order.

"I suppose not," Stiger said, studying this side of the river as he wiped sweat from his forehead with the back of his arm. With the trees pressing in on both sides of the road, there was no room to move the wagons around the herd.

Stiger knew from repeated crossings of this river that the ford itself was quite narrow. On the other side of the river, the terrain opened up. It looked as if the opposite bank had at one time in the distant past been cultivated. There were the remains of a small barn—only the stone foundation and a couple of walls. The rest of the structure had collapsed in upon itself. The ruin was overgrown with brush, several young saplings sprouting from inside the decaying walls.

"Orders, sir?" Varus shifted uncomfortably in the heat. He, like the rest of the men and Stiger, was baking in his armor.

"Stand the men down," Stiger said, resigned to fate. "Might as well have them eat their rations and refill canteens."

"Ah, yes, sir," Varus said, and Stiger sensed the man seemed a little uncomfortable.

"You have something to say?" Stiger asked, looking down on the corporal from his horse. This was the first time he had been assigned Varus's file to help with escort duty. The other file was led by Corporal Durus, whom Stiger could stand less than Varus. "Say it, man."

"We are in enemy territory, sir," Varus said. "I recommend we set a watch and bring as many of the wagons up and together as possible in the event of trouble."

"The Rivan have retreated north," Stiger said.

"Their army has, sir," Varus said. Stiger noticed the corporal's careful tone. "They would only need a handful of men to strike at our supply trains."

Though he was in a sour mood, Stiger nodded slightly. What Varus said made sense. His military tutors had mentioned time and again that good officers listened to their sergeants and corporals. Uneducated and uncouth though he may be, there was no doubt in Stiger's mind that Varus knew his business of soldiering. If Varus was concerned, then perhaps Stiger should be as well.

Stiger glanced back down the road, narrowing his eyes against the brightness of the sun. There was just enough room along the road to double up the wagons side by side.

"Very well." Stiger let out an explosive breath and turned back to Varus. "Bring the wagons up as much as possible. Detail a watch and some men to refill canteens."

"Thank you, sir," Varus said, and Stiger noticed a look of relief on the corporal's face.

"Do we have any scouts with us?" Stiger asked.

"Yes, sir. One with each file."

"Send them out into the forest to look for evidence of the enemy." Stiger pulled out one of his own canteens from a saddlebag and unscrewed the top. Taking a deep pull of the warm, stale water, he looked unhappily at the mass of cattle ahead. "Might as well put the scouts to some use."

Varus was silent, and Stiger looked over at him.

"Anything else, corporal?"

"No, sir."

"Good," Stiger said. "Dismissed."

Varus saluted and left to pass along Stiger's orders.

Stiger nudged his horse forward, skirting around the edge of the cattle moving upriver, away from the animals and their stench. The drovers shouted and cursed the animals as they prodded them toward the river crossing. So far, they had managed to get only a handful across. Stiger had a sneaking suspicion he had a long wait ahead. For a fleeting moment, Stiger considered ordering his men to hurry the animals across, but then dismissed the idea. His men had just marched several miles, and it was gods awful hot out. They needed a break, and this was as good a place as any to take one.

The river was shallow, anywhere from two to five feet deep, perhaps a little more, and slow moving. The water was clear. Stiger could see right down to the rock-studded bottom. Any fish that had been about had been driven away by the commotion of the cattle. They made an awful racket.

Stiger dismounted and led Nomad to the water's edge. Upstream from the crossing, he found a small tree to loop the reins loosely around. Nomad would be able to drink at will. Stiger drained his canteen in one swallow and then refilled it. He drank some of the cool river water and refilled the canteen again before returning it to a saddlebag. He then went and found a rock on the river's edge that was in the shade and sat down, his back against a tree that grew up right next to it.

Even in the shade it was hot, though the proximity to the water cooled the air somewhat. Stiger closed his eyes and dozed for a bit. After forty-five minutes, Varus reported that the scouts had found no evidence of the enemy. Stiger accepted the report, and then settled back in to wait.

It took over an hour and a half before the last of the cattle were splashing their way across the river. Stiger had impatiently mounted up and called his men to fall in as the last of the animals were driven over. The first wagon had rumbled off, but what should have been quick work turned into a painful nightmare.

The cattle had churned the soft river bottom into a morass of sucking and clinging mud. The wheels of the wagon almost immediately sank deeply into the river bottom and became stuck fast. Stiger considered unloading each wagon and carrying the supplies across, but that would have taken too much time. Instead it proved quicker for the men to push and pull each heavily loaded wagon across, straining with the effort as the river bottom tried its best to keep them from succeeding.

Stiger sat astride Nomad along the edge of the crossing and watched it all as the men worked, becoming muddy and weary. As he waited and fumed impatiently, Stiger glanced down at the dried mud and disturbed grass along the outer edges of the narrow ford. It was heavily marked with evidence of previous crossings. Since he had taken up his post with the Third, Stiger had made this crossing at least a dozen times without incident. Watching his men struggle to work each wagon across, Stiger realized that he had just learned something of importance about river crossings and the time they could suck up. He mentally filed it away.

"All lessons come with a price," Stiger said wryly as he recalled a saying his father had been fond of using.

Two

Stiger crossed after the last wagon, Nomad splashing easily through the water and quickly across. The drovers had moved their herd to one of the abandoned farm fields away from the water's edge, allowing the animals a graze and themselves a well-earned break. The supply train was lined up along the road. The teamsters were clustered in small groups, playing dice or talking.

Stiger sourly surveyed his men, who, after their back-breaking work of moving the wagons across, looked extremely un-legionary-like. They were caked in mud and grim, and clearly tired. Stiger gazed up the road and was itching to be off. It was the middle of the afternoon, and he knew with certainty there was no way he would make it back to the legionary encampment this evening. The comfort of his cot would just have to wait. They would all be sleeping on their arms tonight. Worse, Stiger's captain would not be terribly pleased with his tardiness and would take it as another sign of his lieutenant's lack of competence.

"Varus," Stiger said when the corporal approached, just as muddy and bedraggled as his men. Varus had lent a hand at the back-breaking work of moving the heavy wagons across the river. "Have the men clean up before we march."

"Yes, sir," Varus replied, clearly not surprised by the order. He turned and called out to the men, who began moving back toward the river.

The added delay was unavoidable. The high standards of the legion had to be maintained. If a senior officer happened upon them in such a state, Stiger would find himself in serious trouble. And so, the men cleaned up while the heat of the day burned slowly away, and Stiger stewed about lost time. In the end, it took another forty minutes for the men to bathe in the river and tend to their kit.

By late afternoon, the supply train got back on the road. Stiger continued onward until dusk. He briefly considered pushing on through the darkness, but the road was poor and riddled with potholes. The risk to man, beast, and wagon was just too great.

He recalled a large open field just a few miles beyond the river. This, he felt, was a suitable place to make camp for the night. The field, like all of the others for miles around, had been burned by the enemy some weeks before. Stiger estimated that the campsite was roughly six hours from the main legionary encampment. With luck, he could be there by noon the next day.

Stiger had the wagons circled up just off the road. Fresh tufts of grass poked out from the charred remains of the field, though it no longer stank too badly of smoke. Varus sent men into a stand of trees to chop some wood, enough for several fires, while the rest of the men cleared space to lay their blankets and sleep. Despite the wagons being heaped high with supplies, the legionaries would subsist on their cold, pre-cooked rations. Stiger had made sure that they had left the legionary encampment with two days' worth of rations. The last two times he had made a supply run, Bruta had delayed him sufficiently so that what should have been a single day run turned into a day and a half.

Stiger tied up Nomad to one of the wagons and threw some hay down in front of his ever-greedy horse. Stiger's tutors had imparted a responsibility to care for his horse and equipment before he tended to his own needs. He had also been taught to rely upon himself to do the work and not servants or slaves, though many officers preferred to use the men as manservants. Stiger had that option available to him, but the lesson had taken and he was reluctant to rely upon another.

"Sir," Varus called.

Stiger had removed the horse's saddle and was brushing the animal down thoroughly. His armor, which he still wore, would come next.

"What is it?" Stiger called back, feeling weary from a long, hot day. Varus was on the other side of the camp, standing on one of the wagons and looking off into the distance.

"Riders emerging from the woods," Varus called back and pointed away from the road. "That way, sir."

Tiredness forgotten, Stiger hurried over to where the corporal was, climbed up the wagon, and stood on the driver's bench. There was a patch of forest around four hundred yards distant. A body of horsemen—of which Stiger quickly counted twenty—was emerging from the trees. The sun was setting in the direction of the riders. It was unclear whether they wore the red of the empire or the blue cloaks of the Rivan. Stiger very much hoped they wore the red.

"Get the men formed up," Stiger ordered curtly, suddenly feeling nervous and exposed. "Inside the wagon circle."

"Form up!" Varus roared. "Shields, helmets, and spears."

The men rapidly scrambled for their shields, protective canvas covers thrown aside as they drew them out. While the men assembled, Stiger glanced around. There was the work detail in the trees about fifty yards away, gathering wood.

"Send a runner to the wood detail," Stiger ordered Varus. "They are to remain hidden in the trees."

"What if we are attacked?" Varus asked.

Stiger shrugged, glancing back at the horsemen. "They are on their own then."

He did not think the detail could get back in time, should the riders decide to attack. They were safer staying put. Stiger had studied cavalry tactics. If the horsemen turned out to be the enemy, and were armed with lances and swords, Stiger's men would be relatively safe behind the wagons. After all, he outnumbered them. If, however, they were armed with bows, then it would be a different matter. The enemy horsemen would be able to stand off and pepper him with arrow shot, at least as long as the light lasted.

"Corvus," Varus called to one of the men. "Run to the wood-gathering detail and tell them to lay low until we know if that bunch are friendly."

"Yes, corporal." Corvus, one of the youngest in the Seventh, set off. He slithered under one of the wagons and moments later was gone, dashing off toward the stand of trees where the detail of men worked, oblivious to the oncoming danger.

"They are moving toward us, sir," Varus said unnecessarily.

Stiger remained silent. He was frightened more than he cared to admit. He was concerned that, should he speak, he might betray his nerves and disgrace himself. So he said nothing and simply watched.

The riders formed up into a double column and slowly rode toward them. Stiger tried to remember if the Rivan employed horse archers but could not recall. He wished he had paid closer attention to his tutors. Then, Stiger saw the red cloaks of legion cavalry and the distinctive imperial standard being carried by one of the riders. He breathed out in relief as the troop of cavalry rode closer. They were from an allied auxiliary cohort.

"Stand the men down," Stiger said to Varus, his voice a little shaky.

"Stand down," Varus called.

"Lieutenant Fulvius," the commander of the troop introduced himself as he called for a halt some ten paces from the wagons, "of the Third Cogaron Cavalry Cohort."

"Lieutenant Stiger, of the Seventh Imperial Foot Company."

The lieutenant's eyes widened slightly before narrowing. "We're on patrol from an outpost fifteen miles from here." Fulvius gestured vaguely back the way he had come.

"Have you found anything?" Stiger asked. The Fulvius family was of the senatorial class. They were not exactly enemies of his house, but were not allies either. It was a gray area, and one of which Stiger was sure they were both well aware.

"We came across a path a few miles back that had evidence of a large body of horsemen moving through the area," Fulvius said. "The tracks looked fresh, perhaps a day or two old, but were headed north."

"I see," Stiger, said and then remembered his manners. "Would you care for a cup of wine?"

"Very kind of you," Fulvius said, inclining his head. He spared a glance behind him at the setting sun before turning back to Stiger. "Unfortunately, I am afraid I will have to pass. We were due back at sundown. Exploring those tracks took us farther afield than I anticipated."

"Another time then."

"Safe travels, lieutenant," the cavalry officer said, nodded respectfully, and wheeled his horse around back the way he had come. His troop followed neatly after him. Stiger watched them for a few moments, then turned back to Varus.

"Let's get some fires going, and I think setting a double watch might be in order."

"Yes, sir," Varus said.

With the departure of the friendly cavalry, the men returned to the business of setting up camp. The wood-gathering detail returned with sufficient fuel to keep several fires going. And so, as the light died, the men settled in for the night. Stiger enjoyed some of the wine he had purchased, finding it quite good. It reminded him of the more comfortable life he had known back in Mal'Zeel. He was surprised that he actually felt a little homesick as he laid out his blanket near a fire that had been set for him.

The capital was an exciting place, with a much faster pace of life than the one he had seen with the legions so far. Entertainment was readily available, with the best being the chariot races, seconded only by the gladiatorial games. He had loved those sports.

Stiger took a long breath as he recollected better times. He missed the food, which was a sight better than the slop the legions provided. Most of all, though, Stiger missed his friends. He had a few, but treasured them nonetheless. Now, in service with Third Legion, he had no one else he could count on save but himself. Stiger finished the wine he had been drinking and decided to turn in.

The night air brought on cooler temperatures, which was a relief, and Stiger wrapped himself up in his blanket. He used a rolled-up tunic for a pillow, shifted around until he found a comfortable position, and then closed his eyes and drifted off into sleep.

❧ ❧ ❧

The night passed peacefully. Despite that, Stiger slept poorly, worrying about a possible attack and arriving overly late at the encampment next morning. He had left orders that he be woken well before dawn. After a quick, cold breakfast of precooked rations, Stiger had the supply train back on the road, creaking and clattering away as the first streaks of light brightened the sky. He was eager to return to the encampment, despite the dressing down that was surely waiting.

"Sir." A legionary drew his attention, pointing behind them. Stiger had been riding at the head of the column, alongside Varus's file. He turned in the saddle and looked backwards. The road was straight at this point, cutting through a small scrub forest that was beginning to encroach closely on the road.

Looking back, Stiger saw, to his consternation, that his wagons, one after another, were pulling off to the side and coming to a stop. Before stopping, the teamsters were driving their wagons into the scrub brush, at which the mules balked, leading to additional cracks of the whips interlaced with curses until they complied.

Stiger saw the reason a moment later. A double column of cavalry was coming up, with a carriage following closely behind. The cavalry and carriage were forced to wait for each wagon to slowly move aside.

"Get the men out of the road," Stiger snapped to Varus and also moved his horse aside as the troop and carriage approached.

"About bloody time," a cavalry lieutenant Stiger did not know barked angrily at him.

"Excuse me, sir?" Stiger asked, surprised at the open hostility. Though after the weeks of abuse from his peers, he knew he should not be too shocked at such treatment. Perhaps the other officer simply knew who he was and felt free to heap on the abuse.

"You heard me," the lieutenant said, drawing his horse up. The cavalry troop continued to ride by, horses hanging their heads in the heat. "You could have gotten off the road a little faster."

Stiger ground his teeth but said nothing. He turned to look as the carriage rattled by, catching a brief glance of an older man and a woman looking out at him. Then the carriage was past them, bouncing up the road, following after the escort troop of cavalry.

"Sir," Stiger directed himself to the cavalry lieutenant, who had remained behind. "If you would kindly get a move on, I would like to get my wagons back on the road and rolling."

The cavalry lieutenant shot Stiger a furious glance, dug his heels into his horse, and galloped off after the carriage. Stiger watched for a moment, thoroughly irritated, and then turned on Varus.

"Get the men bloody moving," Stiger fairly shouted at the corporal. He was angry, and embarrassed. Though he knew it was unfair, he was taking it out on Varus anyway.

"Yes, sir." Varus snapped to attention and saluted. He began to shout at the men to reform into a marching column.

Word was passed back down the supply train to move. Slowly, almost painfully, they got back on the road, crawling toward the main encampment of Third Legion.

Stiger kept his horse still as the supply train moved by him. He was in a thoroughly unpleasant mood and did not feel like sharing the road with anyone. Besides, none of the men were fit company for a nobleman. Before the end of the train reached him, he nudged Nomad into a walk and rode slightly behind, off to the side of one of the wagons.

An hour later, the road emerged into a rolling set of hills, the wagons slowly climbing and descending under the mounting heat of the day. The sun was almost directly overhead, and it was quite oppressive. Stiger took a quick drink from his canteen and then replaced it in his saddlebag as Nomad dutifully continued to plod along. The heat was so brutal that his horse hung its head as it clopped along, mile after mile. Stiger was considering calling for a break when a shout ahead drew his attention. The wagon he had been riding next to rumbled to an unexpected stop.

"Sir," the teamster called, having had word passed back to him. "You are needed up at the front."

Stiger kicked his horse into a trot and quickly made his way to the front of the supply train. Nomad did not seem terribly pleased at the increased pace and whinnied in protest. The lead wagon had stopped just short of the crest of another small hill. To the front of the wagon, Stiger found Varus organizing his file into a line of battle. The men had also discarded the canvas covers of their shields, an ominous sign that set Stiger's heart beating a little faster.

"What's going on?" Stiger demanded of Varus, who simply gestured to their front.

Stiger nudged Nomad forward a few steps to the crest of the hill and brought his horse to a stop. He found himself looking on the melee of battle. Down the other side of the hill was the carriage and cavalry troop that had passed them by earlier. They were under attack by a large force of cavalry, perhaps three hundred yards distant.

The cavalry wore the blue cloaks of the Rivan.

A good number of the defenders were down or had been unhorsed. The sounds of the fighting reached him clearly, and Stiger was surprised he had not heard it as he rode up.

"Looks to be around forty of the Rivan bastards," Varus grunted. Stiger did a quick count himself and found that the corporal was correct. Though in the chaos of the fight there appeared to be more. "They are pressing our boys hard, sir."

Stiger nodded in agreement, but was not really sure what he could do. His tutors had taught him infantry never attacked cavalry. It simply did not happen.

"Sir," Varus said, an urgent tone in his voice. "We need to help our boys."

"Right," Stiger said, the corporal's words jolting him into action. This was his chance to secure some of the glory he so craved and deserved. "Send word for the other file to come up at the double. We will take this file down and attack the enemy. As soon as the other file is up, they are to follow and engage. Understand me?"

"Yes, sir." Varus turned and spoke to a legionary who set his shield and spear down. The man immediately sprinted away toward the rear of the train.

Stiger glanced over his assault line, still hidden behind the crest of the hill. Twenty men organized into four ranks of five looked fairly insignificant. He then looked back down at the fight. He idly wondered if the disagreeable lieutenant he had encountered earlier was still alive.

"Corporal," Stiger said with sudden inspiration. "I want two ranks. That's all. Quickly now."

Varus reorganized the men into two ranks, which made the assault line look larger and—Stiger hoped—more intimidating. Once it was done, he unfastened his helmet from a tie on the saddle and put it on. Stiger secured the strap tightly and drew his sword. He looked back on his men. Each held a short spear and shield with grim expressions on their faces. He glanced back down at the fight. The enemy cavalry, engaged with the carriage's escort, were distracted. It wasn't like he was assaulting an organized and prepared formation. Stiger's appearance would hopefully surprise the enemy. The spears would serve well, Stiger hoped. If the opportunity came for a toss, where there was no risk of hitting friendly forces, he would take it.

"Sir," Varus drew his attention. "Would you care for one of the teamsters to hold your horse?"

Stiger studied the corporal for a moment. It was a gentle and subtle rebuke, which surprised him. Varus was right, he decided. He was an infantry officer, and in battle his place was afoot with his men. Stiger dismounted and beckoned for a man to take his horse. The man quickly led Nomad over to the nearest teamster and handed the reins up.

"Very good." Stiger used his free hand to check the tightness of the strap on his helmet. "Advance."

The line started forward and within five steps reached the crest. Then they were over it and on their way down the other side at a steady, measured pace.

"Seven levels," one of the men breathed, seeing the action below for the first time.

"Quiet in the ranks," Varus barked. "Another word and I will personally make sure you will be up to your elbows in shit, mucking out the latrines after we make it back to camp tonight."

There were no more comments after that.

Stiger, studying the fight as they closed, estimated that about half of the friendly cavalry were down. Several had been unhorsed and fought afoot. Screams and the clash of sword on sword filled the air. Bodies littered the ground.

Wounded crawled from the fight, while others writhed or thrashed about in agony. Horsemen wheeled around, trading blows. Horses whinnied and screamed.

Stiger saw the horses that had been pulling the carriage had both been cut down. An injured horse broke from the press and thundered away past Stiger and his men, a badly wounded Rivan cavalry trooper clinging desperately to its neck.

Stiger's nerves increased the closer they got.

This was his first fight.

He hands were sweaty on the hilt of his sword. His mouth was dry. Stiger suddenly found he was unprepared for the fight ahead. He offered a quick, silent prayer to the High Father, asking that the great god grant him glory this day. Stiger also prayed for strength. He begged that he not turn coward, for he really felt like doing nothing other than running.

What Stiger took to be an enemy officer abruptly pointed in their direction and shouted a number of orders. They had finally been seen. The enemy cavalry pressed their attack, clearly intent upon cutting the defenders down before Stiger and his men could intervene.

"At the double," Stiger shouted, understanding that he had do something. It also occurred to him that as long as the enemy were focused on the carriage and its escort, the horsemen would not pose a threat to him and his men. The sooner they closed and joined the fight the better. "March!"

The pace increased, and the distance closed rapidly, armor jangling and chinking as the assault line closed on the enemy.

"Slow march!" Stiger called when they were fewer than ten paces from the enemy. "Close up."

The legionaries came back together in a solid line.

"Ready shields," Varus snapped. The shields thunked together.

Several of the enemy wheeled about and attempted to close on Stiger's legionaries. All they found was an impenetrable shield wall that bristled with short spears. The horses shied back, fighting against their riders' commands. A legionary lunged forward and jabbed out, found flesh. The horse screamed in agony. It reared up, dumping its blue-cloaked rider before the line of legionaries, then turned and ran madly in the other direction. The man died under a number of spear strikes.

Another horse was jabbed by multiple spears and went down, crushing the rider. Stiger stood off to the side of his line, slightly behind his men, as they coolly moved forward and into the fight. He was impressed by their calm and discipline, though he knew he should not be. They were mostly all hardened veterans with years of service behind them.

Stiger realized with an abrupt shock that he had left his shield back with the supply wagons. He cursed his stupidity as one of the enemy, seeing an officer off to the side of the legionary line, wheeled his horse about and drove forward, cavalry sword leveled for the kill.

Stiger crouched and made ready to spring aside, when one of his men at the end of the line casually stepped forward and drove his spear into the beast's chest. The force of the horse's momentum ripped the short spear from the legionary's hand as the horse collapsed to the earth, spilling the rider into the dirt. The legionary calmly drew his short sword and jabbed downward, killing the trooper before the man could even struggle to his feet. The legionary glanced over at Stiger and grinned before turning back to the action.

A strange-sounding horn blasted three short notes, then repeated again. The enemy cavalry immediately broke off the fight, pulling their horses around. They galloped away, making for a stand of trees some twenty yards to the left.

"Spears," Varus called to the men before Stiger could even think to give the order. "Release at will."

With grunts of effort, Stiger's men threw their spears. It was a ragged toss, but five of the deadly missiles found their mark, striking down horse and man alike. Stiger saw another wave of spears come down amidst the enemy a few heartbeats later. This toss had come from his second file, led by Corporal Durus, who had been at the rear of the supply train. They had just started down the hill.

Four more of the cavalry were struck down. One enemy trooper, whose horse was down, kicking about in the dirt on its side, stood and began dashing for the safety of the trees on foot. Another stood with an injured leg and began to limp painfully away.

"Send five men to dispatch the survivors," Stiger ordered Varus, gesturing with his sword at the horsemen who had been downed by the spear toss. An injured horse screamed and thrashed in the dirt. The animal's back legs no longer worked. "Also, kindly put the wounded beasts out of their misery."

"Yes, sir," Varus said.

Stiger watched the rest of the enemy cavalry make it into the trees and disappear. A few moments later they could be seen riding up a small hill beyond the trees and disappearing again over the top.

Stiger glanced around. None of his men appeared to have been injured or killed. He turned back to the carriage—a pile of bodies forming a ring around it. It was a right mess. Several of the cavalry escorts had dismounted and were moving amongst the bodies, putting any of the enemy they discovered alive out of their misery. A few were even searching the bodies for loot. A number of rider-less horses milled uncertainly about.

"You men," Stiger called to his men who were looking about at the carnage. "Gather up those horses."

At least the enemy's mounts were prizes of war. The legion would pay good money for them. The men would get a small portion, and so would Stiger. He received an allowance from his father, but that was barely enough to make ends meet. A little prize money would be more than welcome.

"You are not as slow as I had initially thought."

Stiger turned and saw the cavalry lieutenant he had met earlier approaching on foot. The lieutenant's armor and face were spattered with dried blood, but he looked unhurt. He flashed a good-natured grin at Stiger and offered his hand.

"Lieutenant Aquila Carbo at your service, sir."

Stiger took his hand and returned the grin. It was the first real respect he had been shown by a fellow officer since he had come north. The Carbos had once been allies of his house, but after his father's fall from grace, nothing was certain.

"Lieutenant Ben Stiger."

"Stiger you say?" Carbo asked, with raised eyebrows. "I was not aware there were any Stigers still serving." The lieutenant paused for a moment. "Lucky for me there are."

"Lucky," Stiger repeated quietly. He noticed that his hand had started to shake slightly. He placed it upon his sword hilt to keep the trembling from showing.

"I would like to apologize for my deplorable behavior earlier," Carbo said formally. "I trust you will forgive me?"

"Lieutenant Carbo," a firm voice called from behind, saving Stiger from having to respond. "Whom do we have to thank for our timely rescue?"

Carbo and Stiger turned. Another legionary officer, this one wearing the rich blue cloak of command, was striding confidently toward them. He also was splattered with blood and clearly had been involved in the fighting. Stiger stiffened to attention and offered a salute to the general.

"Enough of that, son," the senior officer said with a raised hand. "Today, I owe you my life, and for that I am grateful." The general paused and briefly surveyed the death around him. "Though, I would hazard we have a spy who tipped the enemy off...a nasty business, this. He will have to be found."

"General Treim," Carbo said. "May I introduce Lieutenant Ben Stiger."

"Stiger, eh?" the general asked, and Stiger realized that he was speaking with the new temporary commander of Third Legion.

"Yes, sir," Stiger said.

"You did well," General Treim said. "Are you in my legion?"

"Yes, sir," Stiger said. "Seventh Company."

"Excellent," Treim said. "I like men who can fight and are not afraid to pitch in. Carbo...how many men do you have left who can ride?"

Carbo glanced around and quickly counted. "Around eight, sir."

"Well, enough of this damned carriage," Treim said. "Get me a horse. We are only seven or eight miles from the encampment. We shall ride the rest of the way." The general paused and frowned. "The fact that the enemy moves so freely near our own encampment makes me wonder what our cavalry is doing."

"Yes, sir," Carbo said, and then hesitated. "What of Livia?"

"My daughter?" Treim turned back to the carriage, and then to Stiger. "Bring my carriage and my daughter to the encampment, son."

"Yes, sir," Stiger replied. "She will be safe with me, sir."

"I don't doubt it. Make sure you don't forget the carriage too. It was rather expensive and my daughter is fond of traveling in it."

"Sir." Stiger gestured toward the hill where the enemy had disappeared. "Are you certain about riding off? What if that bunch comes after you?"

"I rather doubt they will try," Treim said with a heavy breath. "After this, they have to know we will send out a force after them. Besides, we will ride hard for the encampment. They will not expect it. Yes, I think we shall be quite safe."

"Yes, sir," Stiger responded neutrally, not so sure he felt as confident. But it was not his place to question the decisions of his general.

Stiger watched as a cavalry trooper approached the coach and helped General Treim's daughter out. She wore a pale blue dress. Stiger was struck by her beauty and figured she was near his age in years. Livia had long blonde hair weaved into a single braid hanging down her back to her waist. Her green eyes looked on with distaste at the death and injury that had been wrought around the carriage.

"My dear," General Treim said. "See, I told you everything would be fine."

"Yes, father," she said with a voice that was clear and fresh, though fluttered with an understandable nervous tremor. Stiger, in that moment, thought her very brave.

"This is Lieutenant Stiger," Treim introduced. "My daughter, Livia Domana."

"I am pleased to meet you," Stiger said, offering the girl a small bow. She did not share the same last name as Treim, which meant he had adopted her.

"Stiger?" She cast an interested look in his direction. "Stigers still serve the empire?"

"Yes, my lady," Stiger said, stiffly. "The emperor gave me his blessing personally."

"Lieutenant Stiger will see you safely to the encampment," Treim said. "I will ride ahead with Carbo. There is business I must attend to."

"But, father," she said with an alarmed look. Stiger saw General Treim's face harden. She must have also seen it as well, for after a moment's hesitation, she bowed her head in acceptance, but not before glancing back at Stiger. Stiger realized that she desperately did not want her father to leave. Yet she would not embarrass him with a public protest either. She would endure as asked.

There was strength in this girl, he thought.

"You have my word of honor," Stiger said to reassure her, "that I will see you safely to the legionary encampment."

"Thank you, lieutenant," she said, turning her beautiful green eyes upon him. "That will be a comfort."

Carbo led a horse over to Treim, who mounted with a smooth, practiced manner. He looked down upon Stiger and hesitated a moment.

"Mount up," Carbo called to those of his men who still could.

"Lieutenant," Treim said with a quick glance at his daughter and then around at the remains of the fight, which had centered around the carriage. "Make sure the wounded are cared for and brought back to the encampment. Also, bring back the dead."

"Of course, sir."

"I was friends with your father, you know," Treim said suddenly, which Stiger had not known. "I also fought against him."

Stiger said nothing, feeling he was on dangerous ground.

"If you are half the officer Marcus Stiger was, then I shall be pleased," the general continued, his new horse side-stepping nervously. The general tightened his grip on the reins and the horse stilled.

"Yes, sir," Stiger said, straightening.

"I shall be watching you, Stiger."

With that, the general kicked his horse forward into a trot and left Stiger with his daughter, and the aftermath of the fight, to deal with.

"They will ride in my father's carriage." Livia stamped a foot in the dirt of the road. "And that is that."

Livia had suggested using the carriage as an ambulance, but Stiger had protested, not thinking it proper. She had firmly insisted. Stiger considered her for a moment. The general's daughter was around five feet, four inches tall. Her blonde hair looked radiant under the bright sunlight of the day, and the serious and determined look upon her face made her only that much more beautiful to him. He found his heart beating a little faster as he contemplated her.

"Very well," he said, conceding defeat. "The seriously wounded will ride in the carriage."

"Excellent," she said, clearly pleased at having won. "Now, find me a horse."

And so, Livia was mounted on one of the captured horses. She seemed capable enough at handling the animal.

Stiger pulled himself up onto Nomad's back and did his best to avoid her gaze as he shifted about in the saddle to get comfortable.

"Hup there, hup," the teamster called to his mules, clicking his tongue. A crack of the whip followed. The wagon rattled forward, and with it Stiger's supply train was once again moving. Ahead of the wagon, Varus's file marched in a neat column. Durus's file waited patiently at the rear for the last of the wagons begin moving.

The legionary cavalry troopers killed in the fight had been lashed atop the supplies still neatly stacked on the wagons. The wounded who were able shared a seat with the teamsters, walked, or rode one of the captured horses. Those more seriously injured rode inside the general's carriage, at Livia's insistence.

Stiger watched as another wagon clattered into motion, following the first.

Two of the captured horses had been hitched to the carriage. One of the animals was injured, a sword cut along its rump. Varus had insisted the injury, though it bled freely, was not serious. The carriage, driven by a legionary who had some experience with carts, began to move. Groans could be heard from inside as it bounced through a large pothole. The ride to the encampment would be a torment for the wounded, but there was no alternative. He could make them no more comfortable.

The enemy dead had been dragged off to the side of the road. Stripped of any valuables, they would be left to rot. Stiger felt no compulsion to give them a proper burial. On account of the general's daughter and the wounded, he felt duty-bound to return to the encampment as speedily as possible.

He waited a moment more, and then nudged Nomad into a walk. The general's daughter did the same. They rode for a time in silence. Stiger noticed that she kept glancing his way, as if she wanted to say something. For some reason he could not name, she made him uncomfortable.

"You are truly a Stiger?"

He looked over at her warily and nodded.

"Your brother is Senator Stiger?"

He nodded again, wondering where she was going with this line of questioning. Would she treat him with disdain and contempt? It was becoming all too familiar.

"You must be Ben, then?"

"I am," Stiger replied, taking a deep breath. "Younger brother to Senator Maxentius Manutius Stiger."

"Ben is such an odd name." She threw him a mischievous smile.

Stiger glanced back over at her, and he thought her a bit talkative for having just survived a near encounter with death. Though he knew he had done the general a service, he wasn't yet sure how he felt about what he had just been through.

"Ben is short for Bennulius."

"You do not like that name?"

"No," he said. "I prefer Ben."

"Then I shall call you Ben," she announced, sounding pleased with herself. "You shall call me Livia."

"As you wish," he said. Stiger was once again struck by her beauty as she rode next to him. Yet she was also the general's daughter, even if only adopted. He had to be careful around her. "Livia it is."

"Though we are beyond the frontier, I see no reason why we cannot be civilized."

"I agree," he said. "It has been too long since I shared company of one so fair."

She had the grace to blush and offered him a coy smile, which he found pleasing.

43

"Such a gentleman," she said. "I had feared encountering only equestrians and brutes amongst the military. It is a pleasure to find a fellow noble of the senatorial class serving in my father's legion."

"To be honest, I had not expected to encounter a lady of your standing either."

Even though his family had been in disgrace, Stiger suddenly found once again that he actually missed the refinements of Mal'Zeel. There were people there who could be counted on to treat him with respect and courtesy, as Livia was now doing. Without realizing it, he longed terribly for such civility.

Then again, there were those in Mal'Zeel who desired nothing more than the ruin of his house and family. It was an interesting contrast, and one he had hoped to put behind him for the simpler life of a soldier. How mistaken he had been.

Stiger wiped sweat from his brow. The heat of the day was broiling him in his armor. He glanced over at Livia, who was looking over at a farm off the side of the road that had been burned. The barn had collapsed in upon itself, and now only the soot-scorched stone walls that made up the foundation remained. The farmhouse had been reduced to mostly ash and a few charred beams. The fields, like all of the others he had seen, had suffered the same fate.

"I would very much like to thank you for rescuing my father and me." She turned to look over at him. "It was very dashing of you."

"I was simply in the right place at the right time. It was what any other officer would have done."

"But it wasn't any other officer," she said, pointing a finger at him. "It was you."

"Yes," he admitted, not sure what else to say.

"Then I am in your debt."

Stiger looked over at her sharply and pulled Nomad up short. She stopped her horse as well, a curious, almost impish expression upon her fair face.

"You are not in my debt. I only did my duty," he said.

"I say that I am, for which I will be eternally grateful."

Stiger frowned, and then he noticed a mischievous smile upon her face. What an interesting woman, he thought. Two hours ago she had been in mortal fear of her life, and now she was teasing him and enjoying it immensely. Some of the other women he had known back in the capital would still be crying their eyes out.

"Perhaps you just might be able to discharge any debt you feel you owe me," Stiger said, a slow smile creeping onto his face. Her delicate eyebrows rose slightly.

"How?"

"I think I might settle for the courtesy of your refined company over dinner one evening," Stiger said. "Yes, that would settle affairs equitably. How does that sound?"

"I would like that," she said quietly. "Some evening soon, I hope?"

Stiger felt a sudden thrill that was mingled with a chill as he looked back at her. Livia seemed like the kind of woman who got what she wanted, when she wanted it. He nudged Nomad back into a walk, and she did the same. How would her father react to her spending time with a Stiger?

"I would warn you in advance that the food at the encampment is not up to the standards to which you are accustomed."

"I will have to settle for good conversation then," she said.

"I do have a few bottles of fine wine from Venney, though," Stiger admitted, more pleased with his recent purchase.

"Sounds wonderful."

Stiger looked over at her and suddenly saw her pale.

"What is it?" he asked as he looked away to steer Nomad around a large rut in the road.

She did not immediately reply, but looked down at her horse's neck. He sensed something darker on her mind and considered asking again. Instead, he decided to respect Livia's silence. She would speak when ready. He turned back to the road. For some time there was only the sound of the clopping of the horse's hooves, the creaking and grinding of the wagons, and the distant sound of the men from Varus's file to the front of the column talking the miles away.

"My real father fought under your father's command," she said abruptly. "He died during the civil war."

Stiger glanced over at her, and his mood darkened. Had she been playing with him up to this point? He expected to find recrimination and anger. Instead, he saw only the sadness of one who had lost, and terribly so. He could see it plainly reflected in her eyes, the pain of losing a loved one. The lightness that had been on the air between them had fled. Saying that he was sorry seemed inadequate.

"I lost everything," she said, and her voice trembled ever so slightly. "Our lands and estates were taken by the senate and emperor. My mother, in grief, killed herself, and I was left alone to fend for myself."

"I..." Stiger stuttered, feeling terrible.

"I tell you this not because I wish you to feel sorry for me," she said, and there was heat in her voice. "I tell you so that you know the truth. My family supported yours because what your father was doing was right."

"You did?" Stiger was dumbfounded. He blamed his father for the family's plight, and here before him was another who had suffered much worse. How could that be right? How many others had suffered a worse fate? How could she still support the man?

"We did," she said. "I do not want your pity, just your understanding."

Stiger was silent as he gathered his thoughts. Dark and hard memories surfaced.

"I lost my mother and sister." Stiger found he needed to clear his throat. It was still difficult for him to speak of.

"I'm sorry," she said, and Stiger sensed that she meant it.

They said nothing more for some minutes as they rode, each lost to their own thoughts.

"It has worked out well for me," she said after a time. "Shortly after our lands and estate holdings were seized, I was taken in and adopted."

"By the general?"

"Yes," she said. "He was friendly with my father and took me in as his own, when no one else would. Had he not done so, I would have ended up on the street." She paused a moment, and a tear traced its way down her cheek.

Stiger's heart ached for her.

"My new father is a good man," she said. "In a year or so I will be permitted by the priesthood to dispense with my old name, Domana, and take my new one, Treim. Where once my future was bleak, now it is bright...as, I suspect, is yours."

Stiger turned away and glanced around at the landscape. They had emerged onto wide open grasslands. The road cut through the land in an undeviating straight line. He could see for miles in any direction. Though he judged it unlikely, should the enemy cavalry make another appearance, they would be seen with plenty of time to prepare. Stiger felt there was little to worry about, and he relaxed somewhat.

Besides, once the general reached the encampment, he would call out the cavalry to hunt for the band that had attacked his party. The enemy, if they had any sense, would be well on their way to the safety of their own lines.

"Well then," Stiger said, deciding to change the subject to a more pleasant topic. "Should you desire, I shall be honored spend time with you when duty permits."

"I had hoped you might," she said, and the mischievous little smile was back. He eyed her for a long moment, wondering once again what the general would think.

THREE

"I am sorry, sir," Stiger said, standing stiffly to attention. Sweat beaded his brow, but it was not from nerves. Stiger had resigned himself to this dressing down. He was sweating because the tent was hot, almost unbearably so. For some reason the captain had kept the tent flap closed.

"Sorry?" Captain Cethegus poured himself a drink from a freshly opened bottle of wine. The cork had been tossed onto the captain's camp table. The captain placed the wine bottle back on the table and sat down on his stool. He leaned forward, resting an elbow on the table as he took a sip from his cup. Cethegus looked up at Stiger with an unhappy expression. "Sorry? You are sorry for taking two entire days to return with supplies from the depot? Is that it?"

"We were unavoidably detained, sir," Stiger said, attempting for the third time to deliver his report. "If you would allow me to ex—"

"I don't think I will," Cethegus said, cutting Stiger off. He took a generous sip from his cup of wine before placing it down hard on the table. "Quite frankly, I am sick and tired of your excuses. No other lieutenant takes two days to make that supply run for their company. Seven levels, man, the depot is barely twenty miles away." The captain became silent and frowned deeply. He then wagged a finger at Stiger. "There is really nothing that comes to mind that would excuse your utter incompetence."

Stiger stood still, staring above the captain's head at the back of the tent. Though he wanted to, he did not respond, and that took some effort. Instead, he burned with shame. This treatment was so unfair. If he could only explain, but alas, he understood the captain wanted no explanations. The captain was indulging in what was becoming one of his favorite pastimes, Stiger bashing.

"You have heard a new general has arrived to take command of the legion?" Cethegus asked, taking another sip at his wine. The captain slurred his words slightly and Stiger realized he had been into the bottle for some time. It did not bode well for what was coming.

"Yes, sir," Stiger said. "I have heard."

"Good," Cethegus said, and his voice fairly purred with satisfaction. He set the cup down. "Both of us are relatively new to the company. The men are of good quality, with most being veterans." Cethegus paused and looked up at him, seeking Stiger's agreement.

"Yes, sir."

"I have always felt that the number seven has been my lucky number." The captain paused to chuckle at that, but Stiger could not see the humor. The captain sobered quickly when Stiger did not share in his joke. "Lieutenant, it is my intention to make the Seventh the best company in the legion."

"Yes, sir," Stiger said neutrally.

"Good," Cethegus said. "Then you can understand why I can't have a disgrace of a lieutenant making me look bad. You set a very poor example, not only for the men, but for your fellow officers. Do you understand my meaning?"

"Sir?" Stiger asked, some of the frustration leaking into his voice as his face colored.

Captain Cethegus seemed not seem to notice.

"I should never have left my estate and family," Cethegus muttered to himself as he poured more wine into his cup. "I gave up a comfortable life for this? All I wanted was a leg up on a political career and here I am in the middle of a real war."

"Sir?" Stiger asked again.

"It may have escaped your notice, but you are the laughingstock of the legion," Cethegus said, looking up, gaze focusing. "You need to shape up and quickly, lieutenant, or I will hand you your balls in a grass-thatched basket."

Stiger said nothing as Cethegus picked up his cup and took another sip from his wine. The captain contemplated his lieutenant a moment. Stiger sweated and fumed in silence under his superior's gaze.

"What do you think the general would say?" the captain finally asked him.

"Of what, sir?" He was on dangerous ground with his captain and wanted to be clear on what he was answering.

"Of what, sir?" Cethegus's mocking tone became hostile. "Seven levels, man, you took two days to make a simple supply run. How do you think the general would feel about that?"

"I think, sir," Stiger grated out slowly as he considered his answer. His shame and humiliation had shifted to a sullen, smoldering anger that was threatening to explode. After a moment, he gave a mental shrug, deciding to set aside his fear of the consequences and let the dice fall where they may. He took a deep breath and continued in a quiet but firm tone. "I think, sir, that General Treim would be more than understanding."

"You do, do you?" Cethegus demanded, coloring with anger at the response he apparently felt was insolent, which

Stiger had intended it to be. "Why in all of the gods' great names do you think that?"

"On account of the service that I and the Seventh rendered him, sir."

Cethegus leaned back on his stool and contemplated Stiger with narrowed eyes.

"What possible service could you have rendered our general?" Cethegus asked curiously, leaning forward. The captain rested his elbows on his camp table, which creaked at the movement. Cethegus held his cup in one hand, his chin in the other.

"The general and his escort were ambushed, sir," Stiger said. "My two files drove the enemy off. We saved the general's life, sir."

"When was this?" Cethegus asked, setting his cup down and sitting up straight. His look became piercing.

"Today, sir," Stiger said, the anger he felt leaking back into his voice. "If you had allowed me to report properly, I could have explained."

At first, Cethegus said nothing. He flashed a dangerous look at his lieutenant.

"Go on," Cethegus demanded, his entire demeanor changing to one of sudden interest. "Explain what occurred."

"We were delayed in picking up our supplies from the depot due to complications with...ah, the supply captain's staff," Stiger said, struggling to keep the bitterness out of his tone. "By the time the wagons were loaded and we were able to get rolling, much of the day was gone." He chose not to mention the cattle that had delayed them further. "The condition of the road was poor, making traveling at night risky. As such, I was not willing to risk the animals or damaging the wagons."

Stiger paused for a heartbeat to take a breath and gather his thoughts.

"The men were also tired, sir. I felt compelled to camp overnight in a field. The next day, today ... sir, we set out before first light. Due to the delay at the depot, fortune smiled upon us as we came across the general's party a few minutes after they had come under attack. I formed up Corporal Varus's file and we attacked the enemy. I am pleased to report I was able to drive the enemy off without too much difficulty. General Treim set out for the encampment on horseback shortly after the fight ended with the remainder of his escort. Before he did so, he ordered me to bring his carriage and daughter back to the encampment. We were also instructed to tend to the wounded and dead of his cavalry escort, taking them back with us as well. Unfortunately, this all took some time, and we were delayed even further, sir."

Cethegus leaned back in his chair and studied Stiger for a long moment. It was almost as if the captain wanted to disbelieve his lieutenant's report. When Stiger thought back on it, it did seem a little improbable.

The silence in the hot tent stretched out. "We had two casualties," Stiger continued, filling in the silence. "Both minor injuries, a light cut and twisted ankle. We also managed to capture ten horses, sir." The silence returned to the tent and continued to grow. Stiger wondered what fresh abuse the captain would find in his report to toss back at him. It had been like this ever since Stiger had arrived to take up his appointment to Seventh Company. Whenever the opportunity presented, the captain went out of his way to find fault with his lieutenant.

Stiger took a deep breath and waited for it to come. He was tired. He simply wanted to retire for the evening to the comfort and security of his tent. He was also hungry, and that meant a trip to the officers' mess, a place Stiger had begun to avoid whenever possible.

"You may go," Cethegus said abruptly, voice harsh and cold.

Surprised, Stiger snapped to attention and offered a salute before turning to leave.

"I will have Sergeant Geta bring you the company books," Cethegus said, and Stiger groaned inwardly. Reconciling the company accounts meant a least an hour, perhaps as many as two, of additional work. By rights the job was the captain's, but it had been foisted off on him.

"Yes, sir," Stiger said, turning back at the tent flap. "I will see them done before I turn in. Good night, sir."

"Good night, lieutenant," the captain said in the same cold tone.

With that, Stiger stepped out into the growing darkness. It had felt good to put one over on the captain, but at the same time, Stiger wondered what price Cethegus would extract upon him in petty revenge. He sighed. At least the general had thought he had done well today.

Several dozen feet to his right, the company sergeants and corporals from both Seventh and Tenth Companies were supervising the unloading of the supply train. Stiger paused to watch a moment. The air had cooled, but it was still uncomfortably hot. He glanced over at his tent with longing, then turned in the opposite direction, heading for the officers' mess. With the company books soon needing attention, it was going to be a long night, and he was hungry.

The officers' mess was located a few yards away. There were no walls, only a canopy for protection against the elements. A number of rickety tables and chairs were scattered about. Several lanterns lit the mess with a dull, sullen glow. Insects buzzed about the lanterns with frenzied interest. It was late for most, so there were only few of his peers about, which pleased Stiger. A couple of officers sitting off to the side smoked while they played a quiet card game. A small group diced a few feet away. He did not fit in here.

Those playing dice looked up with mild disinterest as he passed before one said something under his breath. The others chuckled with amusement as they watched him pass. Stiger ran a hand through his hair and continued on, pretending not to notice.

A cook wagon was backed up to one side of the mess. Around the wagon were several fire pits that were slowly being allowed to burn themselves out. A pot hung over one that had been recently fed, a cook's assistant stirring the contents. Like a long lost friend, the smell of cooking meat greeted him as he approached. Two slaves were working around the wagon, cleaning pots, pans, and bowls.

"How can I help you, sir?" the cook's assistant asked, looking up. He continued to stir the pot.

"I need something to eat. What do you have?"

"I still have some beef stew left." The cook's assistant gestured toward the pot hanging over the low-burning fire that he was stirring. "All of the fresh bread is gone, but I have some ale, sir."

"I will take stew and ale to go," Stiger said curtly.

"Very good, sir." He set about ladling a healthy portion of stew into a well-worn wooden bowl. He handed the steaming bowl to Stiger and then went to draw a mug of ale. Stiger took the mug and, in the gathering darkness, made his way back to his tent.

Though he was part of Seventh Company and Third Legion, Stiger felt as if he did not belong. It was almost as if he had been rejected, not only by his peers, but by the men as well, and it bothered him greatly. Though if he were honest with himself, he did not very much care for the opinion of the men. He was concerned about what his fellow officers thought. So far they had treated him with cold disdain. Deep down, he had a suspicion that no matter how hard he worked, he would never be able to win them over.

Stiger placed his food on his camp table. His tent was hot, but not unbearably so. It began to cool as soon as he tied the flap back, letting the heat out. Stiger lit a lamp so that he could see better and changed out of his armor, into a fresh tunic. Later, he would clean his kit and then go and find some water to clean up a bit before bed. In the morning, he would perform a proper toilet, which included a shave.

Stiger ate quickly. The stew was watery and poorly made, but he had come to expect nothing more from the army's cooks. Still, it was filling, and after such a hard day he enjoyed it, much more so than the salted pork that seemed to be a staple when the legion was on the march.

There was a cough. "Excuse me, sir."

Stiger looked up and saw Sergeants Geta and Tiro standing in the entrance to the tent. He gestured for the sergeants to enter and moved aside the mess bowl to make room for the company books. Sergeant Tiro followed Geta in.

Both were hardened by years of service. Geta had the look of a man who was simply mean to the core. Tiro, on the other hand, came off as a tough, no-nonsense sort of sergeant, and yet there was something almost fatherly about him.

Tiro was just over five feet in height and built like a stone house. It wasn't that the man had muscles upon his muscles, for he did not. He was clearly a strong and hard man, but that wasn't it either. Tiro had a natural way about him that projected the appearance of strength and confidence.

The two men before Stiger were an interesting contrast, but Stiger did not trouble himself too much with it, as both of the sergeants were below his station.

"I heard from Corporal Varus that you saw some action, sir," Tiro said.

"A minor scrap." Stiger was not willing to go into detail after his dressing down by the captain. He did not think it a good thing if it got back to the captain that he had been bragging. So he was more than content to play things down.

"Varus mentioned you saved the general's party," Tiro continued.

"Yes," Stiger confirmed but did not elaborate. The thought of the general's daughter came to mind. He had enjoyed escorting her back to camp. It had been months since he had spent time with a lady equal to his social rank, particularly someone his own age. She was educated and cultured. He wondered how soon it would be before he could find an excuse to see her again.

"The books, sir," Geta said and placed them on Stiger's camp table before stepping back.

Stiger opened the first book and thumbed to the latest page. He skimmed down the lines of entries, studying each. Sergeant Geta had made a number of notations in his thick, nearly illegible scrawl. These were deductions of income from several legionaries. Each deduction represented replacement equipment, such as new tunics, sandals, and parts of the legionary armor, like leather straps and padding that had worn out. The legion gave nothing for free. The legionary had to pay for it all. Expenses came out of their salaries and pension funds.

"That is a considerable sum for a shield." Stiger tapped the offending deduction next to Legionary Hagan's name with his index finger. "Six silver talons? Is that correct?"

"Yes, sir," Geta said.

"Why so much?" Stiger looked up at the sergeant. "The last I saw, a shield cost no more than two silver talons."

"Supply did not have any readily available," Tiro said. "So we were forced to turn to the merchants. It was the cheapest that we could find."

Among the camp followers there were always a variety of merchants ready to sell their wares for a premium. It was unfortunate for Legionary Hagan that supply had not had a ready replacement.

"Hagan's shield was old," Tiro continued, "and had he been wise enough, he should have had it replaced before we marched north."

"We're pretty far from the border," Geta explained sourly, "and the bloody merchants feel they can charge more than is right."

"I see." Stiger flipped back several pages, where all of Hagan's accounts were individually detailed. He was wondering if Legionary Hagan could afford such a large deduction. Would it put the man into debt? He studied the figures for a few moments. Hagan, it turned out, had served with the legions for nearly twelve years. Between loot disbursements and his salary, the man had built up a very modest pension. The cost of the new shield would eat into it, but he would still have a good bit saved for retirement. Should he survive the next few years, in Stiger's estimation, the man's pension should grow considerably. Stiger flipped back to the current page. He found it ironic that he was learning more about the inner workings of the company from the books than from his daily interactions with the men. Though he detested the work, he took his responsibility seriously, as honor demanded. He signed his name at the bottom with a charcoal pencil. "Very well then."

Stiger flipped to the next page and scanned through the deductions detailed there carefully. Everything seemed in order. There were no large sums being charged to the men. He signed once again, certifying the accounting.

"We took ten horses as prizes and some minor loot," Stiger said, looking up at Geta. "Varus has custody of it all. Make sure they are delivered over to supply and entered into the books."

The horses would need to be delivered to the legion's supply officer, who would reduce them to a monetary value. The general and the legion would take the lion's share of the prize money. Captain Cethegus and Stiger would receive a modest portion, and the company would receive a small amount to be divided amongst the men's pensions.

"Yes, sir," Geta said. "Sergeant Tiro will be happy to do it, sir."

Stiger saw a frown flick across the other sergeant's face, and a hint of a smile on Geta's. Despite their professional attitudes, Stiger had gotten the impression over the last few weeks that the sergeants disliked each other.

Well, Stiger thought, looking up at the two of them, their feelings for each other did not matter to him. In fact, he would prefer to not have them in his tent, let alone his very presence. Just like the men, they were common brutes. These two were likely only smarter and meaner than their fellows and had managed to claw their way as far as they would in life. Geta, who was standing close to Stiger, smelled strongly of sweat, onions, garlic, and cheap ale.

The sooner this was done, Stiger decided, wrinkling his nose in distaste, the better. Besides, Geta was the captain's pet, always hovering nearby Cethegus as if on a tight leash. With surprising relish, the sergeant frequently did the captain's dirty work when it came to punishment duties. The men feared the sergeant with good reason. Stiger had to admit, Geta made him uncomfortable as well.

Perhaps it was Geta who had the leash on Cethegus?

Stiger turned back to the book detailing the company accounts. He signed one last time and then turned to the company general fund. He scanned the additions and deductions, including the men's pay, which was due to be disbursed in a week. He signed here as well, but not before asking a dozen questions to make sure he understood why the sergeants had made certain decisions. After nearly an hour, he was done with the books and, with a stifled yawn, bid the sergeants a good night.

"Sir." Tiro hesitated at the tent flap. Geta had already left.

"Yes, sergeant?" Stiger looked up, irritated that Tiro was taking up more of his time.

"Rumor has it the legion will march in the morning, sir," Tiro said, as if it the orders had already been cut. "Seems our new general wants to take up the pursuit of the enemy. General Treim is an aggressive sort. I understand orders should be coming by in about an hour."

Stiger thought quickly. If true, it meant he needed to begin packing. Stiger was responsible for his personal possessions. The men would break down his tent, table, cot, and chair. All of it would be stowed for transport. Had the sergeant not given him advance notice, Stiger would have wasted an hour relaxing. When the orders finally arrived, he would have had to scramble, staying up later into the night than he had planned, with an early start in the morning and a long, hard day's march ahead. He grimaced at the thought.

"Thank you, sergeant," Stiger said, and found with surprise that he was actually grateful to the man.

"You're welcome, sir." Tiro stepped out into the night and left Stiger alone.

Stiger glanced over at his trunk, where his books were stored. He had been looking forward to relaxing on his cot and skimming through one of the histories he had brought with him. His eyes were drawn to his dusty and dirty armor. His kit required attention, and his personal possessions needed packing. Stiger let out a slow breath. There would be no relaxation tonight.

"Welcome to the army," Stiger said with a chuckle.

FOUR

Stiger put his back against the tree and looked wildly around. The rough bark scraped against his armor. His sword was in his right hand, shield in his left. It was almost completely pitch black out. He could barely see the handful of men who were still with him. Screams, oaths, and the clash of sword on sword rang out from all directions in a confusing cacophony. The wood around him seemed to echo with death.

Stiger's chest heaved as he gulped down air. His heart beat madly, thudding in his chest and ears. He longed to put the heavy shield down, but the thought of the enemy bursting from the darkness around him checked the desire.

"Sir." Sergeant Tiro paused, also struggling to catch his breath. "What are your orders?"

The moon poked out from behind a cloud and then just as rapidly disappeared, the near-absolute darkness returning. Stiger turned his attention to the hard-faced veteran. He knew from the company books the man had served over twenty years. In the darkness, Stiger could barely make out the sergeant's face and form.

The moon shed some of its light again as a cloud passed. The sergeant's jaw flexed as he waited for a response, but Stiger did not have one. He was not even sure what to do.

The Seventh, along with four other companies, had been assigned the task of taking a small wooded area from the Rivan. Scouting had reported that the wood, perhaps two miles long and half that deep, was only lightly held by enemy skirmishers. The assault, a rare night action, had been designed to catch the enemy by surprise and limit casualties with a rapid strike.

Unfortunately, it had not worked out that way.

The assembling companies had been spotted before they could even begin to approach the boundary of the wood. As they had gone in, arrow shot greeted them. The enemy was waiting.

In the darkness, the enemy's fire had been inaccurate. The men's shields had provided adequate protection, and as proof, there had been only one casualty up to that point in Stiger's company.

However, after only a few minutes under fire, Captain Cethegus had ordered the company to charge the wood. Stiger had felt the order a mistake, but said nothing. It had not been his place to question his commanding officer. The other companies had kept formation, even as the Seventh had charged blindly into the woods. Stiger now wished he had spoken up, though he knew it would have had little effect. The captain held little respect for his lieutenant.

"Sir?" Tiro asked. "Your orders?"

Stiger started to mouth a reply, but the sergeant abruptly turned away.

"Sounds worse than it is, boys," Tiro said in a steady voice to the men gathered around them. It was clearly an attempt to calm frayed nerves, and Stiger found it even worked on him. Despite breathing heavily from the exertion of the charge, the veteran sergeant was calm, collected, and confident.

Stiger looked from the sergeant to the men. He counted five others, each a veteran with years of service. All were looking to Tiro for direction, and that bothered Stiger. If they were looking to him, they were not looking out for the enemy, who in the darkness could be literally feet away.

"Turn round," Stiger ordered in a low voice so that it would not carry. "Shields up. Keep a lookout for the enemy."

The men immediately turned around, presented shields forward with swords readied, eyes and ears keen for any hint of the enemy. Stiger was relieved they had done as ordered without hesitation.

"Sir." Tiro stepped forward and lowered his voice. Stiger could smell the older man's sour breath. "The company must be reorganized."

"That, surely, is the captain's decision," Stiger responded hesitantly. He was not afraid to admit to himself that he was frightened. But it wasn't that he was concerned for his own safety. He was worried that if he made a decision, and it turned out to be to a mistake, he would be responsible for getting men killed. Without a doubt, the captain would love the opportunity to rake him over the coals.

Worse, though he had been trained from boyhood, Stiger felt wholly unprepared for the responsibility Tiro was attempting to thrust upon him. In the confusion of the fight, he simply did not know what to do. The captain had ordered the mad charge, but what now? His training, which he had thought more than sufficient, clearly was not enough. He was at a loss.

"Captain Cethegus is not here, sir," Tiro said quietly but firmly. "You are."

Stiger clenched his teeth in frustration and glanced around, more to avoid the piercing gaze of the sergeant. Their mission had been to take the wood so that afterwards the legion could safely move through to attack and secure the bridge over the Hana River. The bridge was supposedly just beyond the other side of the wood. And so, Stiger was here in this dark little forest, with screams and fighting all around.

"You are in command sir." Tiro grabbed at Stiger's shoulder with his free hand and shook him slightly. "At least until the captain can be found."

Oddly, the general's daughter came to mind. During the last five days' hard march, he had managed to see her twice. Though his time with Livia had been brief, she had been exceptionally polite and proper. More importantly, she had not discouraged him from calling upon her.

What would she think of him if she saw him now? Would she be disgusted to find him cowering in the darkness? The thought made Stiger burn with shame and self-revulsion. His behavior was not worthy of a Stiger. He cleared his throat.

"Very well," Stiger said, turning back to the sergeant. He hesitated a moment, unsure how he wanted to proceed. The sergeant certainly looked confident, almost as if he knew what needed doing. "What...what would you suggest?"

The sergeant blinked in surprise. Stiger mentally berated himself for showing weakness before one of the rank and file. He was an imperial officer, and a Stiger. He was supposed to be the one to know what needed to be done, not the sergeant.

"I would reform the men," Tiro said curtly. "There is strength in numbers."

Stiger nodded. He knew he would feel safer with more men around, and he was confident the enemy would be less likely to test an organized force. From the sounds of the confused fighting around him, it appeared as if the enemy had become dispersed too, though in the darkness nothing was certain.

"Reform the men," Stiger ordered.

"Yes, sir." Tiro turned away.

Stiger caught the sergeant's arm. "Use the Old Tongue," he said. Issuing movement orders in the Old Tongue was still taught during a recruit's basic training, but seldom used in practice. Stiger had never understood the reason why, as only the nobility bothered to learn the Old Tongue these days. Now, perhaps he had managed to make sense of the tradition. "That way the men know we are not the enemy calling them to their deaths."

Tiro gave Stiger a long, unreadable look before turning away. In his best parade-ground voice, the sergeant began calling out orders to reform on him. The men stood ready in a ring around him and Tiro should any of the enemy come out of the darkness. The sergeant called out again and then waited. At first, there was nothing. Then a rustling to Stiger's right drew his attention. Two legionaries appeared out of the darkness. They looked relieved. Both men fell in with the others. Tiro called again, and more legionaries materialized. Stiger's defensive ring steadily grew larger.

"Seventh," Stiger called out in the Old Tongue, adding to Tiro's encouragements. "Fall in!"

For several minutes, they continued to call out. The noise of the fighting in the wood suddenly intensified. Stiger estimated that the other legionary companies had finally entered the fight. More men flowed in, and Stiger's defensive ring grew larger still. There was no sign of the captain, though, or Sergeant Geta. In the past few weeks, Stiger had learned that wherever Captain Cethegus went, Geta was usually not too far behind. There was a running joke amongst the men that if the captain stopped short, Sergeant Geta's nose would go up his ass.

"Well, sir," Tiro said after five minutes with no additional legionaries coming in from the darkness. "I think that's about all we are likely to get."

Stiger glanced around, doing a rough head count. He reckoned he had close to fifty men on hand, which was a definite improvement over the five he started with. That said, it was not good either. "Fifty out of nearly two hundred men."

"Yes, sir," Tiro said in a neutral tone. "The rest are likely scattered about. We will find them later."

"This was supposed to be easy," Stiger said to himself. Captain Cethegus had said so when he had addressed the men prior to the assault.

"Nothing in war is easy, sir," Tiro replied quietly.

Stiger had not realized that he had spoken aloud. He mentally cursed himself for showing weakness yet again.

"Form the men into a single line." Stiger pointed with his sword in the direction of what he thought was the river. "Our job is to secure these woods. We will push through until we come out the other side. Perhaps we can set up a blocking position to keep any of the enemy from escaping."

"Yes, sir." Tiro began snapping orders, moving the men around. Within a handful of minutes, he had them formed up into a single rank. Stiger took a position in the center of the line directly behind the men. Tiro joined him. The moon made a showing, lightening the darkness a bit. Stiger saw Corporal Varus on the end of the line to his left and Corporal Tencha on the right. Stiger glanced over at Tiro and received a confident nod.

"Adva—"

Just then, a man came out of the darkness behind them and threw himself at the sergeant. Tiro caught sight of the attack at the last moment and dodged right, but it was not enough. The two men crashed together, going down in a tangle of arms and legs. Stiger stepped forward to assist, but there was an agonized scream. The attacker stiffened before going still. Stiger saw a dagger sticking out of the attacker's neck. Dark blood flowed out from where the steel met skin. Tiro rolled over onto his back.

"Are you injured?" Stiger asked.

"Only my pride, sir," the sergeant responded, looking up with a strained grin. "I've had recruits hit me harder than this fellow just did."

Relieved that Tiro was uninjured, Stiger offered a hand and helped the old veteran to his feet.

"What are you sorry lot looking at?" Tiro growled at the men who had turned around. The sergeant pointed down at the dead enemy. "That sorry piece of shit there is why I train you in hand-to-hand. He's fodder for the worms and I'm still breathing. Now, eyes front and prepare to advance."

The men turned back as Tiro bent down and retrieved his dagger. He wiped it clean on the cloak of the dead man he had just killed, then sheathed it. The sergeant casually retrieved his shield and then looked over at Stiger.

"Sorry to interrupt you, sir," Tiro said in a serious tone.

"Right," Stiger said, and then called out loudly, "advance."

"HAAAAH," the men shouted in unison, and began a steady advance deeper into the wood. The shout temporarily drowned out the sounds of fighting that reached out to them from the darkness. Stiger found it both reassuring and exhilarating. He was leading the men forward.

"Steady that line there," Tiro barked out harshly. "Close up that gap. You could drive a supply wagon through that. Step lively now."

Stiger looked over to see three men step around a large tree, which had broken the cohesiveness of the line. Within moments, Tiro was shouting and calling orders continually, as both the underbrush and trees conspired to break the integrity of the line. Stiger was alarmed as the implications sank home. If the enemy hit them in force, he could find his line easily broken up. Then again, the enemy would face the same problem.

"You there," Stiger snapped, motivated to speak up now that he had seen the danger himself. "Back in line."

The legionary glanced at Stiger and hastened his way through the brush, shield catching. Stiger's own shield got snagged on a low-lying bush, and he had to pull it through with some effort.

"Tighten up that line there," Stiger shouted as he looked back up to see the men before him move around a tree. This was followed almost immediately by a shout and the clash of sword on shield to his right.

The moon slipped from behind another cloud and the darkness lifted momentarily. Stiger glanced over to see a small group of Rivan soldiers attacking a part of his line. In the dim light and through the brush and trees, Stiger could barely make the action out. He judged it likely the enemy did not know how many men he had on hand. Stiger hurried over, following Tiro.

"Lock shields, lock shields," Tiro was shouting, which was followed by a solid thunk as the legionaries brought their curved, rectangular-shaped shields together. Coming up behind Tiro, Stiger counted only five of the enemy.

"You, you, and you." Stiger tapped the men he wanted on the shoulders with his sword, immediately to the right side of the action. They had their shields up as ordered, but there were no enemy to their front. "You men too, push around and into their side."

A dozen legionaries broke ranks and moved forward to hit the enemy from the side, jabbing with their short swords as they came on. The enemy, becoming aware of the danger, tried to back away, but there were just too many legionaries closing around them. They were cut down under a flurry of unrelenting jabs. None survived.

"Nicely done," Tiro called to the men. "Back in line now, boys, back in line. Hurry now."

"Line up," Stiger joined in. "Dress that line properly."

Under Stiger and Tiro's prodding, the line reformed. Stiger gave the order once again to advance. The line continued forward, with both Tiro and Stiger struggling to keep them from becoming too disorganized. Within moments, another group of Rivan soldiers, numbering ten in strength, emerged from the darkness. They were rapidly beat back, losing half of their number before the survivors turned and fled.

Once Stiger had reformed his line, the advance began anew. Soon after, they came across an enemy camp in a small clearing. There were half a dozen low-burning fires that smoked lazily upward, and as many tents. The smell of cooking food and fresh human excrement hung in the air. Stiger spotted an open latrine along the edge of the camp. The entire campsite was devoid of life.

Making a dash into the abandoned camp for the tents, the men broke ranks. Stiger blinked in surprise. No order had been given.

"As you bloody were," Tiro roared at them, enraged.

The sergeant's wrath halted the men, as if they had run into an invisible wall. They turned with guilty looks.

"Who gave you permission to break ranks? Get your sorry asses back into formation before I personally kick them there."

The men sullenly yet hastily fell back into line, looking warily toward the sergeant.

"Any man who breaks ranks again without orders will be on punishment detail for a week," Tiro shouted at them. He turned to Stiger and lowered his voice. "Can't have them looting when we have enemy all about us in these here woods, sir."

With a quick glance around, Stiger nodded in understanding. The sergeant was quite right. Keeping the men under a tight discipline was something that had been drilled into Stiger. The impulsive move might have exposed them to a counterattack had an enemy formation been about. It was something to keep in mind.

Stiger walked over to a low-burning fire. A cast-iron pot with a wooden ladle was hanging over it. He glanced inside and saw a watery stew boiling away. The enemy had clearly left the campsite in a hurry. Whether it was to contest the legionary attack or to flee, Stiger had no idea. Judging from the sounds of fighting ringing throughout the woods behind, he suspected it was the former.

He turned to look back at his men, who were lined up for battle. They were all looking to him, including Tiro. It was an unsettling feeling. Many of the men were much older, and yet these veterans were counting on him for direction. Stiger took another quick glance around the campsite, more to avoid the men's eyes than anything else.

Taking in the enemy camp, Stiger understood it was possible the legions would fail to secure the wood. As such, he knew it was his duty to see that nothing material was left for the enemy.

"Burn it all," Stiger ordered Tiro in a voice that sounded harsher than he had intended. "We will leave nothing of value for the enemy."

"Yes, sir." Tiro turned to two legionaries. The sergeant ordered the burning of the tents, packs, and anything else that was flammable. The men set their shields down and immediately moved forward to carry out their orders.

"Don't you bloody grumble," Tiro shouted at the men, turning on them in a towering rage. Stiger had heard nothing, but clearly the sergeant had. "By the sounds of ya, I'd think you were all wet-behind-the-ears, weak-kneed recruits. I should not have to tell you that before this war is over there will be plenty of loot for all."

Stiger's order had been an unpopular one, and he could understand why. Loot was an essential part of a legionary's life. It added not only to their purses, but also their retirement pensions. Any and all loot would be pooled and reduced to a monetary value. The majority of the men's portion, after the legion and company officers had taken their share, would be set aside for their pensions. The larger the pension, the better off the legionary would be upon discharge. Still, Stiger suspected for many of the men retirement was a long way off, and a few coppers or bronzes in their purse now would be more than welcome during their next leave or visit to the flesh merchants that tagged along with the camp followers.

Stiger shielded his eyes from the brightness of the flames as the tents were set alight. In the darkness, they blazed brightly. Most of the sound of the fighting was now squarely behind them, some distance away. Stiger scanned the darkness in that direction. The farther he had led his men into the depths of the woods, the more isolated they had become. Stiger realized that by pushing through the woods, this was solely his fault.

Tiro walked over to join Stiger. The sergeant had sheathed his sword.

"The farther we push forward..." Stiger said to Tiro, hesitating to finish.

"The deeper we get into it," Tiro finished with an understanding nod.

Stiger said nothing for a moment, but scanned the dark trees beyond the firelight. The men stood in an assault line while the campsite burned, waiting for him to make a decision. He was tempted to turn back and find one of the other legionary companies to link up with. However, if he did turn back, it was possible he would run smack into one of those companies and in the darkness be mistaken for the enemy.

Stiger glanced back over at Tiro. It pained him to seek the veteran's advice. As an officer, Stiger felt he should have all the answers himself. After a moment's more hesitation, he gave a slight shrug. The simple truth was that Tiro was more experienced. Stiger came to the realization that he would be a fool if he did not solicit the man's advice.

"Sergeant, what do you think?"

Tiro seemed surprised by the question and did not speak for a moment as he considered what to say.

"Push forward and out of this damned wood. Let's get to some open ground, sir. We make it to the other side where the river is and as you said...we are between the enemy here in the wood and their own lines." The sergeant paused and then grinned. "Perhaps, sir, we can even take some prisoners."

Stiger thought through the sergeant's advice. It made sense, and it was in line with his own thinking. There was precious little he could do in the wood, other than blunder about and into small pockets of the enemy. And there was, of course, the possibility of taking a prisoner or two, who could then be sold as slaves. There was profit in that.

"I did not join the legions to play it safe, sir," Tiro said.

"I suppose not." Stiger gestured toward the other side of the campsite. He had made up his mind. "We continue on, then. I think that is the direction of the river."

"I believe it to be, sir," Tiro confirmed.

"Let's get the men formed up on the other side of the campsite," Stiger ordered. He glanced at one of the burning tents. The oil that had been applied to weatherproof the canvas was giving off a distinctly unpleasant odor. "We will give them a minute or two to let their eyes adjust to the darkness, and then we continue the advance."

"Yes, sir." Tiro ordered the men to form up on the other side of the campsite. In moments they were reformed, with orders not to look back at the flames.

"Legionary Barus," Tiro shouted. "I can assure you that somewhere, someplace, a village is missing its idiot. Did you know that, legionary?"

"No, sergeant," the legionary responded.

"Don't you look back on the fires, you idiot," Tiro snapped to the legionary. "Keep your eyes to the bloody front and save your night vision for the enemy."

"Yes, sergeant."

Several of the men chuckled at the exchange. Stiger let slip a little grin and felt a lessening of the tension. He had only just joined the legion a few weeks ago, but he had already learned there was always one legionary who could be counted on to do something stupid.

Looking out into the darkness of the woods, Stiger once again felt unsure he was making the right decision. His anxiety increased as he rethought his order to advance through the wood. To hide his uncertainty, Stiger walked down the line of legionaries, casually inspecting them as he did so.

It was an attempt to make the men feel that he had everything well in hand. He felt like a fraud, that his uncertainty was transparent. The men straightened at his passing and gave no sign that they saw through the stern demeanor that he was working so hard to keep in place. Having walked the entire line, Stiger moved to the center and drew his sword. He looked to Tiro, who nodded casually. All was ready.

"Advance," Stiger called.

The company pushed forward, back into the trees. Stiger half expected to run into additional enemy like they had before reaching the campsite. The advance continued for another ten agonizing minutes, the men struggling around the trees and through the undergrowth. Then they emerged abruptly from the woods and out into the open. Stiger marched them ten yards from the wood and then called for a halt.

Moonlight bathed the land in a pale glow, which lit up the river less than a quarter mile away, down a slight slope. There was a wooden bridge, and beyond, perhaps a few hundred yards from the water's edge, a ridge rose to some height. The entire ridgeline seemed aglow. It took him a moment to realize it came from thousands of campfires. The main bulk of the enemy army was encamped on the other side of the river, just behind the ridgeline.

The enemy had prepared for their arrival, for the dark walls of a fortification just across the river rose up from the ground. In the darkness, the fortification seemed ominous and foreboding. Stiger could see the torches placed strategically along the top of the wall. Sentries walked its length.

"Sir," Tiro called, pointing toward the bridge. A body of men were marching across. Stiger glimpsed the movement, a half second before the moon moved back behind a cloud and darkness settled once again over the land. Tiro jogged over to Stiger. "That would be reinforcements to help the bastards hold the wood, sir."

"Coming our way then," Stiger said unhappily, and then glanced back toward the darkened wood where the sound of fighting could still be heard. It seemed to Stiger that the level of fighting had diminished somewhat, but that could simply be attributed to the distance they had come. He had a general suspicion that the legionary companies had the upper hand. Stiger had no facts to support this. It was more feeling than anything else.

He took a deep breath as he considered the situation. If the enemy reinforcement made it to the wood, they might just be able to swing things back in favor of the defenders.

Stiger glanced back in the direction of the bridge and the enemy reinforcements. He wondered if he could delay them long enough to allow the contest in the wood to be decided decisively in favor of the legion. Stiger nodded to himself. If he was aggressive and attacked, perhaps the enemy commander leading the reinforcements would think the wood already lost? It was a gamble, and one that might cause the death of all he commanded.

"Sir?" Tiro asked.

"I am thinking we attack those reinforcements." Stiger was surprised that his voice was firm and under control.

Tiro gave Stiger a long look, as if checking to see if the lieutenant was committed to this course of action.

"If we attack, it will delay any reinforcement of the wood and give our boys back there a chance to decide the issue. We may also convince those fellows coming at us that the woods are already lost."

Tiro mulled this over a moment, and then nodded.

"Max," Tiro called to one of the men. "Do you still have your horn?"

"You know I do, sergeant," the legionary responded. "I lose it, and it comes out of my pay, not to mention the shit punishment detail you would think up."

"Good boy," Tiro said, with a smile. "When I tell you, I want you to blow the signal to advance. You got that?"

"Yes, sergeant," Max replied without question. "The order to advance."

"Sergeant?" Stiger was confused. "Why would we want to alert the enemy we are coming? I doubt they saw us emerge from the wood before the moon disappeared again."

"Sir." Tiro stepped closer to Stiger and lowered his voice so only the two of them could hear. "When they see us, we have Max there blow his horn. It will confuse the enemy, sir. Horns are only used for brigade-size formations."

"You are suggesting that the enemy may conclude an entire brigade is about to emerge from the wood?"

"I am, sir. Seen it done before." Tiro nodded. "If we blow that horn, our boys in the wood may even come to our aid."

The sergeant knew his business, and though he should not be, Stiger was surprised by it all the same. He was also impressed. Tiro was unrefined, uncouth, and, though he could read and manipulate numbers, would be considered uneducated by Stiger's standards. He knew nothing of the classics or refined society. Outside of the army, Stiger would never have stooped so low as to associate with the man. And yet, he was coming to realize that lack of refinement did not equate to a lack of intelligence or competence at one's job. Tiro was a solider, and had been for much of his life. He had been a soldier for more years than Stiger had been alive. Tiro would not have been promoted to sergeant had he not been good at his profession.

Stiger stole a quick glance around at the men, who were waiting patiently for orders. They were brutish, crude, and coarse, just like Tiro. Among the ranks were drunks, thieves, murderers, rapists, and cheats. The legion accepted them all and gave them a purpose, in effect a fresh start at a new life.

Up until this moment, Stiger had looked upon them with disdain, creatures barely above beasts of burden who were hardly worth his attention. They had been mere pawns in his plans to achieve glory for himself and further prestige for his house. Did they have something to offer beyond their lives? Could they be more? It was an interesting thought, and one Stiger planned to think more on should he survive the next few minutes.

"Good idea," Stiger said grudgingly to Tiro. "When we advance, have Max blow the horn for all he's worth. Let's give the enemy something else to think about."

"Yes, sir," Tiro said. "Might I make another suggestion?"

Stiger nodded for the sergeant to continue.

"Form the men into a double line," Tiro said. "That way, should we run into greater numbers, you can move the men of the second rank about more easily to counter a turning movement."

It was another good suggestion. Stiger was again struck by Tiro's experience. He decided that, going forward, he would lean on the sergeant and learn all the man had to teach.

"See to it."

Tiro reorganized the men into a double-ranked assault line. As he finished, the moon once again emerged from the clouds. Stiger could see the enemy again. An entire company had crossed the bridge, organized into a marching formation. Though they were not quite headed toward Stiger, they were moving in his general direction, toward the wood behind him.

The Rivan company was around two hundred yards away. With each step, they were closing that distance. Stiger was fairly confident that the enemy had yet to see him. If they had, they would have halted and formed an assault line.

Once spotted, he hoped it would take them a few moments to become organized. The shock of finding an enemy formation so close should work in his favor. Stiger wished his men had their spears, but Captain Cethegus had ordered the weapons be left behind. The captain's reasoning had been that they were taking part in a night action in a wooded area. There was no need for the short spears, as there would be no massed tosses.

"All ready, sir," Tiro reported in a low voice. The sergeant had quickly and quietly aligned the men in the direction of the enemy company.

Stiger checked the straps on his helmet to make sure they were still tightly secured. Then he drew his sword, feeling its comforting weight in his hand.

"Draw swords," Stiger ordered, just loud enough for the men to hear. "Advance."

They started forward in a slow, determined step, shields presented forward, swords held ready.

Surely, Stiger thought, the enemy should see them. But apparently, even as the moon bathed the land in a pale light, they were not seen. The distance closed. Perhaps the Rivan thought they were a friendly formation?

"Now, Max," Tiro called when they were only fifty yards away. The legionary took a deep breath, brought the horn to his lips, and blew. The horn shattered the night with a sound so abrupt that, even though Stiger knew it was coming, still caused him to miss a step.

The enemy company seemed to hesitate mid-stride. They were close enough that Stiger could see the heads of the enemy come up and snap his way. Someone shouted, and the marching column dissolved.

"Shields up!" Tiro hollered. "We're gonna give them some steel, boys!"

"HAAAH," the men shouted in unison as their shields came up. "HAAAH."

Stiger had placed himself in the center, just behind the second rank. They were moving downhill toward the river at a slight grade, so he had a good view of the enemy. After the initial shock of surprise, the Rivan company was hastily forming a line of battle, with sergeants and officers shoving and shouting men into place. Stiger was impressed with how quickly and professionally the enemy shifted into a proper shield line.

"Keep blowing," Stiger shouted at Max, who had stopped. "I want them to think more are coming."

The legionary blew again, four rapid notes followed by a long one. Stiger's stomach knotted as the two formations neared contact. By his count, his men were heavily outnumbered...at least two to one. He glanced back toward the wood, beginning to question his decision to attack, and blinked in surprise. In the moonlight, men were emerging from the trees, and not just a few. They were in no way organized as they ran full on toward the bridge.

It took Stiger a moment to realize these were the defenders abandoning the wood. The horn! He glanced over at Max. The defenders in the wood must have heard the legionary horn coming from their rear and thought they had been outflanked.

There was a titanic crash to his front, and Stiger whipped back around. His front rank had reached the enemy's shield wall. The two sides were similarly armed and armored, the only difference being the shields. The enemy carried medium, rounded shields painted with a blue star outline. The polished-metal, conical helmets of the enemy glinted under the moonlight as they struck at the legionary shield wall with short swords. The Riven soldiers wore chainmail shirts over their tunics. Dark-blue capes that looked black in the darkness draped down their backs. Like the legionaries they faced, they were a professional force.

The legionaries had locked their long, curved, rectangular shields and pressed forward. At Tiro's urging, the front rank unlocked them just long enough to jab outward with their swords, seeking the flesh of the enemy.

This was Stiger's first proper standup fight. The sight and sound of it was shocking to the extreme. He had learned and studied a shield wall, had even seen it practiced during company drills. But he had never seen one in actual use. He had never had to command one and, at first, was unsure what to do. Tiro was pacing up and down the line, calling out encouragements to the men and occasionally shouting obscenities and threats when he saw something that he did not like.

Stiger's eye was drawn to the left side of his line. The enemy had a detail of men who were moving behind their formation in that direction. It was clear they intended to flank him. He looked over his second rank and saw Corporal Varus waiting his turn to advance to the front rank when the rotation was called. Stiger grabbed Varus by the arm.

"Corporal," Stiger pointed. "Take ten men from the second rank and form a right angle on the end of our line there. The enemy intends to flank us. Hurry, if you would."

Varus called to a number of men, and they jogged over to the end of the line, armor jangling and chinking. They quickly formed the right angle Stiger wanted. Varus arrived none too soon, as the enemy flanking movement hit a few moments later. The corporal and his men were hard-pressed. Stiger joined them at the end of the right angle, lending his shield to the shield wall, and found himself immediately pressed by an enemy soldier.

The feeling of uncertainty and fear left him as he blocked a jab with his shield. The blow was painfully communicated to his arm behind the shield. The pain woke an anger, and he jabbed out, seeking flesh. He threw the frustration and anger of the last few weeks into his attack and screamed at the enemy incoherently. His sword struck a shield hard. His hand tingled with the impact. Frustrated, Stiger slammed his shield at the enemy's, putting his shoulder into it. The two shields connected with bone-shattering force. Stiger's opponent staggered to the side, off balance. Stiger jabbed again, aiming for the man's leg.

The sword punched into the leg, and the man fell back with a scream of pure agony, collapsing to the ground. He dropped his sword and clutched at his ruined leg, which pumped out an astonishing amount of blood. Stiger knew he had dealt his opponent a mortal wound. He stood there a fraction of a second in shock, then the man next to him bumped his shield roughly as he shifted to ward off an attack. Spell broken, Stiger blinked and glanced over the fight along the flank.

"Push," Stiger called to the men with him, for he sensed that it was the right thing to do. "Push them back!"

The line slammed their shields forward and heaved into the enemy, who moments before had been attempting to flank the legionary line. It took only a few heartbeats, but the pressure eased. The enemy soldiers who had been sent to execute the flanking movement took several steps back. Then an enemy officer shouted an order and they fell back and around to their line, leaving half a dozen dead and wounded in their wake. Stiger stepped back, breathing heavily as Varus swung his men around to align properly with the end of the line. He then detached a man to see to the enemy wounded, who did so with a quick thrust of his sword.

Attempting to catch his breath, Stiger glanced around. For the moment, his line was holding. Enemy soldiers from the wood were fleeing in a vast stream toward the bridge. Some cast furtive glances at the two bodies of men locked in a death struggle, but none seemed interested or inclined to stop to assist their fellows. Max still blew on his horn. It was shocking to Stiger at how easily the enemy fighting in the wood had broken to such a simple trick.

"Sir." Tiro drew his attention, pointing. Another body of men was making its way across the bridge. Stiger's heart sank at the sight of additional enemy reinforcements. He glanced back toward the wood and saw, to his relief, a large formation emerging. It must be one of the legionary companies.

"Sergeant," Stiger said and pointed behind them. "Send Max to tell them to hurry."

Tiro called the legionary over and gave him his orders. Max dropped his shield and dashed off toward the legionary company, about two hundred fifty yards off. Stiger turned back to the action to his front. The enemy seemed to be extending their line out farther along both sides. It looked to be another attempt at a flanking movement, one that Stiger would be unable to match. It was not yet set, though, and he sensed an opportunity.

"Sir," Tiro said, stepping close. There was concern in the veteran's voice. "I think we need to do something."

"Push forward hard," Stiger said, without more thought on the matter. Instinctually, just like a few moments before, this felt like the right thing to do. If he hit the enemy now before they set the extensions to their line and pushed into them… "We only need to keep them off balance long enough for aid to arrive."

"Are you sure, sir?" Tiro asked.

"Lock shields right!" Stiger shouted as loud as he could, not willing to waste any more time debating. If this was going to work, it had to happen now.

He was rewarded with a solid-sounding thunk as the men brought their shields together and braced themselves. He had seen this formation drilled, studied it, and understood it in theory, but had never led men in its use, particularly in battle. If he survived the night, Stiger resolved to correct that oversight. There was a great deal he still had to learn.

"Push!"

With a massive effort, the men pushed a half step forward, and the shields unlocked in unison. The swords jabbed out and back. There was a tremendous racket, followed by a number of screams from the enemy, and then the shields locked back into place as the men shifted their weight to the opposite side, preparing to push the enemy line once again.

"Push!" Stiger roared and the men took another half step forward, throwing their weight into their shields. The shields unlocked for a fraction of a second to allow the swords to jab out once again. There was a clatter of swords striking both armor and shield, intermingled with a scream or two. Then the shields relocked. "Push!"

"Keep at it," Stiger shouted, his voice cracking from the strain. The enemy was giving ground grudgingly. "Push!"

"You've got them, sir," Tiro hollered, excitement coloring his voice. The enemy was now giving way, falling back at a quicker pace, and it was not due to his thrust into them.

The enemy commander was calling it quits. Having finally seen the approaching legionary company that had emerged from the wood, it was clear he was seeking to actively disengage. With the stream of Rivan soldiers fleeing the wood, it was apparent that the woods were thoroughly lost and that continued fighting was not worth the risk.

A gap appeared between the two lines, at first a foot and then a yard as the enemy stepped backwards in good order. Stiger was about to order his men to advance when Tiro turned and shook his head. "Sir, I think it might be best to let them go."

"What?" Stiger asked in astonishment. He had the enemy before him, and they were falling back. Why not turn that into a rout?

"Taking the wood was our objective, sir," Tiro reminded him. "We've done that. The enemy outnumber us still. It would not be good should the enemy turn and give us a drubbing in kind, what with that fresh company just over there."

Stiger glanced beyond the enemy company to their front. The second formation had halted and formed a line before the wooden bridge. Stiger took a deep breath, and the protest in his chest died. The sergeant was quite correct. The men were tired, and they had performed well. Stiger's decision to attack had kept the enemy from successfully reinforcing the wood. He had done all he could, and then some. Stiger glanced back and saw the friendly company nearing. He recognized the Tenth's distinctive standard and Captain Lepidus leading his men.

"Very well," Stiger said.

"Halt!" Tiro shouted at the men, who stopped and then automatically redressed their line. The enemy continued to pull back, and in moments, the distance had grown from a handful of yards to fifty. "Sheath swords and stand easy."

Shields came to rest on the ground, and the men gave a hearty cheer. A number of catcalls were sent the enemy's way as the Rivan company, seventy-five yards distant, calmly dressed their ranks to march for the bridge. They had left a number of wounded in their wake, who lay there screaming their pain to the world or begging for help. One dragged his ruined legs behind him as he crawled his way toward the bridge. Stiger returned his attention to the second enemy company. They had also reformed into a marching formation and were beginning to move back across the bridge. Stiger smiled with some satisfaction.

He had won his first victory.

"Lieutenant Stiger," Captain Lepidus greeted as he approached. The captain had stopped his company a few paces behind Stiger's men. The first hints of dawn were coloring the sky. "It seems the Seventh beat us through the wood. I would not have expected that kind of initiative from Cethegus."

"I did not realize it was a race, sir?" Stiger offered the captain a salute.

"I apparently did not realize it was one either." A tight smile escaped the man's perpetually stern demeanor. Lepidus glanced around at the aftermath. There were a handful of legionary wounded and a larger number of Rivan dead, lying sprawled where they had fallen. In some instances, the dead lay in perfect lines, as if they had simply gone to sleep next to one another. Tiro had men finishing off the enemy wounded, including the one who was attempting to escape by crawling away. "Looks like it was a spirited fight. Your first?"

"My first standup fight, sir," Stiger said, suddenly feeling bashful.

"Well." Lepidus gestured across the river. "There are more to come, perhaps even some worthy of a Stiger."

"Sir?" Stiger asked, coloring. He did not like the implication.

"Just a jest, lieutenant," Lepidus said, holding up a hand to forestall any further offense. He glanced over Stiger's men. "Say, where is your captain and the rest of your company?"

"I am not sure," Stiger admitted. "We were separated after he ordered the charge."

"Stupid thing to do...haring off into a darkened wood infested with the enemy," Lepidus said with outward disdain. He spat on the ground. The two officers were silent as they watched the last of the enemy cross the bridge. He then clapped Stiger on the shoulder. "If Cethegus got himself killed, the army will be a better place for it and, I think, the Seventh a happier company."

Stiger was not sure what to say to that. Lepidus spared Stiger one more glance and stepped back to rejoin his men. The Tenth's own lieutenant, Sadeus, had not come forward. Sadeus was Stiger's age, though he had been with Tenth Company for more than a year now. Much like the other officers of the legion, he had treated Stiger with disdain. He was with the men of the Tenth now, watching the enemy march across the bridge.

Lepidus spoke briefly with Sadeus. The lieutenant glanced in Stiger's direction and gave a faint nod of approval.

"Sergeant," Stiger called.

"Sir?" Tiro said.

"Detail several men to search the dead for loot," Stiger said, loud enough for his men to hear. They gave a ragged cheer.

FIVE

The Seventh marched back into the legionary encampment a few hours after dawn. The encampment was a fortified position that was protected by an earthen brick wall and capped with a wooden barricade. The sun was well up, and the early heat of the day beat down upon the weary men of the company. The sentries watched them curiously as the company passed through the wooden gates, snapping to attention and saluting as the officers trudged by.

Stiger's legs ached abominably. He stifled a yawn of exhaustion and lifted his head up. Captain Cethegus marched to the front of the company, Sergeant Geta at his side. The sight of the two of them brought on unhappy thoughts of the last few hours. Stiger's mood darkened.

The enemy had fired the bridge shortly after retreating over it. There had been nothing either the Seventh or the Tenth could have done to stop it. Had they tried to take the wooden span, both companies would have found themselves unsupported and well within bow range from the first of the enemy's defensive ramparts just a few feet beyond the river's edge. So, Stiger and his men, along with those of the Tenth, stood by and watched helplessly as the bridge burned.

Eventually the chaos in the wood behind them had died down. Elements from the other companies that had taken part in the assault emerged from the trees. Reinforcements also arrived, bringing with them pickaxes and shovels, prepared to begin digging defensive positions along the legion's side of the river should the enemy attempt to dislodge them.

In the growing light, the true, fearsome scale of the enemy fortifications had slowly taken shape. There were two powerful lines of defenses. The first ran along the river's edge and the second followed a small ridgeline that was nearly fish-hook-like in shape. Looking across the river at the first earthen rampart, Stiger knew with certainty that the enemy would not attempt to retake this side of the river, at least anytime soon. Their fixed defenses were just too strong. The Rivan wanted the legionaries to force a crossing, and they intended it to be bloody. The defenses were not some fresh construction hastily thrown together. Judging from the grass that grew thickly up to the wooden barricades of both lines, the Rivan had prepared their position months ago. Stiger suspected that a difficult campaign lay ahead, with the river crossing being just the first obstacle.

Stiger and his men had received new orders and marched away, following the Tenth. They had been tasked with helping to clear out any of the enemy still hiding out in the wood. In the early morning light, this task had proven much easier and was swiftly done. They had taken a number of prisoners.

The rest of the company, missing through the night, had also been found. This included Captain Cethegus, Sergeant Geta, and the company's standard bearer. Stiger had been worried about losing the standard. Should the enemy have taken it, the company as a whole would have lost its honor and been broken up. Everyone would have been disgraced and subject to some form of severe punishment, even the officers. The relief was palpable when the standard bearer turned up. The man had had the good sense to join up with Fourth Company after becoming separated in the darkness.

Stiger's men had found the captain wandering the wood with Geta and half a dozen others. Stiger had dutifully given his report, which Cethegus surprisingly accepted without comment or criticism.

"Thank you, lieutenant. I can manage from here," Cethegus had said. Then Stiger had been quietly but firmly dismissed. The captain had said nothing further to his lieutenant since then.

In the end, the cost to the company had come to five dead. Twenty more were wounded, three missing. They hoped that the last would turn up, having simply become lost or attached themselves to another company during the confusion.

As the company marched through the gates of the encampment, he could not recall a time when he had been more physically done in. Simply placing one foot in front of another was a tremendous effort. He longed to sit down and rest, taking the load off his feet. Only his determination not to appear weak before the men kept him going.

When on the march, temporary fortified encampments were carefully erected at the end of each day. They were planned and laid out by engineers, and the legions carried everything that was required to build them. From legion to legion, every marching encampment was constructed exactly the same way. When finished, these temporary camps resembled small tent cities, complete with streets, parade grounds, a trench, and very formidable walls, along with a host of other amenities. The legion could sleep securely in the knowledge that an enemy could not easily surprise and overwhelm the defenders. And so it was that each and every man relaxed upon arriving home, a place that was known to be secure.

Stiger, trudging along, picked his head up. Livia stood just inside the entrance gate, watching the companies that had participated in the assault return. Stiger felt his weariness melt away as their eyes met. She raised a tentative hand to wave and smiled.

Stiger wanted to break off from the company and go to her. Duty kept him in place, trudging along with the men. So he waved back and flashed Livia a tired grin. Her smile grew, and Stiger's heart warmed. At least someone here cared for him, he thought. Then she was gone as the company marched past.

"Company," Sergeant Geta hollered, after they had marched by several streets and come to the company's assigned parade ground. The sergeant's tone was weary, heavy with exhaustion. "Halt... right face."

The men came to a stop and then turned to the right. It was more of a scruffy shuffle than an actual turn. Captain Cethegus stepped out in front of the company. The captain was a small man. His armor was caked with soil. As dirty as he was, it made him somehow seem less impressive.

"Under trying conditions, you men did well. You distinguished yourselves, and made me proud," the captain said. To Stiger, the captain's words seemed insincere. He wondered what the men thought of it. "Sergeant Geta, dismiss the company."

"Fall out," the sergeant called, and the men fell out, moving toward their tents several streets away. The captain cast a disdainful look in Stiger's direction before turning on his heel and stepping off. Stiger delayed a moment, wondering what he had done to earn the look, and then shrugged. He was so tired that he found it difficult to care.

He considered walking back to see Livia, but a glance at his armor and the dried blood spattered across it convinced him that was a bad idea. Stiger was certain he smelled terrible too. He would seek her out in the morning, after he had had a chance to clean up thoroughly and rest.

In the privacy of his tent, Stiger took off his armor. He carefully undid each tie. As his funds were limited, his armor had to last him. His father provided only a small allowance and the legion paid him very little, especially after the officers' mess fee and funeral club expenses were deducted. The funeral club covered the proper handling of his remains after death and paid the cost for a priest to make the appropriate sacrifices needed to appease the gods and help him on his way into the next life.

So he took extra care with his equipment. If he were not careful, the leather fittings, padding, and straps would need early mending, if not outright replacement. He removed his soiled tunic and slipped on a fresh one before sitting down on his cot.

He was still a moment, enjoying the feeling of simply not standing. His feet ached dreadfully, not to mention the muscles in his legs crying out from the strain. Stiger contemplated lying down and going right to sleep, but a sense of duty checked that desire. Taking out a brush, rag, and some fine sand from a bag he kept under his cot, Stiger began the painstaking process of cleaning his armor and kit, slowly removing the blood and grime.

The entire process typically took around thirty minutes. Stiger did not rush. It had been drilled into him that if he took care of his kit, it would take care of him. As he worked, he thought on the man he had killed. Did the man have a family, children? He had not only taken the man's life, but everything the man was, and would ever be. Stiger let out an unhappy breath as he worked on cleaning his armor. Killing felt very different than he had imagined. Had their places been reversed, the Rivan soldier would have happily ended Stiger's life. By extension, a number of men had died due to his orders this night. It all came down to duty, Stiger decided. He knew with a certainty that his duty required him to become a killer and his position in the legions would demand him to order more killing. And he would do what was asked of him.

Once his armor had been tended to, he moved on to his sword. It was splotched with dried blood. As he was finishing up, there was a polite cough at the entrance flap of the tent.

"Yes?" Stiger looked up and found a legionary standing there with a steaming bowl in one hand. In the other, he held a mug.

"Excuse me, sir," the legionary said rather tentatively. "Sergeant Tiro thought you might be hungry."

Stiger sat back slightly on his cot. This was an interesting development. He had always had to go and fetch his own food from the officers' mess.

"Legionary Priscus, from Varus's file, right?"

"Yes, sir." Priscus stepped into the tent. The legionary was a large man, almost as tall as Varus, and yet he seemed uncertain standing before Stiger. He had to duck his head slightly to keep from bumping the top of the tent.

Priscus was a veteran, and if Stiger recalled correctly from the company books, he had served close to twelve years. Priscus handed over the bowl and mug. Stiger glanced down and saw it was a thin beef stew that smelled strongly of leeks. The mug was filled with ale.

"Thank you," Stiger said and found that he meant it. He was moved by Tiro's thoughtfulness and had to clear his throat before continuing. "Now tell Sergeant Tiro to make sure you and the men get some yourselves."

"I will, sir," the legionary said, retreating hastily from the tent. Stiger watched the man go. For a moment, he sat there. Then the smell of the food drew his attention.

Stiger had not realized he was so hungry. He ate greedily, cleaning the bowl, then drank the mug dry in one long pull. He sat there, content, enjoying the feeling of a full belly. Stiger yawned deeply. He rubbed at his tired eyes. It was time he got some sleep.

He let out a groan as he stood, over-stressed muscles protesting with every movement. He put the empty bowl and mug on his camp table. Stiger placed his armor, helmet, and sword on the rug in a corner of the tent so they were out of the way.

Stiger was proud of his rug, which he had purchased from a merchant in Mal'Zeel before he had set out to join the legions. Both the rug and tent were his personal property, and good quality. The rug covered the entire floor of the tent, which itself was high enough at the center for him to stand fully erect. The rug lay atop an oiled tarpaulin base that was tied upward to the interior walls of the tent itself and served to help keep any water out when it rained.

Satisfied he had tended to everything, Stiger lay down on his cot and realized belatedly he had forgotten to remove his boots. He chuckled. They were soiled and in need of cleaning. He considered getting back up to remove them, but was so tired he decided to deal with his boots later. The meal and ale were having an effect upon him. He yawned deeply, closed his eyes, and fell instantly asleep.

"Captain wants to see you, boy," the harsh voice of Sergeant Geta barked out, startling Stiger awake.

Stiger looked up, slightly disoriented. It felt like he had just closed his eyes, though he had the feeling that he had been asleep for some time. Propping himself up by his elbows, he looked at the sergeant. Geta stared back with an amused, almost nasty expression. Sergeant Geta was a big man, more so than Priscus. Heavily muscled, Geta was intimidating, and Stiger had always felt uncomfortable in his presence.

In a flash of insight, Stiger understood Geta's power resided in those who feared him. The sergeant took pleasure in having dominance over others. Stiger realized that he had inadvertently fostered an attitude of disrespect by not standing up for himself. This extended from fellow officers, down to Geta himself, who felt empowered by the captain's protection. Stiger abruptly saw the man for what he was, a bully. Geta had misjudged the situation, for Stiger did not fear him. Instead, Geta angered Stiger.

Stiger had seen combat, and it was not at all what he had imagined it to be. He had killed a man, and that made him a killer. Stiger was too tired to give it much thought, but seeing the sergeant there got him thinking.

Where had Geta been during the fight with the enemy company? What had he and the captain been doing all those hours? Had they been truly lost? Were they shirking?

"What was that, sergeant?" Stiger asked, swinging his legs over and sitting up. Stiger accepted that further sleep would have to wait.

"Captain wants to see you, boy." The sergeant grinned wickedly, exposing rotten and broken teeth.

"That's 'sir' to you," Stiger said in a deathly quiet voice.

The smile slipped from Geta's face, and an angry, malevolent look replaced it.

"Did you hear me, sergeant?" Stiger stood slowly, his muscles protesting with every movement. It was time to turn the tables on Geta. "Would you prefer me to make a charge? Disrespecting an officer is a serious offense. On my word alone, I could have you busted back to the ranks."

Geta's eyes widened as Stiger bent to retrieve his sword, which he slipped on. Stiger's eyes never left Geta's. The sergeant had been attempting to play a petty game of camp politics. Stiger had been born into a political family and had mastered handling such games from a young age. He had let this get out of hand, to the point where a mere sergeant felt free to denigrate him.

It was time to stop being a victim.

Geta was an enemy and would have to be watched. He had always been an enemy, but now that Stiger had just jerked on his chain, he would be an especially dangerous one, politically speaking. Stiger wasn't concerned about Geta physically harming him. Should a legionary be caught striking an officer, the punishment was death. Should one kill an officer, the punishment would see the entire company suffer in the form of a decimation, the killing of every tenth man, whether guilty or not. Though it was unlikely Geta would try to hurt or kill him, such outrages had been known to happen, and Stiger had to be on guard.

Perhaps he could turn the man and win him over? Stiger considered the possibility for a pregnant moment, then discarded it. There would be no winning him over, and besides, Stiger was not even sure he wanted to try. Geta was on Cethegus's side, and the captain cared little for his lieutenant.

"I did not hear you, sergeant." Stiger took a step forward. Geta had removed his armor and was wearing only a service tunic. He had no sword. Though he was unarmed, Stiger was not fool enough to let that deceive him. Geta had risen to the coveted rank of sergeant, and that meant the man was dangerous, armed or not.

"Sorry, sir," Geta grated out, backing up and out of the tent entrance to make way for the lieutenant. "I did not mean to offend."

Stiger followed him out into the midday sun and flashed a smile. "Of course not, sergeant. Now, why did you come?"

Geta was becoming red in the face. "Captain Cethegus has ordered you to report to his tent at once, sir."

"Very well," Stiger said, and then motion caught his attention. He turned.

Corporal Varus was standing just off to the side of his tent. Stiger had the feeling the corporal had overheard their exchange. Geta followed Stiger's gaze, and the sergeant's face hardened.

"Corporal?" Stiger raised an eyebrow.

"Sorry, sir," Varus said. "I did not mean to interrupt. I was just coming to report that Sergeant Tiro has seen that the men have been fed and are bedded down."

"Thank you, Corporal," Stiger said, very much doubting that was the real reason Varus was present. He could see from Geta's expression that the sergeant had his doubts as well. Stiger's eyes narrowed as he considered Geta. It seemed the two sergeants were more at odds than he had assumed. Perhaps it went beyond simple dislike? Then another thought occurred to him. Had Tiro sent Varus to keep an eye out for him? Stiger suspected he had, and his heart warmed at the thought.

"Sir," Geta said, turning to Stiger. "The captain is waiting."

Stiger said nothing, but instead immediately turned and made for the captain's tent, which was just ten feet away, leaving Geta behind. The sergeant, caught by surprise, hastened to catch up. Geta reached the tent just before Stiger.

"Lieutenant Stiger here for you, sir," Geta announced, stepping hastily into the tent.

Stiger followed the sergeant inside. He found Captain Cethegus seated at his camp table. A bottle of wine was open, the cork lying on the floor. The captain had just drained his cup and was in the process of refilling it with an unsteady hand. Cethegus looked tired. His hair was matted from his helmet and his eyes were red-rimmed. Stiger braced to attention and saluted.

"You asked to see me, sir?"

"About bloody time," Cethegus snapped in a voice slurred by drink.

Stiger noticed a second bottle had fallen and rolled off the table, lying on the rug by the captain's feet. Cethegus was a heavy drinker, but this seemed excessive.

"Yes, sir," Stiger said neutrally. He did not relax his position, but remained fixed at attention and made a point to stare directly above the captain's head, at the backside of the tent.

"Sergeant Geta," Cethegus said, "do you think the lieutenant could have gotten here faster?"

"I do, sir," Geta replied. "That I do, sir."

Stiger resisted the urge to turn and look at the sergeant, who moved over to his right.

"See what I am saddled with?" Cethegus slurred to the sergeant, gesturing with his free hand toward Stiger. His other hand held an overfull cup. The captain sloshed wine onto the camp table.

"Sir?" Stiger said, thoroughly outraged. He had just been rebuked in front of a ranker! Stiger's weariness had vanished, and anger heated his face.

"Do you have something to say, lieutenant?" Cethegus swung his gaze back to Stiger.

"I do," Stiger said quietly, and stopped at that. He had not been given permission to speak, so he had just answered the question that had been put to him.

"I don't care what you have to say," Cethegus spat, then turned back to the sergeant. "What do you think the lieutenant was thinking when he took half of my company off to fight the enemy?"

"I don't know, sir," Geta said. Stiger did not need to look over at the sergeant to tell the man had a self-satisfied smirk plastered on his face. Geta was clearly enjoying the dressing down.

"Neither do I," Cethegus slurred and took another long pull from his cup. He set it down hard on the camp table, spilling some of the wine. The captain's angry gaze turned back to Stiger. "Neither do I."

Stiger said nothing. He simply continued to stare at the back of the tent, though his face burned with shame at being dressed down in front of Geta. Cethegus's treatment was unforgivable, and unacceptable. Stiger was fed up.

"As inexperienced as he is, do you think it possible he could have gotten all of those men killed?" Refilling his cup with an unsteady hand, Cethegus turned to look back at the sergeant.

"It is very possible, sir," Geta said. "Very possible."

"See, not a wise move," Cethegus hissed, taking another pull from his cup. "Bold and stupid, just what I would expect from a young pup of a Stiger."

Stiger sucked in a breath but kept his tongue still as he analyzed the situation. Was Cethegus intentionally provoking him to anger? Did he want to bring a charge against his lieutenant? Or was it something else?

Stiger's family was in disgrace, but it was still powerful, and rich. The captain, on the other hand, was from a family that had seen better and more prosperous days. Years before, the captain's family had been extremely powerful. They had even controlled a senatorial seat. These days, the Cethegus house was a minor client of the Har'rian family, making the captain a virtual nobody.

The Har'rians were close to the throne. That said, they were not open enemies of the Stigers. Perhaps that was why Cethegus felt so bold? Did he feel protected? Or perhaps...he was just stupid, and drunk?

No, Stiger thought. That was not it. Something else drove the captain's behavior. His thoughts drifted back to how he had found Cethegus and Geta. Both men had been covered with soil and grim, as if they had wallowed in the dirt after a heavy rain.

Was Cethegus a coward?

Was he heaping abuse upon his lieutenant to cover for his own failures and inadequacies as a soldier and imperial officer? The thought was a surprising one, and for a moment Stiger's anger and outrage faded as he considered the possibility. He slowly breathed out.

"Fresh to the army, and the lieutenant feels he's already a great leader of men," Cethegus continued. "Sergeant, do you think he wants glory?"

"Absolutely, sir," Geta said, and the sergeant's tone smacked of deep satisfaction. "Stigers are well known for their glory seeking."

"That's right," Cethegus belched. "Stigers are known for bloody battlefields and glory hunting. I bet all you wanted was to enhance your family's prestige," Cethegus belched again and waved a finger at Stiger, "at the expense of my men, and all for some glory."

Stiger's anger mounted again. He had seen battle. It was ugly, brutal, and not at all what he had thought it would be. The last fight had shown him that battle was not glorious. Nor was it glamorous, as the tales and stories made it out to be. It was desperate, wretched, frightening ... but, he thought ... necessary. As he stood here in the tent, being verbally berated, his thoughts turned inward. Cethegus continued his abuse, but Stiger did not hear him as his mind raced. His aches and pains, along with the weariness, faded.

Personal glory ... was something that he no longer craved or sought. The thought was astounding. It was as if he had been struck by a bolt of lightning. Stiger blinked.

Growing up, he had been fed a steady diet of old tales passed down through the centuries of Stiger family prestige and glory on the battlefield. His family was one of the oldest and purest bloodlines in the empire, dating back to its founding. He was even distantly related to the first emperor, Karus the Great.

Stiger had naively set out to serve the legions in pursuit of this glory. He had been desperate to prove himself to those who thought he was not worthy of serving the empire he loved. He had been even more desperate to erase the stain on his family name and honor. In his desperation, he had debased himself by taking the disrespect heaped upon him by his peers. He realized that now, and the thought filled him with pure disgust.

He was a Stiger, and did not need to prove anything to anyone. It was as simple as that.

He had foolishly thought that the successful pursuit of glory would erase the stain to his honor, but having met the enemy on the field of battle and kept them from reinforcing the wood ... his reward was further disrespect, abuse, and derision. The captain was treating him as if he had lost the battle!

Cethegus continued to rage at him. Stiger ignored the captain's words. For years he had been ashamed of his family and his father's actions, which had resulted in their shared dishonor. He could not change what had been done, but... what could he do?

Stiger sucked in a startled breath. There was something that he could do, and it all boiled down to service. Stiger knew what must be done. Quite simply, he would execute his duty and serve his empire with honor to the very best of his ability. Through duty and service, not the pursuit of glory, would he work to redeem his family name.

His armor would be his honor, and service his sword.

Stiger would commit himself to this purpose. He would learn everything about his profession that he could. He would become a soldier of the empire, in spirit and mind. His overriding goal and objective now boiled down to service.

Here in Captain Cethegus's tent, Stiger realized that he was at a turning point in his life. He closed his eyes and begged for the High Father's help, offering up a silent prayer. A sense of serenity washed over him, almost as if the great god had granted his request.

Stiger opened his eyes. For the first time in weeks, he felt in control. Cethegus was still ranting drunkenly, heaping further verbal abuse upon him. Geta stood there, almost gleefully agreeing with the captain.

Stiger's eyes left the back of the tent and traveled down to Cethegus. He saw his captain in a new light. The man was weak, small, and petty. Cethegus was attacking a fresh lieutenant, a man under his own command, and leaning upon a lowly sergeant to do so. Stiger had performed the empire a service, and instead he was being flayed for it. Cethegus was a disgrace of an officer, and Stiger felt ashamed at having tried to win the man's approval. Stiger felt disgusted just being in the presence of this wretch.

"No," Stiger vowed to himself. "I will never be like that."

Cethegus stopped in mid-rant and blinked blearily up at Stiger. His eyes narrowed dangerously. "What did you say?"

Stiger had not realized that he had spoken aloud. He locked eyes with his captain, and for a moment said nothing. Cethegus looked away, eyes going to Geta for support.

"Perhaps, sir," Stiger said, "had I been able to locate you, you could have rallied the company and led the men forward yourself. You might have taken that burden from me."

"What?" Cethegus asked, eyes going wide and leaning back in his chair. Through his drunken haze, it took him a moment. He seemed stunned by the implication of his lieutenant's suggestion. "How dare—?"

"Sir," Stiger interrupted in a firm tone, "we were unable to locate you..." he paused and looked over at Geta, "and Sergeant Geta until after the fighting was over." Stiger turned his gaze back on the captain. "Can you tell me where you were? The wood was not overly large. Surely you heard our horn call to advance?"

Cethegus paled, eyes still impossibly wide, and he half stood before sitting back down hard in his chair. He was too drunk to stand. He looked up at Stiger, clearly unsure what to say. The silence in the tent stretched. A fly buzzed loudly around them, breaking it.

"Get out!" Cethegus shouted, pointing a finger at the tent entrance. "Get out!"

Stiger saluted, turned, and, before exiting the tent, spared Geta a disdainful look. He read surprise in the sergeant's eyes, and then anger. Stiger offered the sergeant a knowing wink before stepping past him, out into the sunlight and the heat of the day.

A few feet away, he spotted Sergeant Tiro, who abruptly looked busy inspecting the load in a wagon he had no business with. Yes, Stiger thought to himself as he walked back to his tent, Tiro was a friend. It brought a smile to his face.

Cethegus, on the other hand, was something altogether different. Stiger knew the man was an incompetent drunk... but was he also a coward to boot? He had no evidence to support such an allegation, only a gut feeling.

Geta was anything but a coward. Yet, both men were dangerous. Stiger had thought that by entering the legions, he would see himself free of politics and his family's shame. Instead, he now understood he would never be free of politics. His family shame would follow him wherever he went. He felt a deep sense of burning dishonor at his behavior and resolved to no longer shy away from that either. He would own it.

Stiger ducked back into his tent, removed his boots, and laid down on his cot. The wood supports creaked in protest. He rubbed at his eyes, feeling incredibly tired as the exhaustion washed back over him. Could he succeed? Would he succeed?

"Only time will tell," he said aloud to himself and then closed his eyes, with a deep sense of satisfaction and a new feeling of direction. He rolled onto his side and in moments was asleep.

Six

"Orders for you, sir."

Stiger's eyes snapped open. He propped himself up on an elbow and looked at the legionary who was standing just outside the tent flap, holding it back so he could peer inside.

"What?" Stiger demanded, seriously irritated at having been awoken again. He did not know all of the legionaries from the company by name yet. "What do you want?"

"I have orders for you, sir."

"What time is it?" Stiger sat up, swinging his legs over the side of his cot, and rubbed his eyes.

"Two hours past noon."

Stiger yawned. He motioned for the legionary to enter his tent and took the orders. Breaking the seal, he read and shook his head in dismay. He read them a second time, not quite believing what his eyes were seeing.

"But we were in action all night!" Stiger was outraged. He looked back up at the legionary.

"Sorry, sir," the legionary said, taking a nervous step back from the angry lieutenant. "Sergeant Geta gave me the orders for you. Said they came over direct from headquarters and I was to wake you straight away."

Stiger glanced down at the orders again. They were scrawled out in the rough scratch of the sergeant's own hand. Cethegus was likely too drunk to rewrite the orders himself, or perhaps he was passed out. Stiger read it again, as if that would change the content.

His orders were to take a file of men and scout south along the river's edge for any sign of enemy activity. Stiger yawned again and covered it with the back of a hand. This was clearly a punishment for his actions earlier in the captain's tent. He shook his head and then crumpled the orders. He should have known better.

"Very well." He stood, his entire body seeming to protest. "Send for Sergeant Tiro. Have my horse saddled and brought around."

"Yes, sir." The legionary saluted and left with evident relief.

Stiger grabbed for his armor and slipped it on, shrugging his shoulders about to get a comfortable fit under the weight. He pulled the straps tight before securing them, then laced up the front with practiced ease, making sure the laces were as tight as possible. That way, if it came to a fight, the armor would stay in place and not shift about, throwing off his balance. Stiger's father had purchased the armor from a master smith back in the capitol. It was well made, and if Stiger cared for it, he should get years of use before needing to fully replace it.

"Sir?"

Stiger turned to find Sergeant Tiro, who looked as if he had just been awoken from a sound sleep. The sergeant's face was understandably etched with weariness.

"I have orders to take a file out on patrol."

Tiro seemed surprised by that but said nothing, waiting for Stiger to continue.

"I am to check the river traveling south for enemy activity. Select a file that is not too worn out, and get them formed up. We will be back after dark, so make sure the men draw rations for evening meal."

"Yes, sir," Tiro said, saluting. The sergeant left as Stiger slipped his sword on and secured it in place.

He then glanced down on his soiled boots.

"Well," he said to himself. "At least I did not waste time cleaning them."

Stiger stepped over to his camp table, where he had left a bottle of wine. He uncorked the bottle and took a generous swig. His mouth tasted foul, and the smooth-tasting wine helped wash that away. His checked his haversack. It was still full with his precooked rations from the night before. Salted pork and hard bread. He would need to refill his two canteens, which were empty. At least there would be fresh water available, Stiger thought ironically. He would make sure to fill them when he got to the river.

Stiger glanced around the tent, his eyes lingering on his cot. He longed for more sleep, but that was not to be. Life could be patently unfair at times. He abruptly smiled, recalling his meeting with Cethegus.

Then he remembered his vow and sobered. Whether he liked it or not, it was time to do his duty. He grabbed his helmet and shield, then stepped from his tent. The file that had been selected by Tiro was hastily falling in on the parade ground.

Stiger saw Corporal Varus hustling from a tent. The corporal was still lacing up his armor as he walked out before his men. He had placed his helmet on his head so that he did not have to hold it while he finished securing his armor. Because it was not tied, the helmet tilted to an odd angle and threatened to fall off his head.

"Move your sorry asses," Varus called back harshly to the men, who had yet to emerge from the tents. "The legion doesn't pay you to sleep all day!"

The men were red-eyed and bleary-looking from lack of sleep. They looked just as Stiger felt. Most were fastening their armor, and some were still emerging from their communal tents, where they slept eight men to each.

Varus stopped to properly lace up his armor, holding his shield with his knees. "Sir." He saluted crisply as soon he saw Stiger. His helmet rolled forward over his eyes, and the corporal broke mid-salute to catch it and shove it quickly back into place. Varus brought his hand down to salute fist to chest once again, the shield still between his knees.

"Corporal," Stiger acknowledged the salute, struggling to keep the amusement from his face.

"Would you be wanting the men to have spears?"

Stiger thought on the matter briefly. The enemy was on the other side of the river. It was unlikely the patrol would encounter more than a handful of enemy scouts brave enough to swim across. Judging from the fortifications he had seen, Stiger doubted the enemy would send any significant force across the river. Besides, the orders had stated that there were no known crossings for at least forty miles in either direction. He was simply looking for evidence of the enemy scouting the legion's position.

"No, Corporal." Stiger shook his head. "I do not expect we will need them."

"Yes, sir." The corporal looked relieved.

Stiger smelled coffee brewing nearby and looked around. One of the cook wagons had a good-sized caldron boiling over a fire. "Make sure the men get some coffee before we depart."

"Coffee?" Varus looked around and saw cook wagons. His eyes lit up at the prospect.

"As soon as the men are ready with all of their kit, have them get a cup," Stiger said. His orders had not specified that he leave immediately. The men were sore and weary. A few minutes' delay would not violate the spirit of his orders, and it would help sustain the men on the long march to come.

Stiger stepped over to the cook wagon and motioned for the cook's attention.

"Sir?" The cook was a civilian, one of the many contractors that the legion hired before marching north.

"Coffee," Stiger demanded.

The cook nodded and ladled coffee into a worn, wooden cup.

"Here you go, sir, freshly made."

"Thank you," Stiger said, and then gestured toward Varus's file behind him. "My men will each require a cup as well."

The cook glanced over, then shook his head. "Sorry, sir. This is for the guard detail."

"Make some more then." Stiger turned away, leaving the cook with a helpless expression as the first of his men made their way over to the wagon.

Nomad was led over. The horse's ears perked up when he saw Stiger. Well, Stiger thought, at least I won't have to walk. His legs were stiff and felt like they had lead weights attached.

"Excuse me, sir."

Stiger turned and saw Tiro striding over. The sergeant had his armor on and looked as if he intended to join the patrol.

"Sergeant?" Stiger asked with some surprise. "What do you think you're doing?"

"Coming with you, sir." Tiro's cheerfulness sounded a little forced. The sergeant continued before Stiger could say anything further. "Seeing as how I was somewhat helpful last night... might I offer the lieutenant some more advice, sir?"

Stiger nodded, curious as to what the sergeant had to say.

Tiro drew nearer and lowered his voice. "I would recommend leaving your horse behind. I would not want you standing out, sir."

Stiger glanced over at Nomad, unwilling to part with the promise of riding rather than humping it ten miles out and back.

"It might prove unfortunate," Tiro continued, "should we encounter an enemy scout with a bow and unnaturally good aim."

"You think that possible?"

Tiro shrugged, as if to say, "Better safe than sorry."

"Well," Stiger said, expelling a breath. "Looks like I will be humping it alongside the men."

"As a right proper infantry officer should, sir," Tiro said in the same cheerful manner.

Stiger stepped over to the legionary, who had led his horse out.

"Thank you," Stiger said, "but I've decided I will not be needing my horse."

"Yes, sir," the legionary said. As Nomad was led off, Stiger felt that his horse looked a little crestfallen. He felt the same.

Stiger watched them go and took a drink of the bitter brew from the cup the cook had handed him. It had not been sweetened and was poorly made. But the drink was hot and welcome, despite the heat of the day. Stiger felt cheered by it and rapidly drained the cup.

"Thank you," Stiger said as he signed his name in the log book and then made a notation of his orders to patrol. The officer of the day, Lieutenant Kinsus of Third Company, had kept him waiting an interminable ten minutes before turning his attention to Stiger. It was just one more show of discourtesy that rankled Stiger. He pushed his irritation aside. His focus was now duty and service.

His men stood waiting just outside the gatehouse for their lieutenant to sign them out. Stiger slid the book back in Kinsus's direction across the table. The other lieutenant spun the book around and examined Stiger's signature and notation. He signed his own name next to Stiger's, dated it, and then closed the large log book with loud clap.

"You may go," Kinsus said in a bored tone, and deliberately turned his back on Stiger.

Keeping a check on his temper, Stiger made his way out to the waiting file and gave the order to march. The sentries came to attention and offered Stiger a salute as the file passed through the gate. He dutifully returned their salutes and continued on his way, walking next to the men, with Tiro at his side.

The legion was encamped in a meadow about a mile from the wood where the action had taken place the night before. They marched around two large catapults that were slowly being drawn by teams of oxen in the direction of the river.

They had returned on the road earlier this morning. It cut right through the wood, traveling to where the bridge had been. He decided to take it, as he did not want to make his way through the tree-filled undergrowth of the wood. They had a long and hard march ahead, and there was no need to add to the difficulty.

As the file neared the wood, they came across several companies of allied auxiliary infantry. These were engaged in clearing the wood—removing bodies, weapons, equipment, and any loot that had been left behind from the night before. Besides the piles of equipment and loot, they came upon a line of legionary bodies, laid shoulder to shoulder off to the side of the road. Stiger counted twenty. All eyes from the file were upon the dead as they passed them by. The legionaries' capes had been thrown over their faces so that the dead could not be readily identified. Stiger took a deep breath. There was a good likelihood some of those were men from the Seventh.

"Poor sods," Tiro said, marching at the lieutenant's side, and Stiger found that he agreed with the sergeant. He recognized that he could have easily been amongst them, had it not been for Tiro's prodding that he do something. Seeing an officer's greaves on one of the dead men, Stiger shuddered. Death, he thought, was the great equalizer.

A file of cavalry trotting in the opposite direction passed them by, a colonel amongst them. A lieutenant riding alongside the colonel abruptly reined in.

"Stiger, right?" the lieutenant asked with a smile.

"Carbo," Stiger greeted, recognizing the cavalry lieutenant.

"Stiger?" The colonel pulled up, holding the reins of his horse in one hand. "You are the Stiger the general spoke of then?"

"He is," Carbo confirmed with a grin. "In a very timely manner, he pulled our bacon from the fire, sir."

"Halt the men," Stiger told the sergeant, and Tiro did so with a wave of his hand. The file stopped and rested their shields upon the ground as they were told to stand at ease. They looked on curiously. Stiger ignored them.

"Well then," the colonel said, "a job well done, lieutenant. I am Colonel Aetius, at your service."

"Thank you, sir," Stiger said, graciously accepting the compliment.

The colonel nudged his horse toward Stiger and leaned over, offering a hand. After a brief shake, the colonel straightened back up in his saddle. Aetius looked over Stiger's men with an appreciative eye.

"You have some fine men here," Aetius said.

"They gave a good accounting of themselves last night." Stiger glanced back at Varus's file.

"You were involved in the fighting, then?" Aetius seemed surprised. "I was under the impression that those companies had been stood down for some well-earned rest."

"Yes, sir," Stiger said. "The Seventh."

The colonel cocked his head at that. "I understand you were the first company through the wood?"

"We were, sir," Stiger said.

"You wouldn't be the lieutenant I heard about from Lepidus?" Aetius's eyes narrowed. "The one who led several files against an entire enemy company?"

Stiger nodded, surprised the colonel had heard an account of the action.

"Sergeant," Aetius addressed himself to Tiro, while casually pointing a gloved hand at Stiger. "Last night, were you with this man?"

"I was, sir." Tiro snapped to attention. "We gave it to them bastards, just like they deserved."

"I see," Aetius said with an approving nod, before turning back to Stiger. "Where are you off to, lieutenant?"

"I was ordered to lead a patrol down the south side of the river, sir." Stiger drew out his orders, which he had stuffed in the pocket of his cloak. He suddenly regretted having crumpled them in a fit of anger. He smoothed them out and handed the paper over to the colonel, who clicked his tongue after reading.

"Proceed with your patrol, lieutenant," the colonel said stiffy. "I will speak with the staff officers who issued these orders. When you return, you and these men are to have the next day off. Those are my direct orders. Anyone who desires to contradict them is to see me. Is that understood?"

The men of the file broke out into a spontaneous cheer. Stiger frowned, but he noticed that the colonel seemed slightly amused. It was, Stiger suspected, the reaction the man had intended to elicit.

"Yes, sir," Stiger said. "Thank you, sir."

"Make sure you catch up on some rest." Aetius jerked a thumb in the direction of the river. "There will be plenty of action in the coming days."

"Yes, sir," Stiger said.

"Sergeant." Aetius turned toward Tiro. "Would you kindly look after the lieutenant? It seems we may have an officer of some worth here."

"I plan to, sir," Tiro said with a glance over at Stiger. "I plan to."

Stiger colored and saluted. The colonel nudged his horse down the road, following the cavalry troop, which had not stopped.

"Good show, old boy." Carbo grinned at Stiger, and then nudged his horse forward after the colonel. "I say, good show!"

Stiger could not help but return the grin. After weeks of abuse from his fellow officers, he suddenly felt much better. His resolve to do his duty to the best of his ability was only reinforced. Stiger watched the two officers ride off, then nodded to Tiro.

"Forward," the sergeant hollered, "march."

The bridge, which had been a long wooden span, was now a charred ruin, and had collapsed into the river. Only a few beams and pilings were still visible. Much of the debris had been carried down river. The causeways on both sides of the bridge looked remarkably undamaged. The river moved quickly around where the bridge had been, attesting to the shallowness of the water there.

Directly across the river, the first enemy fortifications sprang upward in an earthen rampart topped with a wooden barricade. Enemy sentries walked the wall, gazing curiously across the river at the legionaries. Every fifty feet, an archer's tower with a shielded platform rose up and above from behind the defensive wall. The second line of enemy defenses was a more formidable position. It ran along a small, natural ridgeline a few hundred yards behind the first wall.

From what Stiger could see, along the ridgeline there was a deep trench, followed up by the rampart that ran at least a mile in either direction. The position's strength impressed Stiger, and he knew without a doubt the legion would be expected to storm it.

The enemy was firing no artillery, simply looking on at the legionaries from across at least a hundred yards of water. Only their sentries could be seen along the barricade, nothing beyond. It was almost surreal. Stiger felt it was like the calm before a storm. He took this as an encouraging sign though. Perhaps the enemy did not have any artillery.

The legion and auxiliaries on their side of the river had been far from idle. Hundreds toiled away. They had thrown up the beginnings of their own rampart. Looking over the growing earthworks on the legion's side of the river, Stiger could not understand why they were making the effort. He assumed, however, that General Treim had a good reason.

Several legionary artillery pieces had already been brought up. These sat idle, while their crews worked at constructing defensive positions around their machines or toiled with pickaxes and shovels to level the ground.

Of the machines that had already been maneuvered into position, a group of engineers were busy placing small white flags in the earth to their front. These flags ran out in straight lines toward the river.

For the moment it was peaceful, but Stiger suspected that would not last long, at least until all of the legion's artillery had been brought forward. Then the fury of the legion would be brought down upon the enemy defenses. He was interested to see what that would look like.

Stiger turned the march southward. They paralleled the river, which was to their immediate left. Within a short time, both the enemy across the river and the artillery had been left behind. The area they marched through had once been fertile ground, populated with small farms and plantations. All of that was now gone. What had been here just a few weeks before had been razed. This was now an empty, desolate land, burned by the Rivan. Even though the locals living here had been the enemy, Stiger found it depressing.

"This is the way of war," Tiro said. "Either we do it, or the enemy does it for us."

Stiger's eyes were on the burned remains of a house. A small farm, judging by the stone boundary walls that hemmed in a modest field. The inhabitants hadn't had much, but now had much less. Stiger wondered where they had gone. After a moment, he shrugged. Though he did not like what he was seeing, there was nothing he could do about it. Besides, the plight of those who had once lived here was irrelevant to him. Though he found himself caring, he had a job to accomplish, and he would do it.

"The Rivan brought this war upon themselves," Tiro said, when Stiger did not reply. "They started it by continued raiding across the border. Their sack of the border city of Din'esh pushed us into this war. They deserve what they get."

Stiger looked over at the sergeant and considered the man. He was a commoner who could read and manipulate numbers. He had served the empire for many years with enough distinction to rise to the coveted rank of sergeant. If Tiro survived to his retirement, he would receive a healthy pension, and a considerable plot of land.

The land would likely be in a recently conquered province, centered around a veteran's colony. Tiro would be able to buy a number of slaves and farm if he desired. He would also have the option to sell his plot to a land speculator. Either way, he would live out his years in comfort and security amongst other retired legionaries, as long as he didn't squander his funds. It was everything the average legionary desired, or so Stiger had thought. As he considered the man, he wondered ... did Tiro want more? Could he be more? The last few days had opened his eyes to the men of the ranks.

"What if this had been your farm?" Stiger suddenly asked the veteran.

"My farm?" Tiro shot Stiger a hard look. "My farm, you say?"

"Yes," Stiger said. "Say, after retirement, this is your family's plot, what then?"

"I don't have a family yet, but..." Tiro rubbed his jaw as he thought for a moment. A fierce look crossed the sergeant's face. "I would fight the invaders, and kill all I could. I have seen it happen, during the campaign in the Wilds. The locals took to the forests and made us pay, but we repaid them back in kind."

Stiger nodded at that and glanced around. There was a stand of trees ahead. Tiro followed Stiger's look, then glanced over at the file in marching formation.

"Perhaps, sir," Tiro suggested, "a skirmish order?"

It had not been Stiger's intention to suggest such a change by glancing toward the trees. Stiger simply nodded, and the sergeant barked out an order. The formation loosened up and spread out. Men specifically called on by Tiro pushed out to the front and sides of the file, eyes watchful for the enemy and any hints of a potential ambush.

They were moving along the river, the banks tall with grass. The river was around a hundred yards across at this point, slow-moving and deep. From the looks of it, the water level rose significantly when it rained. Stiger wondered how low it got in the dry season.

Besides the ruined bridge, were there other places one could cross? If there were, it might be possible to flank the enemy's fortified position, thereby making a contested crossing unnecessary. Stiger sighed softly with regret. He was only daydreaming. Had there been a viable crossing, the cavalry scouts would have found it already.

The file passed through the stand of trees without incident, coming to the remains of a large plantation. The fields had been burned, the buildings razed. Stiger thought about taking the time to explore to see if there was anything of value that could be salvaged, but then disregarded the idea. The legion was lacking nothing in terms of supply, and there was no need for foraging. Besides, any loot would likely not be worth the effort and could only serve to delay them further. The men were already tired. The sooner the patrol finished, the better.

He wiped at sweat dripping down his brow and into his eyes. Marching in full kit was taking its toll. Stiger glanced around. They had marched into a large open field several hundred yards long and just as many wide before the next stand of trees. Ahead, a single, large isolated oak tree provided abundant shade. It was the lone occupant of the field and had grown up just a few yards from the river's edge. Stiger thought it was a perfect place to call a break. They would be able see anyone coming with plenty of time to form up.

"Sergeant," Stiger said when they came up to the tree. "We will take a thirty-minute break."

"Yes, sir." Tiro called to the men to halt and fall out.

"Make sure the men refill their canteens." Stiger recalled that his own were dry. "And set some sentries."

"Of course, sir."

Stiger leaned his shield against the tree. He left Tiro and made his way carefully down to the riverbank. There were several rocks that traced a path a few feet out into the river. Stiger stepped from one to the other, until he came to a large flat one. He removed his helmet and ran a hand through his sweaty, matted hair. Setting the helmet down on the rock, Stiger knelt down and refilled his canteens. The river water was cold to the touch. He splashed some water on his face and enjoyed the cool feeling. He thought about taking off his boots and putting his feet in the water, but then dismissed the idea. He had best stay with the men, should something happen.

Stiger made his way back to the file and to the tree where he had left his shield. He sat down and leaned his back against the bark, armor scraping slightly against it. Stiger stifled a yawn as a warm breeze rustled the leaves above. He took a long pull from his canteen. The cold water felt wonderful. Leaning his head back against the rough bark of the tree, Stiger closed his eyes.

"Excuse me, sir."

Stiger jolted awake, and he realized with alarm that he had dozed off. He looked up and found Tiro standing before him. There was no recrimination in the older man's eyes.

"I think it's time we get the men up and moving," Tiro said, and then lowered his voice. "I hope you don't mind, sir, but I let the men rest another ten minutes. It seemed like they needed it."

Stiger glanced around. Several of the men had also taken the opportunity to catch up on some sleep, while others diced and talked quietly amongst themselves. The sentries Tiro had posted faced outward, watchful and alert.

"Very well," Stiger said, stretching and stifling a yawn. "Get the men formed up."

"Time to fall in, ladies," Tiro called. "Nap time's over."

The men pulled themselves to their feet. Those who did not stir or move fast enough received a good-natured kick from the sergeant or the corporal. Skirmish order was set, and shortly they were on the move once again, armor and shields jingling and chinking with every step.

"How far do you think we've come?" Stiger looked to Tiro, who had once again placed himself by Stiger's side.

"From the ruined bridge back there?" Tiro jerked a thumb backward.

"Yes."

"I'd say around four miles, sir," the sergeant said, and that squared with Stiger's estimation.

"Another six to go then," Stiger said, cracking his neck. His helmet was literally becoming a pain in his neck. He considered taking it off and securing it about his neck like the men, but decided against it, as it would only transfer the weight and discomfort elsewhere.

"That's why the gods blessed the infantry with feet, and not hooves, sir," Tiro commented. "We always get there, just not as quickly."

Stiger chuckled at that. He was really beginning to like the old sergeant.

A thick line of trees stretched from the river's edge to their right in a near straight line for as far as the eye could see. It was a deep, dark, and impenetrable-looking forest, nothing like the small wood they had fought in the night before. There were no visible roads or paths into it. The forest just seemed to spring up before them. Stiger found it unsettling.

"I wonder how deep it is," Stiger said to Tiro.

Varus stood next to the sergeant, holding his helmet in his hands. The corporal's short-cropped brown hair was matted. Sweat dripped down his brow.

"I dunno, sir." Tiro frowned as he surveyed the tree line.

"How far do you think we've come?"

"I reckon near about nine miles." Tiro glanced over to Varus, looking for confirmation. The corporal nodded, but said nothing.

Stiger agreed with that assessment. The afternoon heat had seemed to increase with each mile, and Stiger's legs ached with a dull throb.

"Should we turn back?" Tiro asked. "It will be difficult going in there, sir."

From what he could see, the forest was thick with under-growth. Though he wanted to agree with his sergeant, his orders were to patrol ten miles south from the bridge. It would be easy to turn around, and no one other than Tiro and the file would be the wiser. Stiger reflected on that for a moment, and glanced back the way they had come.

"I don't think so," Stiger said after a pregnant pause. He'd made an oath to the High Father to do his duty to the best of his ability. Stiger knew he would be justified in turning back, but something urged him on. Weary from a long night and little sleep, followed by a hard march in the heat, Stiger felt anyone else would have turned back. Two days ago, he suspected even he would have. But not this time.

"We continue on."

"Are you sure we should, sir?" Tiro glanced at Stiger, then eyed the seemingly impermeable forest again. "It will be very easy to become turned around in there."

"Not if we stick within sight of the river." Stiger gestured at the water off to their left and then grinned at his sergeant. "Besides, it will be cooler in the trees, and we will be out of this damned sun."

"There is that," the sergeant agreed unhappily. "Forward."

The file pushed up to the tree line, and then into it.

Stiger found it difficult going, particularly with his shield, which seemed to snag on every branch and bush. At first, it was as if the forest itself were resisting their intrusion, with each step a challenge.

Once in the trees, though, as he had suspected, it became much cooler. But the effort of moving through the trees and undergrowth negated the coolness, as Stiger and the men expended more energy fighting their way forward. After a few minutes of struggling, Stiger noticed that, ten feet from the river's edge, the forest underbrush thinned considerably. It was, he suspected, a result of repeated flooding when it rained. Regardless of the reason, he directed the men to move there, and the going proved much easier.

A quarter mile in saw them stumble upon a small trail that led from the river back into the forest. Stiger stopped the men and examined the trail, which traveled around a hundred paces deeper into the forest before disappearing around a bend. Stiger saw Varus studying the ground around his feet. Curious, he moved over to the man.

"These tracks are somewhat fresh," Varus said, kneeling down to examine them. "Cows, I think."

"Cows, here?" Stiger asked, surprised, and looked down where the corporal was kneeling. The grass and dirt had been clearly disturbed by a number of hooved feet. Stiger remembered the cattle tracks at the crossing of the small river, back during the supply run when they had encountered the drovers who had delayed them. The tracks did appear similar.

"Probably a village, or perhaps even a plantation up that way," Tiro said, gesturing down the trail. "I'd say they drive their cows this way to the river for watering."

Stiger glanced toward the river twenty or so feet away. It was nearly concealed by the trees, and he could only see a hint of blue. He looked back up the trail and rubbed at his jaw.

"Let's explore up the trail a ways and see what we find," Stiger said, curiosity trumping his exhaustion.

"Yes, sir," Tiro said unhappily as Varus stood.

"You think we should head back?" Stiger asked the sergeant.

"It's been a long night, sir, and an even longer day," Tiro said with a sigh. "The men are tired."

Stiger could not disagree with that, and then something occurred to him.

"Corporal." Stiger turned to Varus, who looked over. "Have you seen any signs of our cavalry? The scouts? Any tracks?"

"Once we entered the forest?" Varus shook his head.

"The pampered and spoiled cavalry," Tiro spat on the ground. "It's more likely they skirted the tree line, following it around to the other side."

"Then it is possible," Stiger said, thinking aloud, "that we are the first legionary force to explore this forest?"

Tiro's eyes narrowed and he nodded, suddenly looking around with some concern. Stiger could almost read the man's thoughts. There could be enemy about.

"I want to see what's up the trail," Stiger said firmly, deciding the issue.

"Yes, sir," Tiro said, and then hesitated.

"Sergeant? What is it?"

"Sir, as you know, I fought in the Wilds. Instead of taking the entire file, why not send a couple of men to explore. Two men will be a whole lot quieter."

Stiger thought about it. The campaign in the Wilds, a heavily forested area had become legendary amongst the legions. Tiro had survived that ordeal, which meant he had seen hard action. The sergeant's advice was sound.

"Right then," Stiger said and looked at the corporal who had identified the tracks. "Varus and I will go. Rest the men here."

"Sir?" Tiro said, alarmed. It was clear he was not pleased with the lieutenant heading off with only the corporal as protection. "Are you sure about this?"

Stiger felt some irritation at his orders being questioned and ignored Tiro. Instead he turned to Varus. "We leave our shields here."

Stiger leaned his against a tree, happy to be rid of the heavy encumbrance. Varus, apparently realizing that Stiger was serious, set his shield down as well. The corporal did not look too terribly thrilled to be leaving the security of the file, but he knew how to follow orders.

"If we are not back in forty minutes, come looking, and make sure the men stay quiet."

"Yes, sir," Tiro said, gravely.

"Let's go," Stiger said to Varus, and they set off, leaving the file behind.

The trail led them on a meandering path through the woods, as if whoever had cut it had not known what a straight line was. Stiger was unsure how old the trail was, but he was sure that it had taken some effort to make. The trail was not maintained as a well-traveled path might be, but it looked as if it were regularly cleared to keep it passable. Perhaps animals were even permitted to graze along it to keep the grass and undergrowth from growing too high.

Neither Stiger nor Varus said anything as they walked, carefully listening for any hint of the enemy. They followed the trail for a half mile until it led them to a small fenced-in field that, like the trail, had been cut right out of the heart of the forest. At the far end of the field was a farm with a good-sized barn. Unlike all of the other buildings they had passed, these were undamaged. Around the fenced-in field and buildings, the wall of uninterrupted forest continued.

"What do you think?" Stiger asked the corporal as they crouched down behind some brush so that they could not been readily seen by anyone who might be about.

"I think, sir, that no one is home."

"How can you tell?"

"No smoke from the farmhouse," Varus said, gesturing with a hand, "and no animals around. Whoever lived here left, probably in fear of what we would do to them."

Stiger realized that the corporal was right. If someone were living here, a fire would be going day and night. Smoke was an indicator of habitation, and the chimney on the farmhouse belched no smoke.

"Let's go explore." Stiger started out into the field. Varus hastened to catch up.

"The fields aren't enough to maintain more than a handful of cows, sir," Varus told him as they neared the farmhouse. Stiger looked over at the corporal, wondering how he knew that. Varus shrugged. "I grew up on a dairy farm, sir. Cows need a lot of grass, and feed."

The farmhouse, a one-story building with three rooms, was abandoned. After examining the outside, they went in. The fireplace held only ash, and the stones that lined it were cold to the touch. Whoever had lived here had eked out a modest living. There were only a few meager possessions left, and none worth taking. Whatever else there once was had been carried off with them.

Stiger and Varus exited the farmhouse and went around the side, past a cord of neatly stacked firewood, to the barn. Besides a brown cat prowling for mice, there were no animals. Behind the barn, another small trail cut farther into the forest. Stiger was disinclined to explore it.

"Nothing and no one here," Varus said.

"How old would you say those tracks are?" Stiger asked the corporal, a thought coming to him.

"The ones we found on the trail?" Varus asked, to which Stiger nodded. "A week...maybe a few days more?"

"Which way were the tracks headed?" Stiger glanced around the farm. Sure enough, he spotted a well no more than ten feet from a wooden watering trough. Next to that was a feed bin.

"I think toward the river, sir," Varus said after reflecting on it a moment. "Likely to water the cows."

Stiger studied the field. The fencing went completely around the field, with the only gate near the farmhouse, not by the entrance to the trail. He studied the well and watering trough again. There were several large buckets sitting next to the trough.

"Come on," Stiger called and started walking quickly back the way they had come, eager to check the trail for tracks. Varus watched for a second, not understanding, and then hurried to catch up.

"What's wrong, sir?"

"I think," Stiger explained, "this trail might just lead to a ford."

"A river crossing?" Varus asked with skepticism. "Truly?"

"If I am right, and I might not be," Stiger said, looking over at Varus, "it may mean we can avoid having to directly assault the enemy fortifications."

"I bet," Varus said as he climbed over the fence penning the field in, "the general would be pleased if you were right, and so would much of the legion."

Stiger pulled himself up and over the fence, then froze. Out of his peripheral vision, for a split second, amongst the trees, he thought he saw someone. He glanced to the right, but no one was there. He narrowed his eyes and scanned the trees. There had been someone there, dressed in greens and browns. He was sure of it.

"What is it?" Varus asked, noticing Stiger had stopped.

"I thought I saw someone," Stiger said, drawing his sword, "just over there."

He pointed to the trees to their right, just ten feet away. Varus drew his sword as well. Stiger led the way to the spot. He saw no one. He strained to listen, eyes scanning the trees. All he heard were birds calling to each other and the tree limbs swaying with a gentle breeze.

"No tracks, sir," Varus said, having examined the ground. "Are you sure you saw someone?"

"No," Stiger admitted, questioning himself. "I thought I saw someone out of the corner of my eye."

"We're all tired, sir," Varus said. "By rights we should be in our tents and not out here."

Stiger nodded and sheathed his sword. He scanned the trees once more. He saw nothing out of the ordinary. Though...he could not shake the feeling that they were being watched. Shrugging, he chalked it up to nerves and lack of sleep.

"Let's go." Stiger set off for the trail without a glance back. Varus sheathed his sword and followed.

Stiger found the file where he had left them. The men were sitting down and resting. Tiro had placed sentries. They offered Stiger a hasty salute. With Varus in his wake, Stiger moved past them toward the river. Tiro had been dozing. A legionary nudged him awake. The sergeant looked up as Stiger strode past him with a purpose. Tiro stood and followed.

Stiger reached the riverbank and looked down. Sure enough, there were cow prints in the grassy bank. The tracks led right down into the river itself. There were impressions a few feet into the water. He looked across the river to the other side, which was just as tree-covered as this side. The riverbank was high, though he thought he could detect a hole in the tree line directly opposite from where he stood now. He squinted and held a hand above his eyes to shield them from the sunlight as he scanned the far bank. Though grassy like this side, it looked to have been marked up somewhat.

"What is it, sir?" Tiro asked him.

"I think this is a ford," Stiger said, pointing to the opposite bank. "There looks to be a continuation of this trail on the other side of the river. Don't you think?"

"Could be," Tiro said, with some skepticism. The men, curious as to what was going on, had gathered behind. "That water looks right deep."

Stiger glanced down at the tracks in the mud again and considered what Tiro had just said.

"You wouldn't know it, but cows are surprisingly good swimmers," Varus said, having come up behind them. Stiger shot the corporal a look to see if the man was making a jest. Varus looked serious. "Good cows could make it across this if they did not have to swim too far."

Stiger studied the river and the far bank for a moment more. He removed his sword and laid it off to the side in the grass. He then started unlacing the front of his armor.

"Sir," Tiro protested, "you can't be serious. Send one of the men first, a good swimmer perhaps?"

"I am going myself," Stiger said firmly. It was his theory that this was a crossing, and as such, he had decided to take the risk upon himself. He also counted himself a good swimmer. "Besides, it's gods awful hot out. A swim is just the thing to cool down."

Stiger finished undoing his armor. He handed it off to Varus, then took off his boots. Without the armor, he felt incredibly light on his feet and for a moment marveled at the feeling. He slipped his sword back on, and then noticed Tiro had also taken off his armor. The sergeant looked up at him and grinned.

"I think you are quite right, sir," Tiro said cheerfully. "A swim on a hot day like today sounds just fine."

Stiger felt relieved that he was not going alone, but did not let that show. Once Tiro was ready, both men entered the water.

The cold was a rude shock. Stiger's feet rapidly began to ache. He put the pain from his mind as his feet sank into the soft, muddy bottom of the river. It felt slimy and disgusting on his skin. The current, despite its slow-moving appearance, was fast but manageable as they worked their way deeper. The water rose rapidly from their calves to knees and then waists. The farther they went, the stronger the flow tugged at them, threatening to drag them from their feet.

Stiger glanced back and saw the entire file watching them intently. Stiger thought he could even read concern in the eyes of the men. He idly wondered if it was for both of them, or just Tiro, who seemed to be a more popular sergeant than Geta.

The water level went from their waists rapidly to their chests and then just under their arms. Any deeper and it would be up to their necks. Both men moved carefully, lest they lose their feet and be carried away.

"We're almost halfway," Tiro said. "If this gets any deeper, I fear we will be swimming."

"I know," Stiger said with some concern as his feet bumped painfully into a large rock. He turned to look back at Tiro a couple feet away. "Just a little farther and it should start to get shallower."

"You think—ahhh!" Tiro lost his footing, head immediately sinking beneath the surface. The sergeant's hands flailed, splashing water into Stiger's face.

Stiger made a grab for him, while at the same time hooking a foot around the submerged rock he had just inadvertently bumped into. His hand caught hold of Tiro's woolen tunic. Stiger hauled back as hard as he could. The sergeant's arm caught his fast in a vicelike grip. Stiger felt himself being pulled forward, foot slowly slipping against the slimy rock. He strained to hold onto the rock, but it was no good. They were seconds from being swept downriver, then Tiro found his footing. Supporting each other, they were both able to stand safely and firmly.

A cheer sounded from across the water. Tiro looked around at Stiger. Both men broke out in relieved grins before laughing.

"Thought I might have to swim there for a moment," Tiro said. "Thank you, sir."

"You can thank me when we are both safely across," Stiger said. He released hold of Tiro and continued working his way carefully across. A few feet farther, sure enough, the depth of the water began to lessen, from their chests back down to their waists. They staggered the last few feet to the shore. Breathing hard, both collapsed onto the grassy bank on the far side. Once again, the men of the file cheered.

"I would not have thought it so." Tiro propped himself up on his elbows and looked back across the water. He waved the men down to keep them from cheering again. "How did you figure it out?"

"The marks on the bank," Stiger said, gesturing around them. He explained briefly about the abandoned farm. "And there was a good-sized well, with a watering trough no more than ten feet away, complete with buckets for hauling water. There was no reason to run the cows down to the river for water, not when you could just as easily draw from the well." Stiger paused to catch his breath and looked back the way they had come. "This crossing is likely only used when the flow of the river drops."

"Makes sense," Tiro said.

"As the legions neared, whoever lived at that farm brought their cows this way when they fled across the river. Varus thinks the tracks are only a few days old, and besides, he said so himself, cows are surprisingly good swimmers."

"The gods' fortune then." Tiro nodded, breathing heavily, and then laid his head back on the grass. "They smile on the empire and frown on the Rivan."

"If it had rained, well..." Stiger said, "those tracks would have washed away, and I would never have seen it."

Stiger stood and stumbled up the steep riverbank. He was curious to see if the trail continued on this side of the river. Sure enough, there was another trail just over the side of the bank.

"We need to report this," Tiro said, looking up at Stiger.

"Yes, we do." Stiger rubbed his jaw. "But first, I want to do a little exploring."

"Exploring?" Tiro pulled himself slowly to his feet, a concerned look in his eye. "I'm not sure that's such a good idea, sir?"

"I want to find out if the enemy knows about this ford," Stiger said, turning around to face the sergeant. "We need to see if there is any evidence of patrols about."

Tiro glanced back across the river, clearly pondering what his lieutenant had just said. Stiger wondered if he would object, but then the sergeant turned to Stiger and nodded wearily.

"You are right, sir," Tiro said in a resigned tone. "We shouldn't go too far, though."

"Of course. Only a little ways, I think."

"Wait for us," Tiro hollered across the river to Varus. The corporal gave a thumbs up in reply.

Barefoot and feeling every stone and stick underfoot, Stiger continued up the riverbank and stepped onto the trail. He glanced back up the river, trying to judge how far the tree line went, but could not see the end of it. He figured, when they marched back, he would be able to see how far it went before ending. Moving slowly and as silently as possible, the two men padded up the trail in silence, intently listening to the sounds around them.

After a short distance, the trail abruptly ended. Crouching low and staying undercover, both men were faced with a large meadow beyond. It was fenced in but completely empty of livestock. The fencing looked old and in many places had completely collapsed. Stiger looked carefully around, but could see no evidence of anyone about, nor any domesticated animals. The grass growing in the meadow was at least waist high. It was good grazing ground and it was a wonder that it was not being used. In the distance to the north, he could see a large smudge of smoke—enough that it could be a settlement.

"A plantation?" Stiger asked Tiro. "A small settlement?"

"Something, a village perhaps. Certainly not a town, sir," Tiro said. "Perhaps three or four miles off."

Stiger nodded.

"I don't think we should go out there," Tiro added. "If a cavalry patrol comes across us, we'd be dead."

"Let's work our way in the trees then, heading north," Stiger suggested, and Tiro reluctantly nodded.

Staying in the trees, both men moved rapidly, careful where they put their bare feet. Having gone a tenth of a mile, they came across another trail that headed back toward the river. This one was larger than the one they had taken from the ford.

"I don't think we should explore it," Stiger said, though he longed to see what was down the trail. Perhaps there was a farm or something? Since crossing, he had found a reserve of energy he had not known he had left. His exhaustion and aches had vanished, replaced by the excitement of discovery.

"We should head back before we are discovered, sir."

Stiger nodded, then they both heard voices and the sound of feet from father down the trail. They looked at each other before quickly moving back into the brush. They had gone perhaps five feet when Tiro's forceful hand pushed Stiger roughly down to the ground. Stiger turned around to face the trail and made himself as flat as possible. Tiro did the same.

Stiger lifted his head to look. Through the brush and undergrowth, he could see two enemy soldiers walking up the trail as if they did not have a care in the world. They each carried several canteens that dripped with fresh water—more canteens than two men needed. It looked as if they had fetched water for an entire file. Both were deeply engaged in a conversation as they neared where Stiger and Tiro hid. Both spoke a foreign tongue.

Not taking his eyes off of them, Stiger's hand reached for his sword, only to have Tiro's hand clamp down forcefully upon it. Stiger looked over in surprise at the sergeant, who slowly shook his head before returning his attention back to the enemy soldiers. Tiro released his grip, and Stiger turned to watch the enemy. Keeping himself pressed tightly to the ground, Stiger dared not move a muscle. He held his breath as the two soldiers moved by less than five feet away. They continued past, walking out into the meadow and heading in the direction of the smoke.

When they were gone, Stiger slowly sucked in a breath and eased himself up.

"Sorry, sir," Tiro whispered, coming to a crouch. "Had we killed those two, their fellows would have come looking for them."

Stiger was ashamed that he had not thought it through himself. There had been no enemy soldiers watching the ford they had found, so it stood to reason the enemy did not know about it. Had they killed the two, a search might have revealed their presence, and the existence of the ford. Again, Tiro had proven his solid thinking and wisdom. There was a lesson here, he realized.

"Right," Stiger whispered. "I think we have pushed fortune beyond any reasonable measure. Let's head back."

"Yes, sir," Tiro said, looking relieved.

The two men quickly and carefully retraced their way back to the trail and then followed it to the ford. Across the way, Varus looked relieved when they appeared. Without any hesitation, both Stiger and Tiro plunged into the river. They carefully worked their way across. Stiger found the cold of the water just as shocking as before. His feet once again ached abominably from the frigid water, but he put it from his mind as he concentrated on making the crossing safely, lest he be swept away like Tiro almost had. Before he knew it, the water level was receding.

"Get the men back and out of view," Stiger ordered before he had even made it ashore, wishing he had thought of it sooner. "The enemy is on the other side, and we can't risk being seen here."

Stiger and Tiro made their way up the bank and followed the men out of view. As Stiger put his armor back on, he glanced up at the sky through the trees. The light was beginning to dim significantly. He had already known his patrol would return well after dark. Due to his exploration, they would return much later than he had thought.

"We have to get back and report this," Stiger told Tiro and Varus as he dressed, feeling an urgency. If the legion could get a significant presence across the river without the enemy being wiser, it would completely unhinge the enemy's fixed defensive position. The general, Stiger reasoned, might be able to achieve surprise, attacking the enemy from the flank. Perhaps there was even an opportunity to destroy the enemy army. The potential of his discovery was exciting, and Stiger was eager to be on his way.

As soon as they were ready, Stiger had the patrol move out. He pushed them hard, allowing only two stops for short breaks. At one of the stops, the men were permitted extra time to eat their rations. They made it back to the legionary encampment late into the night, with the moon high in the night sky.

"Sir," Stiger said. "We must pass this right up to the general."

"You don't tell me what to do," Cethegus snapped back, badly slurring his words.

At the captain's tent, Stiger and Tiro had found Cethegus in a very poor state, deep into the bottle.

"But, sir," Stiger said, "this is important. We found an unguarded ford across the river. There is no need for a—"

"Silence," Cethegus yelled, getting to his feet and staggering slightly. "Get out!"

"The general must be informed," Stiger said firmly, thoroughly outraged at the captain's response to his discovery. This was critical information that could directly affect the campaign.

"And he will be," the captain hissed, his face going livid with rage. Cethegus abruptly took a deep breath, and a calculating expression crossed his face. "You and your men are not to speak of this. Leave this matter to me. That is an order."

"Sir?" Stiger said, outraged.

"Now get out. Your very presence—like curdled milk—turns my stomach."

Tiro grabbed Stiger's arm and pulled him away.

"Lieutenant, it has been a long day," Tiro said quietly. "The captain has stated his intention to report this to the general. You have what you came for."

Stiger glanced at Tiro, then allowed himself to be led away. At the tent flap, he turned and saw Cethegus pour himself another drink before sitting back down at his camp table. The man did not seem moved to urgency by Stiger's information, and for a moment Stiger considered taking the matter back up again. Instead, he let the tent flap fall back into place and stepped out into the moonlit darkness.

Stiger was thoroughly disgusted. He shared a momentary glance with Tiro, who, Stiger realized, was just as unhappy. Stiger looked in the direction of the headquarters tent. He knew that Colonel Aetius would listen to him, but if he did that, he would be violating the chain of command and his orders. Cethegus had ordered Stiger to leave the matter with him. Besides, he thought, if he went to headquarters, it would only make things much worse between him and the captain.

"Let it go, son," Tiro said quietly. "You've done all you can."

Stiger hesitated, then nodded. A male slave carrying a bucket of water walked by them, head bowed, gaze locked firmly on the ground. Stiger's eyes narrowed as he watched the slave pass out of earshot. Stiger looked back at Tiro. He recalled what General Treim had said about there being a spy.

"See that the men keep their mouths shut as the captain has directed," Stiger said. "We can't afford word to reach the enemy."

"Yes, sir," Tiro said. "I will."

Stiger glanced back at the captain's tent, then turned away for his own tent.

SEVEN

"That's not how you do it," Sergeant Tiro shouted at a legionary as Stiger looked on. "Is it?"

"No, sergeant," the legionary responded, looking straight forward as the sergeant got in his face.

"Then why are you doing it that way?"

"Dunno, sergeant," came the reply.

"How long have you been in the legions?" The sergeant's voice was as smooth as newly purchased silk.

"Almost five years, sergeant," the legionary said.

"In five years," the sergeant continued, purring, "have you been taught proper foot placement when standing on the line?"

"Yes, sergeant," came the reply again.

Stiger looked on, watching the exchange with more than passing curiosity. Since he had joined the legions, this was the first proper training that he had paid more than a cursory attention to and, for that matter, actively participated in.

He was certain that his assignment to give this training his "personal attention" was another punishment thought up by the captain. Contrary to Cethegus's intentions, Stiger saw it as an opportunity to learn, and he was keen to do so.

Stiger's eye was drawn toward the captain's tent. This was the second day since he had reported the discovery of the unguarded ford. After taking a day off to recover and rest per Colonel Aetius's orders, Stiger was back to work. His legs still ached a bit, but all in all he was rested and fresh.

Though it was nearly midday, the captain had yet to emerge from his tent. From what Stiger had gathered, Cethegus had been deep into the cups the previous night. The captain had shared several bottles of wine with an officer from another company. Stiger had heard them singing badly late into the night. With any luck, Stiger thought, the captain would not manage to pull himself out of bed until after the training had completed. The less Stiger had to do with him the better.

"Oh, so you have been taught proper footwork?" Tiro fairly cooed, drawing Stiger's attention back.

"Yes, sergeant."

"Then," the sergeant exploded, "why in the all of the gods' great mercy are you not using what you've been taught?"

"Sorry, sergeant."

"Sorry, sergeant?" Tiro shouted in the legionary's face. He jabbed a thumb at the man to the legionary's immediate right. "Sorry sergeant will get you, and your mate here, killed because you were not using what you were taught."

"Yes, sergeant."

"One hour mucking out the latrines tonight," Tiro said, eyeing the legionary for a long moment. "Mess it up again, and it will be four."

Tiro took a step back and paused. He looked over the file of men, all of whom stood at attention, waiting.

"Proper footwork is the foundation of a solid shield wall. Screw it up, and people die." The sergeant paused again to let that sink in before turning to Varus. "Corporal Varus, continue to exercise your file."

"Front rank," Varus snapped. "Ready shields."

Tiro stumped over to where Stiger stood. Stiger and Tiro had been moving from file to file, examining the work being done. The company had been broken up into individual files. Each corporal was running the same shield drill designed to practice both proper footwork and shield placement.

The men were using practice shields and swords, both designed with an eye toward being much weightier than the real thing. Stiger had learned from Tiro that the men hated both with a passion. The heavy practice equipment was designed with the intention of strengthening the men's arms, so that when they used the real thing, they could do so with ease.

Tiro absently tapped his vine-cane against his open palm a few times as he watched the men work. Stiger had not seen the sergeant with it before today. Very few sergeants bothered to carry the canes anymore. In the old days, well before Stiger's time, a vine cane was the symbol of the emperor's trust placed in the hands of a legion's centurions. The Midisian reforms had changed that with the dissolution of the centurionate. Though sergeants were authorized to carry vine canes, the legion no longer provided them free of cost. A sergeant, should he want one, had to purchase it. They were not cheap. And so, predictably, the tradition had begun to die.

Tiro was one of the few who still carried one, and he seemed to take pride in it. Stiger could well understand. The cane represented a sacred trust, in that the emperor entrusted each sergeant with a small measure of imperial authority.

"Footwork is just that important, sir," Tiro told him, lowering his voice so that only Stiger could hear. "All it takes is one man to screw it up, and the shield wall can break. I've seen it happen. Trust me, sir, we don't want that to happen."

Stiger nodded but said nothing as he continued to watch.

"See that man, fourth from the left?"

"Yes," Stiger said, looking to the man Tiro had indicated.

"His hands are in the proper place," Tiro explained. "The man to his left has mucked it up."

Stiger's eyes narrowed as he studied the two, probing to see how the hand placement differed. With the backs of the men to them, he could not see what Tiro saw. Then it hit him.

"His shield is a fraction higher than the man to his left," Stiger said, turning to the sergeant. "That is how you can tell."

"Right," Tiro admitted with a sly grin as Varus pounced on the man whose shield was out of alignment, verbally berating the offender. "This is why we drill, and often."

"So that the men are as near perfect as possible."

"Right again, sir," Tiro said. "As we've been pursuing the enemy, we've not had regular drilling. Without it and the attention to detail, the men become rusty. Worse, they become careless. It is easy for them to pick up bad habits." The sergeant hefted his vine cane for Stiger to see. "If we keep beating it into the men, well, when the company comes up against the enemy, we are better prepared than they are. It's that simple."

Stiger nodded in understanding. It made sense to him. They began walking through the drilling files. Half a dozen times, Tiro stepped aside, handing out advice, praise, and punishments as he saw fit. He even bashed his vine cane against a legionary's shoulder, which caused the man to drop his sword. Tiro spent five enraged minutes bawling the man out for dropping the weapon. Stiger had never before heard such profanity, especially delivered in such a colorful, creative manner. The sergeant went from questioning the circumstances of the legionary's birth to asking why the man's mother had not smothered him in his crib to save Tiro the trouble of having to deal with his stupidity. Stiger was forced to hide the amused smile that tugged at the corners of his mouth as the sergeant continued to rage at the man.

Tiro rejoined Stiger. "They need a healthy fear of us, sir." The sergeant spoke in a relaxed tone, as if the previous five minutes had never even occurred. Stiger realized that Tiro's tirade had been a clever act. "In battle, their fear of punishment, along with their fear of letting their comrades down, helps to keep order, and discipline."

"So they fear you?" Stiger asked.

"Of course they do, sir...but they also trust me."

The two concepts did not seem to be mutually compatible in Stiger's thinking. Tiro must have seen this, for he continued.

"Too much fear, and the men can become brittle. That is why we sergeants must be fair, and just. We must be sparse in our praise, but fair in our punishments." Tiro paused and glanced around at the men training about them. "A man screws up, sir...he should expect a punishment. It is the way of things. Disciplining a man for something he did not do...well that, sir, is bad business and is sure to ruin morale. The men trust that I will not discipline them without cause. They trust that I will be there to help them through difficult times, such as battle, drawing strength from my example...you know, sharing the dangers alongside them."

Stiger thought on that for a moment and continued walking.

"Is Sergeant Geta fair and just?"

It was Tiro's time to be silent as he considered his answer. "I am not convinced that the men trust Sergeant Geta … yet. He arrived a few weeks ago, with Captain Cethegus. Both are new to the company."

Stiger scratched at an itch on his cheek. It was as he had thought.

"How long have you been with the company?"

"Fifteen years," Tiro said proudly. "Five as sergeant, and more before that with another company."

That meant the sergeant had seen a lot of officers come and go. Stiger wondered how Cethegus stacked up against the other officers Tiro had served under. He was half tempted to ask, but realized it would be an unfair question. Instead, he stopped to watch another file work their way through the drill.

Nearby, there was an extra practice shield lying on the ground. Stiger stepped over and glanced down at it. He had studied shield walls as part of his own training. Studying was one thing. He had seen one in use against the Rivan a few nights before. But until today he had not been part of an organized training. He realized that, though he could lead men into battle, he could not join a shield wall and be a truly effective participant.

His thoughts turned to the future. Stiger reasoned that the time might come, during a desperate moment, when he would be required to join a line of battle. He bent down and picked up the practice shield, testing its heavy weight. He looked over at Tiro.

"I want to learn proper handling of a shield in a line," Stiger told the sergeant. A few days ago, such a statement would have smacked of weakness, an admission that he did not know his business. Stiger felt that if he were going to master his trade, it stood to reason he should start with the basics.

Tiro seemed genuinely surprised. He hesitated a moment before saying anything, glancing around at the men. He looked back at Stiger, eyebrows raised. "Now, sir? Or later?"

"Now, I think," Stiger said, knowing it was highly irregular for an officer to take training alongside the men. Stiger swallowed. He forced his pride down and then added with more conviction. "Yes, now."

"Are you sure, sir?" Tiro asked, giving Stiger another chance to change his mind and back out.

"If I am to lead these men in battle," Stiger said, "I had better know what is proper, and what is not. Don't you agree?"

Tiro looked like he was trying to think of a reason to object, but then shrugged. He spun around to the nearest file. "Adorjan, Hagan, on me."

The two legionaries broke formation and double-timed it over to the sergeant. Both snapped to a position of attention. Stiger could read the concern in their eyes. They were undoubtedly wondering what they had done wrong to merit the sergeant's attention.

"The lieutenant will be learning the basics of a proper shield wall, as in fighting as part of one," Tiro explained curtly. "You two, on either side of him."

The two legionaries cast sideways looks at Stiger, but quickly stepped to either side and aligned themselves. They were so close Stiger could smell their sweat and foul breath. He cleared his throat, resolved to continue. This was necessary.

"Now, sir, it looks easy, but it takes some getting used to," Tiro said, and so the instruction began. The sergeant was patient and polite, but also firm and unyielding. Stiger was shown how to stand and move with the shield. He was quickly walked through each position a shield was to be held in for a number of different formations. There were half a dozen of these that were more commonly practiced from tortoise, or *testudo* in the old tongue, to the wedge otherwise known as the *cuneus* formation.

He was shown how to properly hold his arm with the shield in specific positions for each of these formations and instructed where his sword should be at all times. Then came the line formation and the drill the men were now practicing. Stiger knew each formation intimately. However, he learned very rapidly that intellectual knowledge gained through reading was far different than actually doing it.

Tiro pointed out when Stiger did something wrong, which was more frequent than Stiger would have liked. It was surprisingly difficult, more so than he had anticipated. He worked hard at it, seeking to attain the proper form and technique, more often than not failing to achieve either.

After twenty minutes of work, Stiger was covered in sweat. Thirty minutes in, he was breathing heavily. When Tiro called a halt an hour in, Stiger was exhausted. The practice shield seemed to weigh more than the cornerstone of one of the grand temples in Mal'Zeel.

Tiro sent Adorjan and Hagan back to their files without a word of thanks. Breathing hard, Stiger watched them go. Neither man was as winded as he was. Stiger then turned back to the sergeant.

"Harder than I expected," Stiger admitted, having set the shield back down on the ground.

"Yes," Tiro said, and Stiger thought he detected a slight hint of satisfaction on the sergeant's face. "It is."

"Most officers don't realize that, do they?" Stiger had bent over with his hands on his knees, attempting to catch his breath. He looked up at Tiro before straightening back up.

"Most officers," Tiro said carefully, "would not wish to learn how to work within a shield wall, sir. Common legionary work is..."

"Beneath them?" Stiger finished.

Tiro nodded at that, but said nothing further.

The sergeant was quite correct. Some of Stiger's peers would think he had lessened himself by working alongside the men. With a vicious stab of resentment, Stiger decided their thoughts were of no concern to him. He had sworn a vow to the High Father. Stiger was a soldier. He would do his duty to the best of his ability, and that involved learning everything he could about his profession. Stiger was more convinced than ever that the more he learned, the better he would be at fulfilling his vow. Tiro had a lot to teach, and Stiger intended to be an apt pupil.

"Nevertheless, we will work at this again..." Stiger paused to catch his breath. "Each time the men drill at shield wall, until I master it."

"Yes, sir," Tiro said.

The men were given a thirty-minute break to eat their lunch and recover. Stiger went to his tent and changed into a fresh tunic. He poured himself a drink of water from a pitcher and drank it down in one pull. Then he ate his ration of salt pork and hard bread. He felt like taking a nap, but resisted the urge. In the end, he pulled out a book from his trunk.

On his way out to join the legion, he had been lucky enough to meet an Anesian trader who had a copy of *Scara's History of the Legion,* a very rare book. Stiger had purchased it for half a silver talon, and had not regretted the purchase or the reduction to his meager funds.

Sitting down at his camp table, he carefully unbound the book's tie and ran his hand across the hard leather cover, enjoying the feel. He opened the book to where he had left off a few nights before. Stiger bent his head and began reading, rapidly becoming absorbed.

Scara's *History of the Legion* had been written well before the Midisian Reformation, and Stiger found it fascinating. The first part of the book was a treatise on how a legion should be organized, pre-Midisian, of course. The second half specifically followed Legate Scara's campaign against the Haranan, detailing the man's battles, experiences, and observations. It was all thoroughly interesting, as it covered much that was close to Stiger's heart. He had read it twice over now, and each time he picked up something new. It was that good a book.

Judging his time up, he closed and rebound the book carefully before returning it to his trunk. Would he ever lead a legion like Scara? He already knew the answer. His father had taken care of that. Shaking his head, Stiger went in search of Tiro.

As he stepped out of his tent, Stiger glanced over toward the captain's tent. There was still no sign of Cethegus. Not for the first time in the last two days, Stiger wondered what the general had made of his discovery of an undefended crossing.

The preparations for a direct river assault were still moving ahead. Much of the legion's artillery was now in place or being moved into position, directly in view of the enemy. Stiger assumed this was a blind, designed to convince the enemy that the main assault would come where the bridge had been. Still, he had expected that someone from headquarters would want to talk to him, but there had been nothing, only silence. Stiger figured the general had dispatched scouts of his own to verify the report, and as such had not needed to question him. With an unhappy shrug, he continued on toward the parade and drill ground.

He arrived as the men were reforming. Stiger made his way over to Tiro. The sergeant was looking casually on, as a spectator might watch a sport. He turned and saluted at Stiger's approach.

"A bit of sword drill," Tiro said with a grin. "Ain't nothin' better for strengthening the arm and tiring out good legionaries."

Stiger agreed. He well remembered his own instruction at the use of the gladius, the legionary's sword. His father had paid for the very best instructors, and Stiger had suffered through hours of grueling drill until he was not only proficient, but had proved himself an expert with the short sword. It had been exhausting work. Wielding a sword was not an easy thing. Five minutes spent at the task could wear one completely out. Hours at it built strength, endurance, and competence—not to mention callouses.

Spending hours drilling with a sword is the making of a man, one of his tutors had been fond of saying to the young Stiger when he had flagged.

Movement to his right caught Stiger's eye, and he turned. A priest was making his way through the ranks, moving toward Stiger and Tiro. The priest was older and short, perhaps just under five feet in height. Though he wore the loosely fitting robes of a traveling friar, he looked built like a prize bull. His face was hard and grim as a veteran legionary's on the eve of battle. The priest was unlike any Stiger had ever seen. He actually looked like a soldier, but Stiger knew that could not be.

"Did you call for a priest?" Stiger asked, looking over at Tiro. It was not uncommon to invite a priest to bless the company and hear the men's confessions.

"No," Tiro said, frowning.

"The captain or Sergeant Geta then?" Stiger suggested.

"Not Geta," Tiro said, spitting on the ground. "He isn't the religious type."

"Lieutenant Stiger, I presume," the priest said, to which Stiger nodded. The priest offered a hand. Stiger found the priest's grip rather firm. "Excellent, I am Father Griggs."

"It is a pleasure to meet you, Holy Father," Stiger greeted cordially, and then the name caught his attention. "Griggs, I know that name."

"Yes," Griggs said, his hard expression cracking with a pleased smile that touched his eyes. "My family holds senatorial rank."

Stiger was surprised by this. "And you gave that up for the priesthood?"

He could not understand why a noble would willingly surrender his station in life to become an ordinary priest. Many nobles were truly religious, but this was different. Joining the priesthood meant renouncing everything that came with family, including wealth, privilege, and station. It was a vocation that the noble families of the empire simply did not consider for their second and third sons.

"I felt called by the High Father to join his ministry," Griggs said with a gentle nod. "Being the first born, well let's just say my decision was not easy on my family, but in life anything worth doing never is."

Stiger was not sure what to say to that, but then noticed the men formed up and waiting for orders. He glanced over at Tiro, who had been watching the exchange with interest. "Sergeant, if you would kindly get the men drilling..."

"Yes, sir." Tiro saluted smartly. The sergeant stepped past Stiger and around the priest, bellowing at the men.

"I apologize if my words gave offense," Stiger said, realizing that he may have offended an honest man of the cloth. "It was not my intention, I assure you."

"Trust me, my son, I was in no way affronted," the priest said with a chuckle. "I get that sentiment a lot when I encounter members of the senatorial class."

"What brings you to us today?" Stiger decided to change the subject to safer ground. It really was none of his business why this man chose to serve the cloth over family. "A blessing for the company?"

"What brings me? Why you, I am afraid," Father Griggs said, and then turned to look over the men who were breaking up into their respective files for drill. "Though, if you wish, I could offer the High Father's blessing over your men."

"Excuse me?" Stiger said, turning fully to face the priest. "What business do you have with me?"

"Oh nothing official, per se." The priest waved a dismissive hand. "I was dining with Colonel Aetius this morning, and he mentioned how you managed to save the general's life the other day. It was an interesting tale, and I thought it might be worth meeting you. I do very much enjoy becoming acquainted with interesting people."

"I see," Stiger said, not believing a word of it and wondering why a priest of the High Father saw fit to lie to him or, at the very least, try to mislead him.

"The colonel also described your action in the wood." The priest surveyed the men preparing to execute a sword drill. He looked back over at Stiger. "I say, standing off an entire Rivan Guard company, and with only forty or fifty men. Very impressive, though I am afraid I've heard some of your peers suggest it was a little foolhardy."

"The Rivan Guard?" Stiger asked, confused. The Guard were the Rivan king's own. They were considered the elite of the enemy, the equivalent of the emperor's Praetorian Guard. Surely he had not fought the Rivan Guard? Perhaps the priest was just having a bit of fun with him. "What do you mean the Rivan Guard?"

"You did not know?" the priest asked, clearly surprised, and Stiger abruptly realized, to his embarrassment, that he had thought poorly of the man just moments before. The priest had not thought to lie or mislead him. Then his eyes widened at the implications, and the priest laughed at him good-naturedly. "How could you not know?"

"It was dark," Stiger said, rather weakly. The truth was more rooted in a fact he was not keen to admit to. Stiger would not have known one of the enemy's elite had he seen one, which, of course, he had.

The priest grinned again. "I understand the entire legion has been talking about nothing else but the young Stiger who took on the Rivan Guard and shoved them back over the river. I might have exaggerated a bit on the entire legion, but you take my meaning."

"It did not happen that way," Stiger protested, aghast that he was the talk of the legion and that this priest had gone out of his way to simply meet him because of this supposed feat.

"Well, you don't have to admit that to anyone else." The priest leaned forward conspiratorially. Despite the hardness to his face, the priest's eyes were alight with amusement, clearly enjoying the young officer's discomfort. "Such things usually become the beginning of great tales."

Stiger stared at the priest a moment, then chuckled. "So, they are talking about me, are they?"

"I am afraid," Father Griggs said with a slight shrug, "much of the officer corps can't decide if you were brave, trying to grab some glory for yourself, simply foolhardy, or plain stupid. I am, of course, reserving judgment until I get to know you better."

Stiger looked hard at the older man and realized that he was being teased. Here before him was the kind of man who enjoyed good gossip. Stiger usually hated the type but for some reason he could not explain found himself warming to the priest.

"Lieutenant Carbo, whom I am exceedingly fond of," the priest added, "thinks very highly of you and has argued in your favor."

"I suspect they will just have to keep guessing," Stiger said, and actually laughed with the priest. The officer corps of the legion had gone out of their way to avoid and ostracize him for weeks, but now they were talking about him. Stiger wasn't sure this was an improvement, but it was somewhat amusing.

"That's the spirit." Father Griggs thumped Stiger on the back. The blow was impressively strong, and Stiger winced slightly. He glanced over at the man, surprised by his strength. "Keep the entertainment going."

Just a few feet away, Sergeant Tiro began bawling out a legionary at a level that a deaf man would have been able to hear. Both Griggs and Stiger turned at the explosive diatribe. They watched for a few seconds, neither speaking. Sergeant Tiro was dishing it out for the entire world to hear. Stiger felt somewhat embarrassed that Father Griggs had to witness such profanity.

"Should you be agreeable, I would not be against a blessing for the company," Stiger said, attempting to draw the priest's attention from Tiro. "They are good men, and I am sure they would welcome the opportunity, especially considering that we will likely be going into battle again soon enough."

Father Griggs looked back over at Stiger. "Very well, I shall preform a blessing for your men."

"Thank you, Father," Stiger said. "Now, if you will be good enough to excuse me, I must get back to my men."

"They fear you," Father Griggs said, all trace of amusement gone.

"Who?" Stiger said, turning back to the priest.

"Your men." The priest wagged a finger around at the drilling company.

"I am an officer," Stiger said. "I hold their very lives in my hands, whether it be by discipline or in battle. I suppose it is only natural."

"It goes beyond that. You are a Stiger, though a young pup of one at that." Father Griggs paused for a heartbeat, and his look became somewhat sad. "My son, you come from an old and powerful house. Your family's name runs deep with the legions, very deep."

"They fear my family name?" Stiger asked in surprise.

"They fear you because of your family name," Father Griggs said, eyes hard and penetrating. "They fear what you represent."

"And what is that?" Stiger asked, not liking the turn the conversation had taken.

"It is said that where a Stiger goes, death follows closely on his heels," Griggs said.

Stiger had heard the saying before and had always been somewhat proud of it. To him, it meant Stigers bringing death to the enemies of the empire. But now, well, he was not quite sure what to think.

"These men," Father Griggs continued. "They fear that in search of greater prestige for your family ... honor for your house and glory for yourself ... you will freely purchase it with their blood. In essence, you will sacrifice them on the altar of your great house's name. That is why they fear you."

Stiger stood there, mute, not quite sure how to respond. He recognized truth when he heard it, but his first impulse was to deny it. Instead, he remained silent as he thought through what the priest had just said. He recalled what Tiro had told him about trust. Perhaps it was the same for officers as well. He had to earn his men's trust, just as Tiro had.

"I recently made an oath to the High Father," Stiger admitted quietly, not sure why he felt compelled to do so. He paused briefly, locking eyes with the priest. "I swore that I would execute my duty and serve the empire with honor to the best of my ability. I do not seek glory, not for myself... not anymore. I seek service."

The priest closed his eyes a moment and nodded before opening them again. Stiger wondered what the priest was playing at. Did the priest think he was a paladin imbued with the High Father's spiritual magic? Why the cheap theatrics? It seemed beneath the man.

"I sense that your heart is true, and in the right place." Griggs took a deep breath and let it out slowly. "I shall pray that it turns out as you say."

Stiger did not say anything in reply, but looked away. He had the feeling that he had just said too much. Though he knew that Father Griggs enjoyed camp gossip, Stiger hoped the priest would not repeat what had just been said. Still, it was best to be cautious around people he did not know and reminded himself in the future to be more reticent.

"Sometimes it is hard to remember, but all of these men all about us," the priest gestured around at the entire legionary encampment, "have hopes and dreams of their own, just as a Stiger does. Good officers, like good sergeants..."

Father Griggs paused and nodded toward Tiro. "Look after their men."

Stiger glanced around at the men being put through their drills. The priest was right, of course. Each one was flesh and blood. The only difference between the officers and the men were that they had simply been born to a different station in life. The last few days had seen a huge readjustment in his thinking, and Stiger now saw it plain as day. Men he had viewed as uncouth, brutish louts just days ago he now saw in a different light. There was very little separating him from the men other than birth, upbringing, and education.

As he looked about, Stiger felt the awesome weight of responsibility land on his shoulders like he had not felt before. These men were counting on him, just as he was counting on them. He had sworn an oath to the High Father, and Stiger had a growing suspicion that somehow this simple priest had known. The thought made Stiger go cold, and he paled in the afternoon heat. Had that been Father Griggs's true purpose in coming to see him? Was the priest here to remind him of his oath? Stiger thought hard on Griggs's words. He turned to say something and saw the priest walking slowly away, already some distance off.

"What about the blessing for the company?" Stiger called after him.

"I've already given it," Father Griggs called back over his shoulder. "Lieutenant, we shall meet again. Of that I promise."

Stiger chewed on his lip as he watched the priest walk away. Then Tiro shouted something, and his attention was pulled back to the drill the men were being run through. Stiger had dawdled enough. It was time he got back to work.

"Are you sure you want to continue, sir?" Tiro asked, looking down on Stiger with an expression of some satisfaction.

Stiger rubbed at his shoulder as he sat up in the grass, wincing painfully. The drilling of the company had ended for the day. The men had been dismissed and had gone off to perform a proper toilet, maintain their kits, and have their evening meals.

Stiger, Varus, and Tiro had signed out of the encampment and found a secluded field some ways away to practice hand-to-hand fighting. Most officers never practiced it. Stiger was uncomfortable generating more gossip for the officer's mess tent, so they had gone in search of a secluded setting.

Stiger had received training from his family's tutors, but having seen Tiro in action, he suspected that the life-long veteran was more skilled at hand-to-hand than he was. Stiger had asked for some instruction and Tiro had readily accepted, perhaps a little too enthusiastically. In hindsight, Stiger should have known what was in store for him. He had not been wrong in his assessment of the sergeant's prowess. Tiro seemed to know every trick and was lightning fast, almost inhumanly so. Stiger had yet to land a blow on him.

The entire experience had been frustrating and, he had to admit, humiliating. But Stiger was learning, even while he was taking a beating. Each time he ended up on the ground, he kept in mind that one day, if he kept at it, this training might just save his life. That made it worth it.

Though the sun was setting, it was still almost unbearably hot. He wiped the sweat out of his eyes and glanced back up at the sergeant. Tiro was not even breathing hard.

"Sir," Varus said, clearly amused. "There is no shame in giving in. Tiro does not fight fair."

"Fair?" Tiro scoffed with some amount of heat and turned to the lieutenant, looking down on him with intensity. "Stiger, when it gets to knives...there is you and him...better him go than you. How he dies matters little, as long as it's him. There is no fairness in war. Learn that now, and it will serve you well. You might even live a little longer if you take it to heart."

Stiger nodded at the sage advice. He had to remember that little speech. It was a good one.

"Come on, sir, one more time." Tiro cocked his head.

The sergeant leaned forward and held out a hand, grinning wickedly. Stiger took it and, as Tiro was helping him up, gave a savage pull and put one of his legs in front of the tough veteran's. The sergeant fell forward and into the grass. Stiger rolled to his side and came to a crouch. He swung around with his knife on the defenseless sergeant and was surprised when a hand smacked out, striking his knife hand painfully. The weapon went flying. An elbow found his midriff. Stiger gagged, almost doubling over. Then the world seemed to land upon him, and he abruptly found himself staring up at the darkening sky, with Sergeant Tiro's knife pressed to his throat and the sergeant's grinning face bare inches from his own. After a moment the knife relaxed. The sergeant stepped back.

"Now that...was not fair, sir," Tiro said, chuckling. "I think you are learning."

"It was a good try, sir," Varus said with a huge grin plastered on his face. "Unfortunately, a number of recruits try that very same move, and Tiro here was ready for it."

Stiger began to laugh. Every bruise, bump, and contusion he had received today seemed to ache all at the same time. He winced. There was no offer this time to help Stiger up, so he pulled himself slowly to his feet. He knew he would be extremely stiff in the morning, but the day's instruction had more than made up for it. Between the company drill and the hand-to-hand training, Stiger had learned a great deal and felt the day had been exceptionally productive. Overall, he was well pleased.

"Shall we call it a day then, sir?" Tiro asked, wiping sweat from his brow with the back of his hand.

"Let's go through the moves you taught me one more time, slowly, and then we can head back."

Tiro nodded approvingly. He walked Stiger once again through the three moves he had taught him using a dagger. The sergeant had Varus model the moves a few times so that Stiger could watch. Then Stiger moved through them slowly while the sergeant observed.

"Very good, sir," Tiro said with approval after Stiger had finished the final move. "And remember, if you lose your dagger and find yourself on the ground, throw some sand in your opponent's eyes. Don't hesitate to use whatever you have at hand. All that matters is beating the other bastard."

"Right." Stiger wondered if the sergeant were joking, but he seemed deadly serious. "Well, I think that is enough for the day. I would like to work at this again tomorrow."

"That is," Tiro said, jerking a thumb toward the river, "if the fun doesn't begin first."

"You think that likely?" Stiger asked, raising an eyebrow.

"Rumor around camp is the show will begin tomorrow, sir," Tiro said. "The artillery is finally all up and in place."

"The cooks are preparing pre-cooked rations," Varus added somberly. "That is generally not a good sign."

Stiger gathered up his sword and slipped it on. He was dusty, dirty, sweaty, and extremely tired. He was looking forward to cleaning up and turning in for the night. The prospect of the impending action washed away some of his tiredness. They began to walk back toward the encampment.

"Sir," Tiro said, "have you heard anything from the captain about the crossing we discovered?"

"No," Stiger said unhappily, "not since we reported it."

Though Stiger did not say so, he was extremely concerned that his report had not been taken seriously. He knew that Cethegus despised him and wondered if that had colored the captain's report to command. The fact that Cethegus had likely taken credit for the discovery bothered Stiger little. He just wanted to make sure it had been reported accurately. Stiger once again considered going to command himself and speaking with Colonel Aetius. He thought on it a moment and then decided against it. No matter how much he desired, he couldn't bring himself to violate direct orders and the chain of command.

"If it comes to a direct assault," Tiro said with a glance in the river's direction, "it is gonna be some hot and hard work."

Stiger did not doubt that. Tiro was a veteran and had seen more than his fair share of battles. If he thought it was going to be difficult, then it likely would be. The sergeant was as confident and collected as any man Stiger had ever known. But his words worried at Stiger as they made their way back.

They arrived just as the encampment gate was closing for the night. Stiger signed them in and then went to find his tent. The light died quickly, and with it the heat began to lessen. Stiger lit his lamp, which hung from a hook drilled into the main support pole. Under the dim lighting, he spent some time cleaning up and maintaining his kit. Thinking on what Tiro and Varus had said about the coming action, he checked to make sure everything was at it should be, including his shield and armor.

Stiger poured himself a cup of the wine from Venney. He took a sip and reflected on all that had happened since he had bought this wine from Trex, the wine merchant. That had been just over a handful of days ago, and yet it seemed like an age had passed. He shook his head at the wonder of it all. A lot had happened in just those few short days. Stiger almost felt like a different person. Perhaps he was?

The thought struck him that the next day could very well bring with it a battle. Tomorrow night, would he be enjoying another cup of wine? Or... would he be lying dead and cold out in the dark, waiting for someone to collect his corpse for mass cremation? It was a troubling thought.

There was a cough behind him at the tent flap.

"Excuse me, sir."

Stiger turned to see Sergeant Geta, and his mood darkened considerably.

"What is it, sergeant?" Stiger turned fully around. He casually took a sip of wine from his cup. The sergeant, he was sure, was up to nothing good. Stiger was not in the mood to be bothered with petty games.

"A slight matter, sir," the sergeant said, and coughed. "A disciplinary matter, sir. Two of our boys were caught fighting with men from another company."

After the intensity of today's drill, he was surprised any of the men had the energy to fight.

"Has the matter been referred to the captain?"

"Yes, sir." Geta suddenly looked uncomfortable. "He said to have you deal with it. The captain's down with the chills, he is, sir."

Cethegus was likely drunk, Stiger thought sourly. Yet again, another duty had been passed off to him. He set his cup down and stood, shaking his head slightly.

"Where are the two offenders?"

"Just outside, sir," Geta said, backing out of the tent entrance.

Stiger stepped out into the darkness lit only by the occasional sputtering torch or fire. He saw Sergeant Tiro and the offenders near a post with a torch. The sergeant was speaking to them in hushed tones.

It was unusually quiet, almost too much so. Most of the camp had bedded down for the night, Stiger realized. They had turned in early. That was a troubling sign. Perhaps the rumors were true? Stiger had long since given up frequenting the officers' mess, which meant he was out of touch with much of the camp gossip. The quiet was ominous and only convinced Stiger that there would be action come the new day's dawn.

As Stiger neared them, he saw that the offenders were Adorjan and Hagan, the two men he had drilled alongside earlier in the day. Both were standing to attention. They looked quite a sight. Their tunics were torn and dirty. One had a swelling eye, the other a split lip that still bled freely down his chin. Tiro turned at his approach.

"What do you have to say for yourselves?" Stiger demanded of them before Tiro could say anything. Sergeant Geta had followed and taken up a position on Stiger's right.

"No excuse, sir," Hagan said. "We were fighting."

Stiger had expected some kind of attempt to explain away the fight, and was momentarily put off by Hagan's reply. He had only been in the legion a few weeks, but Stiger had already learned that everyone seemed to have a ready excuse to get out of trouble. Hagan's honesty made Stiger curious.

"Why?" Stiger asked suspiciously. "Why were you fighting?"

"Does it really matter, sir?" Sergeant Geta asked. "Just flog them and be done with it."

Stiger resented the sergeant's intrusion, but he did not react to it. From all indications, there would be a battle sometime tomorrow. If he flogged these two, they would be unfit for duty, and he suspected the legion would soon need every able-bodied man. So, his decision on punishment had to suit the needs of the legion and not what Sergeant Geta desired.

"Well?" Stiger demanded, when neither man said anything.

"They insulted our company," Hagan said.

"Who did?"

"Tenth Company, sir," Adjordan spoke up for the first time, "in the mess line."

"What did they say?" Stiger asked.

Adjordan looked over to Hagan, who nodded ever so slightly.

"In the fight against the Rivan Guard...they said you was just a lucky bastard, sir," Adjordan said. "Sorry, sir, their words not mine."

"They also said they came to our rescue, sir," Hagan said. "Wasn't right of them to say that. We did all the fighting, sir. They showed up late and only got to watch."

"I see." Stiger almost smiled. The two were defending the company's honor and, in a strange way, his too. Stiger saw a look pass between Geta and Tiro. It was gone in a flash, but he gathered the sergeants were also amused.

"Sergeant," Stiger turned to Tiro.

"Sir?"

"Two hours mucking out the latrines," Stiger ordered. The legionaries' shoulders slumped in relief. They would be spared a flogging.

"What?" Geta fairly exploded. "The captain's standard punishment is flogging."

Hagan and Adjordan's eyes snapped to the sergeant in alarm, then back to Stiger.

"The captain left this matter in my hands." Stiger rounded on the sergeant, irritated that he had been questioned in front of the men. "Since it is my responsibility, then I choose the punishment that I deem appropriate."

"The captain won't like it none, sir," Geta said. Stiger knew the man must feel very secure under Cethegus's protection to speak to him that way. Stiger understood he was inviting additional trouble, but dug his heels in anyway.

"Then let the captain take that up with me," Stiger growled, enraged at the sergeant's temerity.

"Yes, sir," Geta said and snapped to attention, apparently coming to the conclusion that he had strayed onto dangerous ground.

"Sergeant Tiro." Stiger turned back. "Punishment is to be administered immediately. Understand me?"

"Yes, sir," Tiro said.

"You two," Stiger said, stepping closer. He actually approved of what the men had done. He just could not condone it, at least publically. He lowered his voice. "Next time, don't get caught brawling in the camp. Got me?"

"Yes, sir," Hagan and Adjordan said simultaneously. Stiger spared both men a glance and then turned around and walked by a seemingly stunned Sergeant Geta. Stiger felt some satisfaction with that, but at the same time knew there would be a price to pay with Captain Cethegus.

"Lieutenant?" A soft voice called to him from out of the darkness.

Stiger turned at the flap to his tent. He had just been about to go in when he saw Livia emerging from the darkness and into the torchlight. She was carrying a lantern. His heart beat a little faster. She wore a flowing light-green formal dress. A female slave followed a few steps behind, likely her escort.

Stiger offered her a slight bow, pleased she had called out to him.

"It is so nice to see you again," she said, coming nearer and stopping a few feet away. Her slave halted at a respectful distance and waited silently, should her master require anything.

"I hope we will be able to spend some more time together," Stiger said.

His eye was drawn to her lantern. It was shaped like a standard lantern, but plated with gold. Behind the glass danced not a candle-fed flame, but a white magical light source that danced and bounced about within. It was no ordinary lantern.

True magical instruments were extremely rare and, as such, very expensive. Families who purchased items like the one Livia held did so to demonstrate their wealth. Stiger's family was no different. His father and brother owned a number.

"As do I," she said, and Stiger's heart soared with those three words.

"Unfortunately," Stiger said, "duty has kept me from calling upon you more than I would like."

"You have been busy." There was a hint of a mischievous smile on her perfectly formed lips. "First you save my father and me, then you take on the entire Rivan Guard. Very noble and ... courageous. One wonders, what will you do next?"

"It wasn't like that," Stiger said, a little too harshly. His face heated with some embarrassment. He should not have said that and was thankful for the darkness. "I'm sorry. It is just that—"

"Perhaps," she interrupted, the hint of a smile still there, "you might find some time to tell me what it was like, then?"

"I," Stiger said and hesitated, not sure what to say. He settled on being gracious. "It would be my pleasure."

"Mistress," the slave spoke up with a cough. "I am afraid your father is expecting you for dinner."

Livia spared a glance behind her at the slave.

"Ah yes, father," she said. "I had forgotten, how careless of me."

"I will call on you soon," Stiger promised, "just as soon as time and my duties permit."

"I look forward to that. I would enjoy a walk or ride through the countryside." With a wink she stepped by him, her slave following. "You still owe me a dinner, you know."

"As soon as duty permits," Stiger said, "I am all yours."

She looked back and flashed him a radiant smile that seemed to light up the night, before turning away in the direction of the command tents. Stiger watched them go. He could smell the faint scent of rosewater on the air. It smelled intoxicating. In moments, both had been swallowed up by the darkness, the magical lantern the only indication of their path. He sucked in a deep breath, and then exhaled slowly.

"A ride through the countryside?" Stiger said quietly. There was a war on and the general was not likely to allow Stiger to take his daughter out of the safety of the encampment. She must have been jesting with him. Chuckling, he entered his tent, spirits raised at the prospect of spending more time with Livia. More importantly, she wanted to spend time with him.

If only duty and Captain Cethegus would permit him that time.

EIGHT

Stiger held his helmet under his arm as he made his way impatiently past the ranks of men drawn up outside the legionary encampment. In his other hand he held his shield. It was dark, the air was cool, and the morning dew was heavy on the grass. The majority of the legion had already marched out, turning onto the road in the direction of the bridge, quickly being swallowed up into the night. Stiger fumed as he waited for Tiro and Geta to finish taking the roll.

"Sir." Sergeant Tiro turned smartly and faced Stiger. "One hundred sixty-four present, seventeen wounded or on the sick list at the hospital. Beyond that, all present and accounted for."

"Very good." Stiger glanced anxiously around. "Where is the captain?"

"Dunno, sir," Tiro answered, glancing over to Geta.

Stiger turned on Sergeant Geta, gritting his teeth in frustration. "Do you know where the captain is?"

"I..." Geta began and stopped for a heartbeat. "I believe he is still getting his kit on, sir."

Second Company marched by them, many sandaled feet sounding almost rhythmic in unison. The captain of the Second glanced their way. Stiger could not recall the man's name but saw the question in his eyes. Why was the

Seventh not moving? The only other company that had yet to fully form up and begin marching for the rendezvous point was the Tenth, and that was because they had been on guard duty.

Stiger cursed Cethegus under his breath. The readiness orders had arrived some hours earlier, but Stiger had only learned about them a little over an hour ago from Captain Lepidus. Wondering why the Seventh was not mustering with the rest of the legion, Lepidus had poked his head into Stiger's tent and woken him. Stiger had, of course, heard the bustling noise of men being assembled, but had assumed it had nothing to do with him, otherwise he would have been notified. Lepidus quickly set him straight.

Stiger had in turn gone in search of Cethegus and found the captain sound asleep on his cot, an empty bottle of wine discarded on the rug. The readiness orders were sitting unopened on the captain's camp table, where he had left them. That had been at two bells. Stiger had opened the orders and read them to the backdrop of the captain's discordant snoring.

He had attempted to wake Cethegus, but the man was passed out drunk. When a gentle approach hadn't worked, Stiger kicked him out of bed, explained what was occurring, and then, in a tower of anger, went to muster the company. He left the captain unsteadily gathering his equipment.

Cethegus had cost them precious time that could not be replaced. Already late, the men had to be rousted from sleep, provisioned according to their orders, and assembled. It had taken time and was made worse because they had mustered so late. The Seventh had to wait behind the other companies, who were already ahead of them in the ration line.

It was now well past three bells, and the sky was just beginning to lighten ever so slightly with the beginnings of dawn. Stiger glanced back toward the legionary encampment. The commanding general would have some hard questions for the officers of the Seventh, and Stiger was not looking forward to that. The shame of what Cethegus had inflicted upon the company angered Stiger greatly. His blood boiled at the thought of it. The man was a disgrace and had no business being an officer.

"Sergeant Geta," Stiger said, struggling hard to contain himself. "Kindly go fetch our captain."

"Yes, sir." Geta saluted and turned to go.

"Oh, and sergeant," Stiger said. "Advise the captain we are marching in accordance with our orders."

"Yes, sir," Sergeant Geta replied in an unhappy tone and continued on his way back through the gates and into the legionary encampment, breaking into a jog.

Stiger turned to Tiro, who was looking at Stiger in astonishment, clearly alarmed at the prospect of leaving the captain behind. Stiger's anger burned hot. They had lost enough time and he would waste no more on a drunk, even if the man was his superior.

"Form the men to march."

Tiro saluted, spun on his heel, and began barking orders. The men responded, and in moments, the company was formed up into a column of four abreast. Stiger gave the order to march. He was anxious to be on his way and fell in alongside the company.

Stiger had considered ordering a quick march, but then decided against such an action. They had a long way to go and he figured there would be fighting ahead. The men would need all of their strength. As they marched by the Tenth, their sister company, Captain Lepidus nodded sympathetically to him before turning back to his own men, who were just beginning to emerge from the legionary encampment and form up.

Sergeant Tiro fell in next to Stiger.

"Are you sure this is wise, sir?" Tiro asked him in a low tone. "The captain will be furious that we left him behind."

Stiger simply reached into his cloak pocket and handed over the company orders to the sergeant. Tiro juggled his spear and shield around, slipping the spear under a shoulder. He opened the paper one-handed. Between the brightening sky and moonlight, there was just enough light to read by. The sergeant read quickly before curtly handing the orders back to Stiger.

"First in the line of march?" Tiro said incredulously. The sergeant glanced up at the lightening sky, now clearly understanding the gravity of the captain's blunder. "The general will not be pleased."

"No," Stiger agreed unhappily, "I expect that he will not be too impressed with our tardiness."

Cethegus had put the entire company in a terrible position. Stiger would be forced to explain the absence of his commanding officer, while at the same time managing to also come up with some clever excuse as to why the Seventh was late. He wondered sourly if he should even bother to try. He ground his teeth in frustration and said no more.

"Sir," Tiro said, once again lowering his voice. They were passing through the same wood they had fought their way through a few nights before. Loud cracks and deep thuds could be heard in the distance. The legion's artillery was already in action. "You don't suppose the general is planning on a direct assault across the river?"

"I don't know," Stiger said, troubled by the thought. Surely, after his report, the general would have taken the opportunity to get across the river uncontested. The legion would be able to flank the enemy's fixed defenses with relative ease. "I just do not know."

They emerged from the wood and were greeted by an incredible sight. Under the brightening sky, the entirety of the legion's artillery was at work on the enemy fortifications just across the river. Catapults both large and small were in operation, along with a large number of bolt throwers that cracked away with surprising rapidity.

Every few seconds, there was a deep thud. This was almost immediately followed by a large white stone ball being hurled up and into the air. The balls, illuminated by the moonlight, whistled ominously as they flew through the air. The round shot came down on the opposite side of the river, slamming into the turf rampart and sending great gouts of dark dirt up into the air. Occasionally, a shot missed and sailed over the rampart and out of view to wreak havoc beyond.

As they marched nearer, the smaller bolt throwers could be seen more clearly shooting their deadly darts at the wooden barricade above the earthen rampart. Already, the barricade was splintered and shredded in a number places. With a least a hundred machines in operation against the enemy, Stiger knew it was a sight he would not soon forget.

Behind the artillery, the legion and all of her allied auxiliary cohorts were in the process of forming up and aligning upon each other in tight blocks. The spot for this gathering of imperial might had been chosen carefully. To their immediate front, the ground inclined on a slight rise that could almost be considered a small hill. The effect was that it hid the flower of the legion's combat power from the enemy's view. Stiger scanned the legion. He did a quick estimation of the number of companies and cohorts assembled. He was alarmed to see all of them present, minus his own and the Tenth.

Stiger's stomach flipped at the thought of what was to come. The general intended to use the legion as a hammer against the enemy's prepared defensive works.

It was madness.

A captain from command, designated so by the blue ribbon tied around his chest armor, waited ahead, standing off to the side of the road. Two other officers, one a lieutenant and the other a young ensign, were with him. Three horses were tethered a few feet away. The captain held a pad and was scratching away in it with a charcoal pencil as the Seventh marched up.

"Ah," the captain said, addressing himself to Stiger after having glanced at the standard. "The Seventh has finally arrived. What kept you?"

"I am afraid I received our orders rather late, sir," Stiger replied, keeping to the truth.

"Where is your commanding officer?" the captain demanded, noticing for the first time that Stiger was a lieutenant.

"I understand," Stiger said delicately, "that he has been delayed and should be on his way. With luck, he will be here shortly."

"Should?" The captain frowned and turned to the lieutenant who had been waiting with him. Silent meaning passed between them before the other officer shrugged.

"Well," the captain said, "you are too late to take the place in the position allotted to the Seventh. First Company now has that honor. The Seventh will be placed in reserve, along with the Tenth, when they arrive. I would like you over there on that hill." The officer waved vaguely to the crest of a small hill a short distance away. "Lieutenant Aeger here will see you to your position. Your name, lieutenant?"

The captain raised his pad, with his charcoal pencil poised to write.

"Stiger."

"Stiger?" The pad and pencil fell away as the captain from command looked back up. His demeanor changed immediately. "I had forgotten you were with the Seventh. I must say, good show against the Rivan Guard. It is an honor to meet you, sir."

"As it is mine, also," Lieutenant Aeger added. Stiger thought he read admiration in the other lieutenant's eyes.

"Thank you," Stiger said, not sure how to take praise from his fellow officers, especially after weeks of being shunned from polite society. "I was just doing my duty."

"I am Captain Tadeas." The captain warmly offered his hand, which Stiger took. "When this ugly business is over, we must share a bottle of wine—a good bottle. I want to hear all about it."

"I look forward to that," Stiger said, and found that he genuinely did.

"Sir," the young ensign interrupted, pointing beyond the Seventh. "Looks like the Tenth is coming up now."

"I am afraid duty calls," Tadeas said with a slightly disappointed sigh. "Lieutenant, if you would be kind enough to excuse me, Aeger here will show you to your position. You should have quite a view of the action when the party starts."

With that, the captain hurried off, the ensign in tow. Tadeas had not even waited for Stiger's salute.

"Sir," Aeger said in a respectful tone, "if you would, this way please."

Stiger shared a brief look with Sergeant Tiro as the company got moving again. The sergeant offered Stiger a grim look in return and shrugged.

Their position was on a hill off to the right of the ruined bridge. They were separated by a good three hundred yards from the bulk of the legion and the auxiliary cohorts, who were still hidden from the view of the enemy. Stiger could see the legion's officers clustered around the eagle, where the general likely stood. General Treim or one of his aids was most probably giving the officers a final briefing and their orders for the assault.

The hilltop was the highest ground on the field and provided an unobstructed view of the action below them and to the left where the bridge had been. The water around the remnants of the bridge gave off the impression of being somewhat shallow. Stiger knew the general would have sent scouts ahead to test the depth of the water before even contemplating an assault at this point, for the legion had with them no boats.

"Tell the men to stand at ease," Stiger said to Tiro. Aeger excused himself and hurried off.

Stiger turned to watch the artillery. The sky had lightened considerably, and it was much easier to see in the early morning gloom. The wooden barricade across the river topping the rampart had been reduced further by the bolt throwers. Entire sections of it were splintered apart or had been ripped clean away. But the rampart was, itself, for the most part untouched, minus a number of impact craters where catapult shot had landed, doing nothing more than disturbing the sod.

The rampart would have to be assaulted and physically taken from the enemy. That would only be the first and easiest step. The greater challenge lay just beyond to the second, more impressive and formidable defensive line, which ran along the crest of the small ridgeline a few hundred yards from the river. Stiger knew, without a doubt, it would be a hot day for the legion.

One of the wooden towers behind the first rampart was hit by a ballista ball. At least halfway up the structure, the ball passed clean through one of the support legs. For a moment, nothing happened, then there was a loud splintering crack that could be heard clear across the river as another support leg under tremendous stress snapped. With a terrible creaking, the tower shivered and heeled slowly over to one side. Several of the enemy who had been on it were thrown free before it came crashing down behind the rampart and out of view. A cloud of dust rose up from where the tower had fallen.

A cheer went up from the men of the Seventh at that.

Stiger glanced over as Sergeant Tiro came to stand next to him. The sergeant looked grim.

"During the fight for the wood," Stiger said, turning to him, "did you know we faced the Rivan Guard?"

"Not at the time, sir," Tiro said. "It was too damned dark, and what did it matter to us? They all die just the same, some harder than others."

That was an interesting point, and one Stiger had not considered. What would he have done had he known? Would it have affected his decision making? Could he have been intimidated into falling back? Stiger considered that such knowledge might have forced him to make different choices.

The two were silent as they watched the artillery firing away at the enemy. It was a one-sided affair, until a large stone ball rose up from behind the enemy defenses. The ball seemed to hang in space for a long moment before it plunged down amongst the legionary artillery, landing with a deep thump that Stiger swore he could feel through the soles of his boots. Other than sending a shower of dirt over an artillery crew and their machine, it did no damage that he could see and barely slowed the crew down in their work.

He now understood why the artillery crews had dug in and erected defensive works around their machines. Another ballista ball, whistling loudly, climbed gracefully up into the sky from behind the enemy's defensive wall. This was followed almost immediately by several more. For a moment, each of the balls seemed to hang in empty space before crashing down amongst the legion's artillery. A number of balls were fired back in reply. These went clear over the defensive wall to strike back at the enemy.

Judging by the rate of fire, Stiger speculated that the enemy had fewer pieces than the legion. That, or they were not as well-trained and proficient at firing as the imperial crews. Either way, it was an encouraging sign for the battle that was to come.

The legionary catapult crews began adjusting their fire in an attempt to hit the enemy machines just out of view behind the defensive rampart. Artillery observers were carefully noting where each enemy shot originated. The observations were then relayed to the catapult crews. With each passing shot, the counterbattery fire appeared to get closer and closer to where the enemy ballista balls were coming from.

"They will stay at it," Tiro said, gesturing with a hand, "until the enemy fire ceases or is reduced significantly. Once that happens, the general will send the first assault wave forward. It could be today or tomorrow or the next day. At that time, the enemy will open up with the rest of their artillery. Our boys will pay the butcher's bill then."

"You think they have more?" Stiger asked the sergeant.

"Yes," came the curt reply. "It is a good thing we were late, sir. I would not want to be in the first wave."

Stiger nodded. If the sergeant were correct, the poor bastards making a first attempt would suffer terribly. Perhaps fortune had been on his side this day after all? It was entirely possible the Seventh, as part of the reserve, would see no action.

However, there would be another price to pay. Stiger was not looking forward to facing the general. Though he might escape punishment, Cethegus likely would not, and the man's disgrace would stain both Stiger and the company.

The sound of many feet from behind drew his attention. Stiger turned to see Tenth Company marching up. Captain Lepidus put his men neatly to the Seventh's left, aligning them carefully. Once his men were in position, they were also allowed to relax like those of the Seventh.

Lepidus walked over. "Stiger," he greeted.

Tiro excused himself, stepping away to supposedly check on the men.

"Captain." Stiger offered the captain of the Tenth a crisp salute. Lepidus returned it.

A moment later, a ballista ball hit a friendly bolt thrower below. The machine and crew disappeared in a cloud of dust, dirt, and debris. It cleared in seconds, revealing the torn and shattered bodies of the crew, one of which was writhing in agony on the ground. The others were still, horribly mangled and missing limbs, including one who was lacking a head. Stiger could not see where it had gone. Of the machine itself, nothing was recognizable but pieces of wood and bits of rope. A muffled cheer sounded from across the river as the Rivan defenders celebrated their success.

"Nasty business," Lepidus commented with distaste. Then a thought seemed to occur to him. He looked around. "Where is Cethegus?"

Stiger considered covering for his commanding officer, but then changed his mind. The truth would come out eventually, and there would be no hiding from it. He would not dishonor himself by lying.

"I don't know," Stiger admitted with a shrug. "I gave the order to march without him, as I did not feel we could wait any longer."

"You left your own captain behind?" Lepidus actually chuckled.

Stiger nodded.

"I am starting to like you," Lepidus said. "I wouldn't want to be in your boots when he gets here, though."

"Should he charge me," Stiger said, "I think he would be hard-pressed to explain to the general why his company had to march without him."

"I agree," Lepidus said. The captain of the Tenth paused a moment and sobered. "I don't believe he will place a charge upon you. Such a move, as you say, would unmask his own incompetence." Lepidus took a deep breath. "That said, there will be consequences for the Seventh being late this day."

"I know," Stiger said unhappily.

"It could be worse." Lepidus pointed down toward the bulk of the legion. "We could be down there, preparing to step off for a river assault that is sure to be exceptionally difficult and bloody."

"There is that." Though Lepidus was trying to cheer him up, he found it was not working. "I might prefer that to disgrace."

"It is not as bad as all that." Lepidus glanced over. "After saving the general's life and how you handled yourself against the Rivan Guard, you won't have anything to worry about."

"You think so, sir?" Stiger asked hopefully.

"I do. If need be, I will speak on your behalf."

"Thank you, sir," Stiger said with some relief.

Lepidus normally had a reserved and hard attitude about him. He seemed to be the kind of officer who demanded excellence and brooked no excuses. Stiger had not known what to think of the man until now, but he was warming to the captain of the Tenth.

"Though our houses are not aligned," Lepidus said, "I think you are an honorable man. Having seen you in action, I daresay you have the makings of a fine officer."

The last few weeks had been hard. Stiger felt moved by the sentiment. He cleared his throat and started to say something, but Lepidus continued.

"Cethegus, on the other hand, will be hard-pressed to weasel out of the trouble he has made for himself."

"Stiger! Where are you? Answer me, you bastard!" The shrill shout drew their attention. Captain Cethegus was making his way up the backside of the hill behind the company. "Stiger!"

"Good luck," Lepidus said with a broad grin. He patted Stiger on the shoulder before stepping off and back to his own company. Stiger could hear Lepidus chuckling softly.

"Sir." Stiger turned as the captain pushed his way through the men. Stiger saluted his huffing, puffing, and red-faced commanding officer, who was followed closely by Sergeant Geta. Neither looked to be in a pleasant mood. "Company is formed up and awaiting your orders, sir."

"Don't give me that formal horseshit," Cethegus hissed as he came right up to Stiger's face. The man's breath reeked of wine. "You left me behind, you bastard!"

"No, sir." Stiger produced the orders he had found in Cethegus's tent. "I followed our orders and led our company on ahead."

The captain made no move to take the orders, but stood there staring at Stiger. A vein pulsed in the man's temple. Stiger read a deep, naked malevolence in the captain's eyes. Sergeant Geta stood behind the captain, but Stiger was surprised to see the sergeant, though angry, appeared uncertain as he looked between the two officers.

"You traitorous bastard," Cethegus breathed after a moment. "I will have you on a charge of insubordination for your actions. We will see what the general has to say about that!"

"Yes, sir," Stiger said coldly. He had taken more than enough abuse from this man, even if Cethegus was his immediate superior. "I, too, would be interested in what the general has to say."

"How dare—?"

"I am confident General Treim will have some hard questions as to why we were not in our appointed position on time. Our spot on the field," Stiger pointed off to where the bulk of the legion was formed up, "was the place of honor for our action in the wood the other night. Our orders say as much. We were late, sir. First Company has taken our place in the line. We are now part of the reserve."

Cethegus paled and shifted uncomfortably before turning to look down at the assembled legion a few hundred yards away. He licked his lips, sputtered for a moment, and looked back on Stiger with an uncertainty that was very satisfying to the lieutenant.

"Sir," Stiger said, bringing voice to his real concerns, "the disposition of the legion would seem to indicate a general assault across the river. There appears to be no move to flank the enemy position."

"What?" Cethegus asked, shifting slightly, a hand coming up to rub his unshaven jaw. "What are you talking about?"

"You did forward my report of the undefended ford?"

"Oh that."

"Did you forward my report?"

"Of course I did," Cethegus snapped, a little too quickly for Stiger's comfort.

"Perhaps it did not reach the general's personal attention?" Stiger suggested. "I request permission to confirm that before the first assault wave goes in."

"No," Cethegus said firmly, running a tremulous hand through his hair. Stiger noticed, for the first time, the captain had come without his helmet and shield. "I am sure the general is far too busy to be bothered with such trivialities."

"Trivialities? But, sir," Stiger protested, "we would be able to turn the enemy's defenses. What if he isn't aware of it? Men will die needlessly."

"What do you know?" Cethegus said harshly, voice rising with each word. "You are a wet-behind-the-ears whelp of an officer with no experience. I doubt you even found a crossing. You probably just saw what you took to be shallow water and made the assumption a ford existed."

"You question my honor?" Stiger hissed at the blatant affront.

"Of course I do," Cethegus yelled back at him. "You were spawned by a traitor. Your house has no honor, and you seriously expect me to trust your word?"

"Since," Stiger said, halting with each word, "my personal honor is insufficient..." He turned, pointing. "Sergeant Tiro and Corporal Varus can vouch to the existence of the ford. The sergeant and I crossed the river, sir. I assure you it exists."

"Enough from you," Cethegus screamed. "I have heard all I care to hear of your nonsense."

"But, sir," Stiger protested again.

"Shut your mouth. That is an order." Cethegus pointed toward the other side of the company. "Post yourself over there, lieutenant."

Stiger stared hard at his captain, incredibly enraged. At first, he took Cethegus's anger to be just that, but the captain's eyes betrayed the man. Cethegus was afraid.

"I will have you physically removed," Cethegus warned him when Stiger did not move.

"Yes, sir," Stiger growled and turned away, fists clenching and unclenching. The entire company had followed the exchange in silence, every eye was on Stiger as he stalked slowly along the front rank to the position the captain had assigned him.

NINE

Three companies moved up to where the bridge had been, around six hundred men in total. They marched in good order—shields to their side, standards to the front—around to the sides of the causeway. An auxiliary cohort of archers followed at a close distance. The men of the Seventh and Tenth gave a hearty cheer as the first company reached the water's edge.

The bolt throwers, which had been cracking away at the enemy barricade, intensified their fire, their bolts coming at a more rapid pace. The catapults continued to lob shots up, over, and behind the enemy rampart. Every few seconds, either the crack of a bolt could be heard or a ballista shot arced upward. The ballista balls had been drilled with a series of holes that made them whistle ominously with their passage through the air.

Return fire from the enemy had been sporadic for the last thirty minutes, which, Stiger reflected, had likely prompted the order to advance. The legion's artillery bombardment had gained superiority over the enemy, surprisingly quickly. The sun had been up no less than two hours.

Stiger watched as an enemy ball landed a few feet to the front of the lead company, kicking up a great splash of water, dousing the men in the front rank. Stiger was grateful for the poor accuracy of the enemy. Despite the errant shot, the officers of the company stepped to the front and entered the water. One of them turned and said something to the assembled men. Stiger found himself clenching his hands in anticipation and forced himself to relax.

A battle cry muffled by distance sounded as the first company splashed into the water and began making their way across. A moment later, a powerful volley of enemy shot arced skyward, hung suspended for an agonizing moment, and crashed down into the water where the company was crossing. The volley was so large the men were temporally obscured from view by the tremendous splash that followed. It was as if the river had suddenly leapt up and swallowed them whole.

"Oh, great gods," Tiro whispered in horror.

In a flash of insight, Stiger understood. The enemy shot that had landed short in the river had been solely for the purpose of determining the range. The enemy had planned well. It was as Tiro had said. The Rivan had brought more artillery than they had initially revealed.

As the mist and spray cleared, Stiger could once again see the men forcing the crossing, moving around the supports and what debris had not been carried off by the river. He was astonished that anyone could survive such a heavy barrage, but, incredibly, the vast majority of the men had done just that. Stiger's relief was tempered by the sight of a handful of wounded struggling and splashing in the water, trying desperately to make it back to the shore. Only one made it. The rest, likely too wounded to put up much of an effort, simply sank from sight, the weight of their armor dragging them down into the river's cold depths.

"A terrible way to go," Tiro said, and Stiger found he could not disagree.

Stiger watched grimly. The men continued to struggle across the river. As they neared the riverbank and were nearly right up to the defensive rampart, a line of archers appeared atop the shattered wooden barricade. These raised their bows into the air, and a moment later a wave of arrows shot upward into the sky. Someone must have shouted an order or warning, for the legionaries below raised their shields over their heads for protection. The arrows crashed down in a rain amongst the struggling mass of men. Several were hit, pitching over or collapsing back into the water, where they were taken by the strong current, disappearing moments later.

Another wave of arrows shot up into the sky. The legionaries continued to struggle ashore as this wave crashed down around them. More men were hit. One simply dropped, half of his still body in the water and half out.

The auxiliary cohort on the far bank fired a massed volley back. It flew up and over at the enemy. The cohort stood lined up in several ranks near the water's edge. Their prefect stood to their side, calmly and coolly directing the action.

When at full strength, auxiliary cohorts numbered four hundred eighty men. In practice, all units were perpetually understrength, but Stiger estimated that there were more than two companies' worth of archers now firing back at the enemy, perhaps four hundred men in total.

Stiger almost cheered when several of the enemy archers abruptly disappeared from view as they were hit. One toppled forward over the barricade and fell down the other side of the rampart, rolling like a child's doll tossed down the slope. A half a second later, a well-aimed bolt from the artillery struck an enemy archer. It was as if a great hand had grabbed and tossed him backward and out of view.

Far from cowed, the enemy archers fired yet another volley at those struggling out of the water. Stiger felt helpless. It was a slaughter, pure and simple. The company standard fell as the bearer was struck down, falling back into the water. A moment later, it was snatched by another man before the river could carry it away. The legionaries continued to scramble out of the water, encouraged on by their officers and sergeants.

Stiger thought he had never seen such bravery, and his heart swelled with admiration as one of the officers plunged back into the river. The officer made his way over to men who were frozen in fear, huddled together and using their shields as cover. The officer pushed, kicked, and prodded men forward. Stiger could see him gesturing and pointing toward the far bank, using his own shield for cover. Surely, Stiger thought, the officer would be struck down, but he was not. His shield was studded with spent arrows like quills on a hedgehog. He got the last of the men ashore, where they clustered against the base of the rampart, shields raised above their heads for protection. The archers above them popped up, leaned over the ruined barricade, and fired directly down at the legionaries below before disappearing from view again.

The next company, which had followed after the first, reached the water's edge and began struggling across, following the same path. The artillery began raining down around them, kicking up great splashes of water. At the same time, the enemy archers switched their fire back to the river, sending massed volley after massed volley into those now wading and struggling across. It was terrible to witness, even more so than the crossing of the first company. Stiger felt sick to his stomach.

He could stand it no more. He glanced around and saw Cethegus watching in horrified fascination, like everyone else on the small hilltop. Sergeant Geta was by the captain's side, just as transfixed. At that moment, Stiger realized that both the Seventh and Tenth companies were silent. No one was saying a word. All eyes were watching those brave legionaries below being slaughtered by the enemy.

"Sir," Sergeant Tiro cautioned quietly, "are you sure that is wise?"

Stiger had not realized he had started moving in Cethegus's direction, but Tiro's words did not cause him to hesitate in the slightest. The sergeant followed. Stiger intentionally ignored the eyes of the men as he made his way back over to the captain.

"Sir," Stiger said. "I respectfully request permission to go in search of the general."

"Denied." Cethegus did not take his eyes from the action below, almost as if he could not. "Get back to your post."

"There is a better way than that," Stiger insisted, gesturing down at the action in view. The men of the first wave had begun to scramble up the steep rampart toward the defensive barricade. With only three companies making the assault, Stiger was confident there was no chance of successfully taking it from the enemy. The third company stood on the far bank and had not yet begun their crossing. "Let the general say no."

"I am saying no," Cethegus snapped shrilly, turning on Stiger. "We have our orders."

Stiger's eyes narrowed. He wasn't sure how he knew, but in that moment he did.

"My report," Stiger breathed, in mounting shock. "You never even passed it along, did you?"

Cethegus was silent a moment. "How dare you question me like that?"

The captain's outrage did not ring with authenticity. Stiger read it in the man's eyes. He saw the doubt, the worry and fear. It only served to confirm his supposition. Stiger took an enraged step toward the captain, and the man flinched before his spine stiffened. The captain stood his ground.

"Get back to your post... or ... or I will have you arrested, and charged."

The threat was a serious one, and for the moment it checked Stiger. He had no proof the captain had failed to pass along the report, only his gut feeling. If he acted and he was wrong, it would be the end of his career in the military, just as it was getting started. Stiger would be disgraced. It would be one more black mark staining his family honor. Clenching his jaw, Stiger turned and stalked off. Sergeant Tiro fell in alongside him.

"Might I offer the lieutenant some advice?" Tiro asked with a hard look.

"No," Stiger grated through clenched teeth, his thoughts raging along with his temper. He stopped, forced himself to calm down. Stiger turned to the sergeant, realizing that he had just been incredibly unfair. He unclenched his teeth and took a deep breath. "Yes, I would welcome your counsel."

"Find a way to get word to the general, sir," Tiro said very quietly, so that the nearest of the men could not overhear.

"You believe the captain never forwarded my report?" Stiger was surprised that Tiro was taking sides. He would have expected the sergeant to play his hand carefully, but then again, Tiro had become his ally after the fight in the wood. And, Stiger suspected, in a strange sort of way, the sergeant had also become a friend, though their respective socials rank would forever keep them at arm's length.

"I do," Tiro said, with a glance over in the captain's direction. "General Treim commanded the Eighth Legion before this. The Eighth fought alongside us in the Wilds. If there were an easier path, he would take it. The general is a good man, sir. He is well thought of by the men and looks after them. We trust him to do the right thing."

Stiger considered Tiro's words as he turned back to watch. He was horrified to see the companies that had crossed were now splashing back through the river, rushing headlong toward safety, completely mixed and disorganized. They were under heavy fire the entire way, coming from both the enemy archers and artillery. Stiger scratched his cheek as he tried to estimate how many men had been lost in the abortive attempt.

Having witnessed the fate of the first two companies, the last company had not even attempted to cross. They had watched from the far bank, but now had turned and were marching back the way they had come. Behind them, the first of the men rushing to safety made it back across the river. Perhaps a third of their number had been left behind. Stiger followed their progress as they moved past the friendly archers in a great mass of confusion. It was very un-legionary-like.

The prefect of the auxiliary cohort had his men spread out, allowing the fugitives to pass through and around his ranks. Once clear, he redressed his line, under fire the entire time. He then gave the order to fall back. They did so in good order. It was an impressive show of discipline and courage.

A few hundred yards beyond, Stiger saw that the entire legion had moved up and was now in clear view of the enemy. Stiger was horrified. Then, it dawned on him why the general had sent such a small force forward. He had been testing the enemy's defenses. Now that General Treim knew what to expect, he intended to throw the weight of the legion across the river.

"It will be bloody," Tiro said. "But the general will break through. They will be successful."

Stiger had his doubts and was about to voice them when he heard hooves. He turned to see a large party of horsemen riding up behind the two companies. One of the riders carried the legion's eagle. It glinted brilliantly under the sunlight. Stiger had no illusions of who rode with the eagle. The horsemen moved behind the Seventh and continued along behind the Tenth until they had an unobstructed view of the crossing. The general had come forward to directly observe the action that was about to unfold.

Without hesitation, Stiger started moving in the direction of the general. So sudden was Stiger's movement that Tiro had to jog to catch up. He could hear the sergeant's hurried footsteps behind him.

"Where do you think you are going?" Cethegus demanded shrilly as Stiger stepped right by his captain.

He ignored Cethegus and continued purposefully striding forward.

"Stop him," Cethegus snapped to Sergeant Geta. "Seven levels, man, stop him!"

"You and you," Geta said to the two nearest legionaries. "Take the lieutenant under arrest. Move, damn you."

Stiger crossed over in front of Tenth Company at a hurried pace. He heard heavy footsteps behind him, then two thuds, which were followed by much cursing. Without stopping, he glanced over his shoulder to see both men down in a tangle of limbs. Sergeant Tiro had neatly tripped them both.

"Oh, how clumsy of me," Tiro said to one of the men who was getting to his feet. "I did not see you there...let me help you up."

The sergeant's idea of assistance involved simply holding one of the men in place. The legionary looked up at Stiger and then the sergeant, who shot Stiger a wink. The man relaxed under the sergeant's firm grip and made no move to struggle. The other man scrambled around the sergeant. Tiro stuck a leg out to trip him, but the legionary dodged it. Stiger sped his pace up, stepping quickly by Lepidus, who was looking curiously at the commotion the men from the Seventh had caused to the front of his company. He made no move to intervene, but simply raised an eyebrow at the lieutenant.

Stiger saw Colonel Aetius ahead. The colonel was the nearest officer to him. The general's party was wholly focused on the legion as it continued to move into an assault position. Stiger reached the end of the Tenth's line. Just then, a hand clamped down on his shoulder, pulling him up short.

"Colonel Aetius!" Stiger called loudly as he was pulled roughly back. "Colonel!"

Aetius turned, and his eyes lit up in recognition. Then the colonel frowned.

"Unhand the lieutenant," the colonel demanded and nudged his horse into a walk. Aetius rode the short distance over. Anger clouded the colonel's face. "Now, what is the meaning of this?"

The words had been directed to Stiger, but the legionary answered.

"Sorry, sir. Captain's orders, sir," the legionary said. "The lieutenant is to be arrested, sir."

"Arrested?" Colonel Aetius asked, aghast. "Whatever for?"

"Dunno, sir," the legionary said. "Just following my orders, sir."

Stiger was about to open his mouth, when the colonel looked beyond him. Stiger turned around and saw Captain Cethegus and Sergeant Geta hurrying forward. Tiro and Lepidus were right behind them.

"Captain," Aetius said. "What is the meaning of this?"

"The lieutenant has left his post," Cethegus explained. "Against orders, sir."

"Is this true, lieutenant?"

"Sir, you have to stop the assault," Stiger said, not even bothering to address the colonel's question. "There is an unguarded ford just ten miles south of here."

"What?" the colonel snapped. His gaze upon Stiger became hawk-like, and he leaned forward in the saddle. "A ford you say? Unguarded? Truly?"

Stiger nodded.

"Aetius?" General Treim rode up, clearly wondering what the commotion was about.

"Sir," Colonel Aetius turned in the saddle to look over at the general. "The lieutenant here says there is an unguarded ford ten miles to the south."

The general's gaze shifted to Stiger. "A crossing? You found a crossing?"

"Yes, sir," Stiger said, gesturing behind him. "Two days ago, Sergeant Tiro and I discovered it, sir."

"My scouts reported that there isn't another crossing for forty or more miles in either direction," the general stated. "I find it difficult to believe they could have missed one."

"It is there, sir," Stiger affirmed.

"Are you sure? You tested it, and crossed to the other side?"

"Yes, sir," Stiger said. "It is a little deep, but manageable. The sergeant here can confirm that."

Sergeant Tiro pushed by Cethegus, who had gone very still.

"Sergeant?" The general looked at the tough old veteran with a raised eyebrow.

"What the lieutenant says is true, sir. As he said, it's a bit deep, but we made it over without too much trouble. We explored for a bit and only came across a water detail, who did not seem to know of the crossing."

The general looked between Stiger and Tiro, then at Colonel Aetius.

"Sir," Stiger said, drawing the general's attention back to him, "we reported this just as soon as we discovered it."

"Then why did I not hear of it?" Treim asked hotly.

"I can vouch that the lieutenant led a patrol south two days ago," Colonel Aetius said. "I encountered him and his men as they were setting out. I even examined his orders."

"And I believe the lieutenant is a man of his word," said another voice.

Stiger looked past the general and saw Father Griggs, mounted on a magnificent horse, riding up next to the general. Father Griggs wore plated mail armor that gleamed brightly in the morning sunlight. The High Father's sigil was emblazoned upon his chest and helmet. A pale blue cloak ran from his shoulders and down around the horse's rump.

The priest's mount momentarily captured Stiger's attention. He had never seen a more perfect and beautiful animal. The horse's coat was as pure as fresh mountain snow, under which muscles moved gracefully. Clearly the good father was no ordinary priest.

A man to the Griggs's left drew Stiger's attention next. He was mounted on a small horse and wore soft green and brown leathers. A richly cut brown cloak draped down the man's back. Surprisingly, under the growing heat of the day, his hood was pulled up, concealing his face in shadow. Stiger could just see the eyes, which somehow seemed unnatural and alien. The look that swept over Stiger was unnerving. Had it not been for the man's cloak, Stiger might have mistaken him for one of the emperor's rangers. But there was no reason for one from the ranger corps to be here, and Stiger's eyes narrowed as he considered the stranger. He felt as if he had seen this man before, but could not place where.

"I have had the pleasure of spending a bit of time with this officer," Father Griggs continued. "If Lieutenant Stiger here says he has discovered a crossing, well, I for one will take him at his word."

The general glanced over at Father Griggs, scowled slightly, and then looked back at Aetius. "Sound the recall, and hold back the assault."

Aetius kicked his horse over to the eagle-bearer and the rest of the general's party. Moments later, a legionary with a horn blew the recall. The crisp sound ripped across the morning air. The legionary waited a few heartbeats, then blew a second time. In the distance, another horn replied.

"To whom did you report this?" the general demanded of Stiger.

"My commanding officer, Captain Cethegus."

The general's gaze turned on Cethegus, who seemed to pale and shrink in upon himself. Stiger thought his captain looked as if he wanted to bolt.

"Well?" the general asked quietly.

"I reported it to command, sir," Cethegus said nervously. "Sergeant Geta here took my report and delivered it himself."

Geta glanced around as all eyes turned to him. He coughed nervously, then drew himself up into a position of attention.

"I delivered it to the clerk on duty at the command tent," Geta said. "As the High Father is my witness, I did, sir."

Stiger saw Father Griggs frown slightly at the sergeant. Only Stiger seemed to notice. Treim said nothing further. Instead, the general dismounted from his horse and reached into a saddlebag. He pulled forth a map, opened it, then knelt down in the grass in front of Stiger. He spread it out on the ground and beckoned both Stiger and Tiro to join him.

"Show me where this crossing is," Treim demanded in a tone that brooked no argument.

Stiger glanced down at the map. It was a rough sketch drawn by a camp scribe of the surrounding terrain for several miles in either direction, ending at the river crossing.

"Sir," Stiger traced his hand down the map, following the river until he came to the forest. "After a short way into the trees, you come to a good-sized trail here. You cannot miss it. The trail travels to a farm somewhere around here. However, if you turn toward the river, it leads to the crossing, which I believe is used to get animals from the farm to market across the river. When we explored the other side of the river, we saw what we took to be smoke from a small settlement or possibly a village. It was more than what you would expect to see from an isolated farmstead, sir."

The general rubbed his jaw as he considered this new information. He glanced over to Tiro with a questioning look, as if to confirm what Stiger had said.

"That's right, sir," Tiro confirmed.

"Well, lieutenant," General Treim said, looking over at Stiger. "It seems the army will march on your word then. I guess it helps that a paladin of the High Father and Aetius vouched for you. Otherwise, I might have disregarded it as the fancy of a youthful, glory-hungry officer."

Stiger colored at the description of himself, but then the words sank in, and his eyes swung over to the priest. Father Griggs was a paladin, a holy cleric in the service of the High Father? The paladin, seeing the astounded look, winked good-naturedly back. Stiger took a deep breath and looked back over at the general.

"It is there, sir."

Hoof-beats from Aetius's horse drew their attention. General Treim stood with the map and walked over to the colonel. Stiger and Tiro stood up as well.

"I was able stop the assault before it could begin, sir," the colonel reported calmly. "The legion is standing by for your orders."

General Treim grabbed the reins of his horse and drew it closer to Aetius. They spoke quietly for a moment. Aetius glanced over at Captain Cethegus. A moment later, the colonel nodded and turned back to the general. Treim then spread the map across his horse's saddle so that the colonel could see. Stiger stepped closer.

"The crossing is here," General Treim said, pointing it out for the colonel. "A short distance into the forest, there is a trail that leads directly to the ford."

"It seems we will have to have a word with our cavalry scouts," Aetius said, and the general nodded in grim agreement.

"The Seventh and Tenth here will start out immediately," the general said, loud enough for all to here but addressing himself to Aetius. "Select five other companies to follow, including the auxiliary infantry cohorts. Secure the crossing and push north. Hit the enemy's line, striking them on the flank as soon as practical."

"I believe I can manage that." Aetius nodded confidently. "It will be good to surprise the bastards for a change."

"When you hit them..." The general scanned the far bank and then pointed to a place where the enemy's fortification ended. "Send a signaler to that bank there. I will have lookouts watching. Once we receive your signal, the entire legion will push off and assault the line before us." The general brought his two hands together in a loud clap. "We hit them from two sides at the same time. With luck, the confusion and surprise will be their undoing."

Colonel Aetius glanced up at the sky. "By my estimation, a march of at least twenty miles... we should hit the enemy's flank sometime around dusk, perhaps even after."

"Then I had best not keep you waiting," Treim said cheerfully, clearly excited. It seemed infectious, and even Stiger felt the excitement in the air.

"Excuse me, sir," Stiger spoke up, and both the general and colonel turned to him. "If we can bring some rope to string between the banks, I believe it will make the crossing go faster."

"Good idea." Aetius turned to one of the general's mounted officers, snapping out orders to fetch a sufficient quantity of rope. The rider galloped down toward the artillery, which was still in action, firing at the enemy. The officer's horse kicked up clods of dirt in its wake.

The general folded up the map and returned it to his saddlebag before remounting his horse. Once settled, he looked down on Stiger. "It seems I keep ending up in your debt, Stiger."

"Just doing my duty, sir," Stiger said.

"Well," the general said, slowly wheeling his horse away, "I shall expect more of the same then."

With that, the general galloped away, moving down the hill toward the legion. The large party of staff officers and dispatch riders that had accompanied him followed. This included the eagle-bearer, Father Griggs, and the strange hooded man in the brown cloak. Only Colonel Aetius remained, looking down from his horse on Stiger, Cethegus, Lepidus, Tiro, and Geta. Lieutenant Sadeus, Lepidus's second in command, had also joined them. The colonel was silent a moment before addressing Cethegus.

"Captain, we shall determine how your report became misplaced after today's action is concluded," the colonel announced brusquely. He then paused and looked over the officers of the two companies. "Get your companies moving. Lieutenant Stiger here will be your guide. Once across the river, begin marching north toward the enemy's defensive line there. The other companies will march just as soon as I can cut their orders. They should be following closely behind you. Though I will likely join you before you go into action, do not wait on me." The colonel paused to take a breath before continuing. "Once across, the enemy will eventually become aware of our presence. We cannot allow them too much time to prepare. Between your two companies, you have nearly four hundred men. Strike at the enemy's flank just as soon as you are able. Is that understood?"

"Yes, sir," Captain Cethegus said in a sullen tone. Stiger noticed a hate-filled glance thrown in his direction.

"I understand, sir," Captain Lepidus said confidently. "You can count on the Tenth."

"I know I can count on both companies," Aetius said. "Now, gentlemen, get your companies moving. We're wasting the daylight."

With that, the colonel wheeled about and galloped off toward the main body of the legion. Stiger watched him go before turning around.

"That crossing had better be there," Cethegus hissed at Stiger, "or I will personally nail you to a cross."

TEN

"You can't be serious," Cethegus said with exasperation, eyeing the forest. "There is no telling what is in there."

"A short way through the trees will bring us to the path." Stiger was barely able to contain the mounting frustration with his commanding officer. Despite attempts to keep to himself, the march south had been painful for Stiger. Cethegus had alternated between periods of brooding silence and abrupt bouts of intense rage where he denigrated and threatened his lieutenant with a wide range of punishments for his failings and perceived slights. Cethegus had even accused Stiger of blatant cowardice. The men had witnessed it all. Stiger felt a deep sense of burning shame and resentment. He'd had more than enough.

"The enemy could be waiting for us," Cethegus said, eyes narrowing as he warily studied the forest, with its thick layer of undergrowth. The captain had ordered a halt, and the men stood loosely in marching formation, shields grounded and waiting. The heat was becoming quite oppressive, and any break was welcome. Cethegus absently waved a fly away.

"Then," Stiger said through gritted teeth, "we shall meet them with shield and sword, sir."

"Don't get cheeky with me," Cethegus barked. "I am barely able to tolerate your continued insolence as it is. I'm of a mind to send you back to the encampment."

"Sir," Stiger said, clamping down hard on his anger. "Our orders are clear. We must make haste."

"You don't tell me—"

"What's the holdup?" Captain Lepidus had come forward. The Tenth was following just behind the Seventh. Like everyone else, Lepidus appeared hot and uncomfortable. He held his helmet under an arm. Sweat ran down the other captain's brow, which he wiped away.

Stiger gave a shrug and gestured helplessly toward his captain.

"Well?" Lepidus turned on Cethegus. "What is the hold up?"

"I was studying the forest," Cethegus said sullenly.

"To what purpose?" Lepidus's tone leaked with irritation.

"The enemy could be waiting for us," Cethegus said, with a gesture at the forest. "They could be waiting in there to ambush us. I think I will send a party forward to scout first. Yes, that is what I shall do."

Lepidus blinked, glancing toward the forest and then back at Cethegus with an incredulous expression. "It is too hot for such nonsense. You have two minutes to move your men forward, or I will march around you." With that, Lepidus turned on his heel and stalked off to rejoin his own company.

Cethegus watched the other captain for a moment before throwing a furious glance at Stiger. He then turned to Sergeant Geta, who had been standing just feet away.

"Order the men forward," Cethegus said in a sullen tone.

The order was given, and Stiger took the opportunity to escape from under his captain's thumb. He was amongst the first to enter the forest. The company came shortly after, crashing through the trees and brush behind him. The sergeants and corporals encouraged the men onward, while Stiger blazed just a few feet ahead. It seemed to take forever, and then suddenly they emerged onto the trail. The relief Stiger felt at finally making it to the crossing was immense.

"This way," Stiger called as the first men burst onto the trail. He turned in the direction of the river, hurrying to the bank. "Ropes! Bring the ropes forward!"

Tiro joined Stiger at the water's edge. Stiger surveyed the opposite bank. There was no indication of any enemy sentries or lookouts. He was cheered by this. With luck, they would be able to get both companies across without detection.

"Sir, ready for another refreshing dip?" Tiro asked, having come up. Stiger looked over at the sergeant and gave a curt nod of greeting.

Two men came up with the guide ropes for the crossing.

"Secure the rope to that tree, and that other one over there," Stiger said, pointing to two trees he wanted. They were close enough to the water's edge that he judged both would be the right height for a crossing. "Make sure you tie them off low enough so that each rope will be around a foot over the surface when secured from the other side."

"Yes, sir," one of the two men said, and they immediately got to work.

"What, exactly, do you think you are doing?"

Stiger turned and saw his captain. Cethegus was looking down upon him from the top of the bank at the edge of the trail. The captain wore a disapproving expression and shook his head, as a parent might at a wayward child.

"I am preparing to cross, sir," Stiger said, thinking that it was quite obvious. He was wondering what the captain's objection would be this time.

"I can see that," Cethegus snapped, eyeing the water and the far bank. He chewed his lip as he looked it over again. "No, I am afraid that a crossing is completely out of the question."

"What?" Stiger asked, stunned. He glanced over at Tiro. The sergeant looked just as shocked.

"It is as I feared. The water is too deep, and moving too fast," the captain declared, placing both hands upon his hips. "I knew this would be a waste of time. Nothing but a fantasy."

"What?" Stiger could not believe what he was hearing. "Are you serious?"

"There shall be no crossing," Cethegus said loudly, then turned around. He scanned the men from his company, who had packed tightly onto the trail behind him. "Sergeant Geta?"

"Here, sir." Geta stepped forward. The sergeant, only a few feet away, had been watching the drama play out. Stiger thought the sergeant looked somewhat nervous. Geta glanced uneasily across the water, down to Stiger, and then back to his captain.

"There is no ford." Cethegus gestured with a vague wave behind him at the river. "It was all a fantasy, a waste of our time and the legion's."

"If you say so, sir."

Cethegus turned in surprise on the sergeant. It was clear to Stiger that Geta believed the crossing existed. The sergeant apparently understood that if a crossing was not attempted, there would be serious trouble, and he wanted nothing to do with it. Cethegus appeared oblivious to this simple fact, but he seemed genuinely perplexed the sergeant was not supporting him as enthusiastically as he normally did.

"Cethegus, what is the delay?" Lepidus had come forward again, roughly shoving men aside so he could make his way through the press. "Why aren't your men moving across the river?"

Cethegus turned toward Lepidus and a frown crossed his face.

"There is no crossing." The captain of the Seventh gestured back down toward Stiger. "The lieutenant made it up."

Lepidus looked to Stiger, who was down by the water's edge, with the two legionaries who were busy tying the guide ropes to the designated trees. No one had ordered them to stop. They were working fast and with practiced ease.

"Is this true?" Lepidus demanded of Stiger, a hard look coming into his eyes.

"I did not make it up," Stiger affirmed, and gestured behind him at the river. "I was just about to cross when the captain here stopped me."

Lepidus studied the water and the far bank before turning back to Cethegus and lowering his voice. "Look here, Cethegus, the crossing seems manageable enough. What are you playing at?"

Cethegus attempted to stammer out a reply, but Lepidus stopped him and stepped very close. The captain of the Tenth leaned forward and whispered something to the captain of the Seventh that only the two of them could hear. Stiger saw Cethegus's eyes go wide, and he turned to look at Lepidus in what Stiger could only describe as pure fright. Lepidus gave Cethegus an even harder look than he had just given Stiger.

"Lieutenant," Cethegus said, a tremor to his voice. "You may begin the crossing."

"Yes, sir," Stiger said. The two legionaries had finished their work. Stiger took the end of one of the ropes, tied it about his waist, and turned to Tiro. "Let's go."

Tiro grabbed a rope end and did the same. He then checked to make sure the other ends of the two guide ropes were secure, giving each a strong tug.

"Best to be sure, sir," Tiro said. "Wouldn't want to have to come back and do it over again."

He gave each rope another tug. Satisfied, he turned back to Stiger, and together they entered the water, the men behind them feeding out the rope. The cold of the water was a shock, especially after being broiled in their armor under a hot summer sun. The only difference from the last crossing was that both men were wearing their full kit, which included armor and shield. They held their shields above their heads, making sure to keep them clear of the water.

The extra weight and drag created by their armor made the crossing more difficult, and they intentionally went slower than they had before. Nearly halfway across, Stiger glanced back and saw Lepidus and Cethegus watching with men clustered behind them. All eyes were on Stiger and Tiro.

Stiger took care to make sure that each foot he placed was firmly planted before taking the next step. With his armor on, the last thing he wanted was to lose his footing. If he did, he might be carried into deeper water, where the weight of it could very well drown him. Drowning was an awful way to go. He decided that if he had to die, it would be preferable to have it happen when he was old and in bed, with a full life behind him. He said a brief prayer to the High Father, asking for his assistance, and continued on with Tiro at his side.

The weight of their armor had an unexpected side effect in that it also helped to weigh them down so they could plant their feet securely in the soft river bottom. Neither slipped or lost their footing. Both men made it safely to the other side. There was a brief cheer that was quickly hushed by the officers on the far bank.

"Well," Tiro said, glancing back the way they had just come, "wasn't that just refreshing? You know, I think we should make an effort to do this sort of thing more often, sir."

Stiger tied his end of the rope off as Tiro moved to secure his. When finished, both guide ropes stretched clear across the river, a foot above the water, as Stiger had intended.

Stiger shot the sergeant a satisfied smile, which was returned. Dripping wet, both men gestured back to indicate that it was safe to cross. Moments later, the first of the men splashed into the water. The men had tied their swords and short spears to their shields, which they carried with one hand. The other hand held on tightly to the guide rope, while helmets hung from ties about their necks.

The crossing was finally underway.

It went smoothly. With the guide ropes, no one was lost or swept away. Men climbed out of the water, soaked and chilled to the bone. Under the brutal heat of the day, they would soon dry and warm up quickly enough. As Stiger watched the company come ashore, he smiled with the satisfaction of a job well done. Third Legion had managed a foothold on the enemy's side of the river, and it was all due to his initiative and energy.

Tenth Company began crossing just as soon as the last man of the Seventh entered the water. Captain Cethegus had dragged himself ashore and promptly ordered the company formed up. He led them boldly forward farther down the path and away from the river. Stiger would have preferred to be at the front, but was instructed to bring up the rear while the captain led the way.

The path was not a long one, and when the company began to emerge from the forest, a shout was called back that the enemy was in sight. Orders were relayed from Cethegus, and the men began hustling forward out of the forest, hastily forming a line of battle twenty across and several ranks deep. Stiger emerged from the forest last and saw what appeared to be an enemy light company moving in their direction, at least several hundred yards off. A number of horsemen were spurring madly away to the north. These crested a small hill and disappeared from view over the other side.

Stiger made his way forward to where Cethegus stood with his two sergeants. The captain appeared deeply troubled. He spared Stiger a disdainful look, and then returned to watching the enemy.

"Looks like bad luck, sir," Tiro grunted. "A few more minutes and this bunch would have been out of view."

"Perhaps they were here as sentries?" Geta asked Tiro.

"I think they were out on patrol," Tiro said. "They were marching north when they saw us come out from the trail."

Stiger wondered why Cethegus had not waited until the enemy was out of view before leading the company forth from the tree line. Then he realized that Cethegus had likely ordered the men forward without having first sent scouts ahead. The captain was not only incompetent, Stiger realized with frustration, he was stupid. A hot wave of anger washed through him.

"Well...now the enemy knows we are here," Cethegus said, with yet another unhappy glance over at Stiger. "They look like they mean to fight."

"They intend to delay us," Stiger guessed. "Those horsemen are likely fetching reinforcements."

"A fight," Cethegus said with a heavy sigh, trailing off before starting again. "A fight seems inevitable."

Tiro looked over at Geta, and though Stiger knew both men disliked each other, they were veterans. Silent meaning passed between the two sergeants, and Geta gave a curt nod.

"Sir," Tiro spoke up, "might I make a suggestion?"

Cethegus looked over at the sergeant, a contemptuous expression on his face. It was almost as if he were going to say no, but then nodded for Tiro to continue.

"We outnumber that light company almost two to one," Tiro said. "We should crush them before any additional reinforcements show."

"I agree," Geta said quickly before Cethegus could reply. "If we wait, we might find ourselves outnumbered."

Cethegus's gaze shifted to Geta. There seemed to be surprise in the captain's eyes as he considered what they had said. Stiger understood that both sergeants had united to deal with the threat before the company. He wondered if the captain realized that.

"They are light infantry, and our men are heavy," Tiro said confidently, throwing disdain for the enemy into his voice. "We should make quick work of them."

"Very well," Cethegus said with another glance at the enemy, who had marched closer and showed no indication of slowing. "I have decided we shall attack. Assume your positions."

Stiger walked to the right of the company with Tiro following, while Geta made for the left and the captain made his way to the center. The enemy company had continued to advance and were much closer now.

"Between you and Geta, that was some fine manipulation," Stiger commented.

"There's been no officer yet born a good sergeant could not handle, sir." Tiro looked over at Stiger with a sly, knowing grin. "Except you, of course, sir."

Stiger looked over at the sergeant and grinned back.

"First rank! Ready shields ... Shields up!" The call echoed up and down the line as the corporals repeated it. "Prepare to throw spears."

The first rank took a step forward, even as the back ranks moved to the rear two steps to make room for a toss. The short spear had been adopted by the legions during the Midisian Reformation, replacing the javelin. It was cheaper, more easily produced, and reusable. Stiger's training had included both weapons.

Personally, Stiger preferred the javelin, as the weapon was deadlier and, more importantly, could not be reused due to its soft, long shank, which bent upon contact. It meant, once tossed, the weapon could not be thrown back.

Stiger drew his sword. He glanced over to his left and down the line. Prepared for a toss, the company looked impressive. Then he turned toward the enemy and studied them. They carried round, medium-sized shields and long spears. Their armor consisted of simple chainmail shirts that stopped just above their waist. Each wore a rough conical helmet with a broad nose guard.

The sun poked out of a cloud, and the polished metal tips of the enemy's spears, held upright, glinted like a thousand flashes of light. Stiger felt his stomach clench as nerves took hold. The enemy was only fifty yards away, then forty ...

"Release spears," Cethegus shouted, and the men gave a near unified grunt as they threw with all of their might. The short spears arced up into the air.

"No," Tiro whispered and shook his head in dismay.

The range was too long, for the spear the legionaries carried was a short-ranged weapon. The enemy raised up their shields and continued their advance without stopping, even as the legionary short spears slammed downward.

Most fell short, imbedding themselves into the grass to the light company's front, but a few that had been better thrown clattered off shield and armor. Pierced through the foot, one man screamed and dropped both shield and long spear as he grasped the shaft of the short spear, which had pinned his foot to the turf. He slowly began to draw it out.

"Close up," the call came.

"Advance," Cethegus shouted, his high-pitched voice breaking slightly.

"HAAAH!" the men shouted in unison, and the company started forward, armor chinking with each step, hobnailed sandals thudding rhythmically down into the knee-high grass. "HAAAH."

Stiger swallowed nervously as the distance closed. Unlike his previous fight in the wood, this was in broad daylight. He could fully see the enemy as the two formations closed upon one another. The enemy looked determined and steady, nothing like he felt. He gritted his teeth to keep from chattering and offered a prayer to the High Father, begging for strength.

"Lock shields," Cethegus called when the two formations were just fifteen feet apart. The legionary shields thunked together, and the sound startled Stiger. Sweat ran down his forehead and into his eyes. The enemy abruptly halted and, in unison, leveled their deadly spears at the legionary company.

The Seventh continued forward, and in the last few feet, Stiger's eyes were drawn to the insects buzzing about the grass and air between the two formations, completely oblivious of what was about to occur. This peaceful meadow with its waist-high grass was shortly to become a place of death.

The two formations met, enemy spears jabbing out first with heavy thunks and a clatter as they struck at the legionary shields, seeking a way past the long, rectangular barriers. The legionaries pushed forward, closing the gap. The spears scraped against the shields as they were thrust either upward into the air or downward into the grass as the shield wall pushed relentlessly forward. There was an agonized scream as a spear found purchase in a legionary's lower leg off to the left.

Then the legionary shield wall met the enemy's in a tremendous crash.

Stiger, standing at the end of the line next to Tiro, found himself facing a spearman who had broken ranks and taken several steps back to gain room to use his weapon. Stiger kept his shield locked with Tiro's, as he had been taught, doing his best to remember his training. The spearman swung his spear around to hit above the legionary shields rather than try to punch in between them. Stiger thrust his shield up, ducking his head at the same time. The spear clattered violently off of the top of the shield. He parted his shield from Tiro's and stabbed toward the enemy. His sword hit the enemy's round shield and was jarringly deflected.

Tiro struck at the same time, expertly aiming for their opponent's exposed leg. The sergeant's sword found purchase and punched right through, driving the screaming man to a knee. Tiro pulled his sword back. Scraps of skin and muscle came with it. The leg wound bubbled and gushed with blood.

Stiger recovered himself and stabbed again, this time carefully aiming for the exposed neck. His sword missed as the man jerked back and away to avoid the strike, but he was not quick enough. Stiger's blade caught him instead underneath his chin in the lower jaw, sword driving upward into the spearman's brain as the head snapped back. Stiger could feel the sword scrape against bone as it went in. He stood frozen in the moment, shocked at what he had just done. Tiro slammed his shield into the spearman, and the man collapsed backward and did not stir.

"Nicely done, sir," Tiro said without looking sideways at Stiger. "Way to use his head."

Stiger was shocked that the sergeant could joke at such a time, but suddenly it struck him as incredibly funny and he laughed, bringing his shield up and stepping over the dead spearman.

Tiro glanced over at Stiger. "It's best to keep your head, sir. Battles need direction and officers are known for occasionally providing that sort of thing."

Stiger nodded at that but, before he could reply, was confronted by another spearman, who hammered his shield forward. Stiger's shield arm ached from the force of the impact. He almost cried out in pain. Instead, he yelled a war cry and shoved back, putting his shoulder into it as Tiro had shown him. The two shields smashed together again and the spearman lost his footing and stumbled backward. The man caught himself, using the butt of his spear for stability, just as Stiger jabbed forward with a thrust and his sword punched into the man's groin. Stiger gave a savage twist to the weapon and yanked back. He punched his shield fully into the man, again feeling the blow painfully communicated to his arm. The spearman went down in a heap, screaming in pain as he fell. Another thrust from Stiger's sword and the man ceased his screaming, silenced forever.

Stiger glanced around. His side of the line had bent slightly around the flank of the enemy light company. This was a result of the longer legionary line and the natural inclination of those not currently engaged to get in on the action. Toward the center, the fighting was intense, with many of the spearmen having discarded their main weapon to draw short swords.

The noise of the fight was incredible. Stiger was surprised he had not noticed how loud it was until this moment. The fear he had felt before was gone. Glancing around the fight once again, he became aware of an opportunity created by the smaller size of the enemy formation.

"You men," Stiger called to the second and third ranks, pointing his sword at them. "Extend the first rank's line. Over here. Quickly now. Step quickly."

The men moved as directed. Tiro looked at him curiously, and Stiger was afraid he might object. Instead, the sergeant helped to get the men where Stiger wanted them.

"We are going to swing 'round and push into the flank of the enemy," Stiger called to the additional length of line he had just created. "Swing 'round!"

The end of the line swung around and into the side of the enemy's formation. Stiger and Tiro joined them at the very tip of the line. The fighting intensified, and both Stiger and Tiro found themselves hard-pressed as the side of the enemy's box-like formation turned and faced them, fighting with grim desperation.

"Push them, boys," Tiro encouraged, and the men responded by throwing their shoulders into their shields. The fighting continued for some minutes, and then one side of the enemy line buckled, folding inward. The entire line before them seemed to shudder. The legionaries, sensing victory, gave a great cheer, and at that the enemy formation completely disintegrated. The Rivan spearmen turned and ran. The abruptness was shocking. But what was more unexpected to Stiger was the wholesale slaughter that followed. The legionaries seemed to Stiger like beings possessed by demons as they cut down and pursued the fleeing enemy with a mad fury.

Stiger stood there for a moment, working to catch his breath as the bulk of the company surged ahead. He rested his shield on the ground, happy to be rid of its weight, and sheathed his sword. Tiro stood only a few feet away and nodded his approval at the lieutenant.

"After them!" Cethegus called shrilly, running with the men, waving his sword high in the air. A number of men, which included much of the first rank, simply looked on as they struggled to catch their breath. Most were leaning heavily upon their shields.

"We have a long march ahead," Tiro said unhappily, his eyes on the captain, "with another fight waiting for us at the end."

Stiger nodded. It was perceptive, solid thinking. Stiger realized that he should have thought of it himself and felt somewhat ashamed.

Stiger watched the heavily encumbered legionaries continue the pursuit out into the meadow after the enemy, who had discarded their shields, swords, and anything else that might slow them down. Stiger saw that the majority of the enemy survivors would escape, while the legionaries would only tire themselves out, the captain encouraging them on to further levels of exhaustion.

"Oh, High Father," Tiro suddenly breathed, looking over to the left. Stiger followed the sergeant's gaze and saw a line of cavalry, less than a quarter of a mile away, with raised lances, the tips of which glittered wickedly under the sunlight. The horsemen were slowly walking their horses forward toward the legionaries pursuing the survivors of the routed enemy light company.

"Sweet gods," Corporal Varus exclaimed, just feet away.

Stiger glanced back at Tiro. The sergeant had gone white in the face and stood stiffly rooted in place. Stiger glanced around at the men. There were perhaps fifty close at hand. The rest were madly dashing after the remnants of the enemy light company. Stiger's mind raced, and he thought on what he had been taught about standing against a cavalry charge.

"We need to reform," Stiger told Tiro urgently. "Let's get the men reformed and then move them into a square formation."

"What?" Tiro said, seemingly shaken back to action by Stiger's statement. "A square, right... ah, sir, we have no short spears."

"We have our shields," Stiger said. The short spears were twenty yards away, lying where they had been tossed. Stiger thought about sending the men for them, but then a thought occurred to him. He remembered standing off the enemy horsemen when he had rescued General Treim. No horse would charge a spear line, he reasoned, particularly long spears. Stiger looked down at the dead and wounded of the battlefield. Crouching down, he picked up one of the enemy's discarded long spears and then stood. "The enemy kindly left these."

"They did, didn't they?" Tiro's eyes lit up and he smiled at Stiger like a proud father. The sergeant bent down and picked up one as well. "Sometimes you just have to love the enemy."

Stiger glanced at the horsemen. They had gone from a slow walk to a trot. Almost in unison, the line of lances with their deadly tips were leveled, angled downward as they closed on the legionaries pursuing the survivors of the light company.

"Grab a spear and reform!" Stiger yelled at the top of his lungs. He turned around, searching for a man with a horn, hoping to sound the recall. Max, the legionary with the company's horn, was with Cethegus. Stiger cupped his hands to his mouth. "Reform! Reform!"

"Quickly now," Tiro called, shoving his spear into the hands of the nearest man. "Take a spear and make me a line. Come on, man, make me a line."

Those nearest, seeing the danger of the horsemen, moved quickly, scooping up spears and falling into line. They looked nervous and shaken.

"Reform!" Stiger yelled at those men still pursuing the enemy. They were so caught up in the chase that they were oblivious to the danger.

"How can they not see them?" a man questioned.

Stiger was wondering the same, but understood their blood was up. Cethegus and more than half of the company were caught up in the moment. It was mad, and Stiger cursed them for the stupidity of it all. Captain Cethegus, a hundred yards away, was still running with them, urging the bulk of the company on. Off to their immediate left, the trot shifted into a strong gallop, the horsemen only sixty yards away from the bulk of the Seventh, still blindly pursuing the running spearmen. Stiger felt sick to his stomach.

"There are at least a hundred of them," Tiro said, having returned to Stiger's side with a spear in his hand. Those who were nearest had formed a solid line behind the lieutenant and sergeant.

Stiger could feel the pounding of the hooves through his boots. The sound of the charge was like thunder in the air. Cethegus and the men pursuing the enemy stopped in their tracks, now finally aware of the danger. Those nearest turned and began to run back toward the safety of Stiger's thin line.

Horrified, Stiger stood frozen, only able to watch in morbid fascination as the charge reached the nearest legionaries. They disappeared under the thundering hooves and leveled lances.

Then the cavalry line swept over the bulk of the legionaries like an ocean wave. The crash of the charge coming home, intermingled with screams, was jarring—shocking even.

Stiger saw Cethegus ridden down from behind as he attempted to run for safety, a cavalry lance taking him squarely in the back. The steel-tipped lance punched through his armor and exploded out through his chest before the shaft broke and snapped off in a shower of splinters. The momentum of the strike threw Cethegus forward. A moment later the captain disappeared from view, obscured by both the charging horses and the tall grass.

Shocked, he looked at the place where he had last seen Cethegus cut down. It was hard to believe that, despite his incompetence and utter unfitness as an officer, Captain Cethegus was gone.

"Oh, High Father." That came from Varus somewhere behind Stiger.

Stiger glanced around at his ragged line of men. All were staring transfixed at the growing carnage just yards away. Stiger estimated he had around fifty men in total, and they looked very shaky. He got the sense they would bolt for the woods if a stiff wind blew their way.

"Form a square," Stiger called harshly, and when they did nothing, he smacked his spear against the nearest man's shield and raised his voice. "Move, or by the gods I will put you on a charge."

"You heard the lieutenant," Tiro roared at the men as only a sergeant could. "Form square."

Under Tiro's guidance, the men Stiger had on hand rapidly reformed into a small square formation, shields pointed outward, spears pointed upward. It was the kind of formation used when an entire company needed to defend themselves against a superior enemy, or when faced with cavalry.

Stiger turned back as the cavalry charge's momentum played itself out, having ridden completely through Cethegus and his legionaries. The horsemen wheeled about and began to ride back toward the survivors, who were pitifully few in number and milled about in shock. The slaughter that followed was brutal. The enemy rode down any who were still alive and on their feet. Only ten men managed to make it back to Stiger's square.

"We can fall back into the woods," Tiro said to Stiger. "Perhaps we should do that now, sir, while those horsemen are distracted. The enemy would be unable to follow us."

Stiger glanced back at the forest. The trees were around fifty yards away. Both men stood outside the square so they could see better. The enemy cavalry rode about, looking for any additional survivors who might be playing dead. Stiger gave Tiro's suggestion some thought before replying.

"No." Stiger firmly shook his head. "I do not desire to fall back on the forest. We have spears and shields. No cavalry can charge a determined square. Besides, they are only armed with lances and swords. There are no bows that I can see."

"But, sir, wouldn't it be safer if we took up position in the trees?"

"It would be," Stiger conceded. "However, the Tenth will be up shortly, and I want to show these bastards we will not be pushed off this field."

Tiro seemed surprised by that. The sergeant looked like he was about to say something. Stiger continued before he could.

"They just slaughtered most of the company," Stiger said, anger tinging his voice. "They will not get the rest of us as easily. We are on guard now. Once the Tenth gets here, they will understand they have no hope of overwhelming us."

"Perhaps we should send a runner to Captain Lepidus then," Tiro suggested, to which Stiger nodded. Tiro quickly dispatched a man, who immediately stepped out of the formation and ran for all he was worth.

Minutes passed. The enemy cavalry seemed completely uninterested in Stiger and his men. They were more intent on looting the bodies of the men they had just killed than continued action. Neither Stiger nor the men liked what was happening, and there was grumbling. Stiger could not blame them. He would use their shared anger to stiffen the men's spines. It was a sight better than the shaky line he had just minutes before.

"We will have our revenge," Stiger said, turning around to face the men. All eyes shifted to him. "Our time will come. Maybe not against these bastards, but there will be more fighting today. I promise you. We will have our revenge."

The men gave an angry cheer. A few of the horsemen looked up at the cheer, but most ignored the legionaries as they continued their looting. They clearly felt no danger from the small square of infantry.

"Silence in the ranks," Tiro called, intent on restoring discipline.

After some time, the horsemen mounted back up and formed up into a line. The line slowly swung around to face Stiger's square, some sixty yards distant. The enemy cavalry formation was incredibly intimidating, and Stiger felt his heart beat faster at the sight of the enemy, lances held high, sharpened tips and helmets glinting under the bright sunlight.

For a minute or two, nothing happened. Then an officer broke ranks and trotted across the field. He rode a beautiful brown stallion and was clearly a man of some wealth. Stiger supposed he was a noble lord of the Rivan. The officer wore an expensively engraved chest plate, along with greaves on his legs and arms. His helmet was topped with a long blue horse-haired plume, the tail of which cascaded down his back. He looked simply magnificent, and Stiger could not help but admire him. The officer came within twenty yards and calmly surveyed the legionaries. The horse stamped impatiently in the late afternoon heat.

"You will surrender," the officer said in slightly accented common. "Or my men will ride you down, as we did those others."

"No," Stiger said, and it came out a growl. "We will not."

The officer laughed lightly, as if Stiger had made a jest. Then his mood changed and he glanced beyond Stiger, standing up slightly in his stirrups to better see.

"It's the Tenth, sir," Tiro whispered. Stiger felt a huge wave of relief wash over him and resisted the urge to turn and look. Instead, he smiled grimly at the enemy officer, who lowered himself back into the saddle.

The enemy officer's face was grave. He gave Stiger a respectful but curt nod, pulled his horse around, and slowly rode back to his cavalry. Only then did Stiger glance around. The Tenth was spilling out of the path that cut through trees, falling into a line of battle. Lepidus, standing to the front of the line, looked confident. The Tenth's captain was everything Cethegus had not been. Lieutenant Sadeus, Lepidus's second in command, stood at his side, looking just as cool and collected.

Stiger turned back to the enemy cavalry. He heard an order shouted, and the cavalry line wheeled about smartly, formed into a double column, and began to slowly ride off to the north. The enemy officer lagged behind a moment, looking directly at Stiger. He drew his sword and gave a salute. The officer then sheathed it, wheeled about, and galloped off to catch up with his men.

"You did it, sir," Corporal Varus exclaimed. Stiger turned to the corporal and saw the relief in the man's eyes. That same look was reflected in the eyes of the men, which were all upon him. Stiger turned around to Tiro and saw a similar look. It surprised him to his core. They viewed him as their savior, even Tiro, who had seen years of hard service. It made Stiger uncomfortable. He cleared his throat, unsure how to respond. He felt anything but a savior, particularly considering that he had been unable to save the majority of the company. In fact, Stiger felt guilty at having survived when so many had not.

Stiger was surprised to see Geta. The other sergeant had been at the back of the square. Their eyes met for a brief moment. Geta broke eye contact first, and looked away.

Stiger took a deep breath. Yes, he felt like a failure. A good portion of the company had been lost, senselessly so. All of it due to Cethegus's rashness and incompetence. They had suffered a staggering defeat. Intellectually, Stiger knew it was not his fault, and yet he found that it did not help.

Stiger turned back to his men and looked them over for a silent moment. He had to say something, he knew...he had to say something.

"No, you did it," Stiger said fervently, turning back to his men, for that was what they now were. "By listening to orders and standing firm, we live to fight again."

"HAAAH!" the men shouted in reply. "HAAAH!"

They fell into silence, all eyes still upon Stiger. Looking over at his men, he felt incredibly moved. He had been accepted. The Seventh was his home. He was home. Despite the loss they had just suffered, Stiger found it was a comforting feeling.

Movement caught his eye. Lepidus was pushing his way through Stiger's men. Stiger cleared his throat again and drew himself up as the captain of the Tenth approached, a thunderous expression on his face.

"Where is Cethegus?"

Stiger glanced out into the field. Lepidus followed his look.

"Shit." The captain spat on the ground in disgust. He was silent for several moments as he surveyed the meadow littered with scarlet-cloaked bodies. Then the captain of the Tenth turned to face Stiger. His expression softened. "I saw your stand against the cavalry. It was one of the bravest things I have ever witnessed."

"I was preserving what I could," Stiger said, feeling again guilty he had been unable to save more.

"Well, you did a fine job of it," Lepidus said, gazing around at Stiger's men, and raised his voice. "You all did." He then turned businesslike. "I will take command of this expedition. Prepare your men to march. We can't spare the time to search and care for any wounded. We have a job to do." He paused a few seconds and glanced back out into the meadow. "We will come back for them."

"Yes, sir," Stiger said and nodded to Tiro.

"Fall in to march," Tiro shouted, and the men scrambled to fall in.

Lepidus hesitated a moment, then patted Stiger on the shoulder before stepping off for his own company.

"Sergeant," Stiger called, seeing the discarded spears lying on the ground where the men had dropped them after the enemy cavalry had ridden off. "Let's hang onto the spears. If we have to scare off another group of cavalry, they might just come in handy.

"Yes, sir."

"What about the captain?" Sergeant Geta said in an unhappy tone.

"What about him?" Stiger turned on the sergeant.

"He is our captain," Geta said defiantly. "We should check to see if he lives, despite what Captain Lepidus just said."

Sergeant Geta's eyes were filled with resentment and anger. If the captain had, through a miracle, survived, Geta would want him tended to. Stiger well understood the man's motivation. Cethegus was Geta's patron, or perhaps, more correctly, Geta drew his power through the captain's fecklessness. The sergeant knew that his stock with Stiger was low and he would find no new ready patron there. Stiger could almost read the calculation in the other man's eyes.

"His incompetence just got more than half of the company cut down," Stiger said, looking away toward the north where the enemy cavalry had ridden off and were now out of view. "We will recover his body later, as Captain Lepidus just ordered."

"Jumped up little shit," Geta hissed under his breath.

"What was that?" Stiger turned on the sergeant. "What did you just say?"

"Nothing, sir." Geta's eyes smoldered. "I said nothin'. Must have been one of the men."

"I will deal with you after this is over," Stiger said, eying the malevolent sergeant for a moment. "That I can promise you."

"Yes, sir," Geta said stiffly and turned away.

Stiger frowned angrily and looked around. He saw Tiro exchanging a look with Varus. Both men's eyes followed Geta. Stiger thought he read deep concern in them.

"Get the men formed to march," Stiger snapped.

"Yes, sir," Tiro said, pulling his eyes from Geta and back to Stiger.

ELEVEN

Lepidus set a hard pace. The Tenth marched before what was left of the Seventh, and even that looked pitifully small to Stiger. He ordered a head count, and the Seventh's absolute strength numbered only eighty-one. The thought of having lost so many men in such a useless manner was thoroughly depressing. Had Stiger not been so tired, it would have bothered him more. Instead, he turned his thoughts to the march and the coming battle.

A handful of enemy cavalry shadowed their march. Somewhere ahead, the enemy would be waiting. Strangely, Stiger found that he did not fear the coming fight. He felt relatively calm about it, resigned even. He was more concerned about letting his men down, those few that Cethegus had left him. Stiger glanced around, looking both up and down the column. There was little, if any, talking. The men moved resolutely forward, some with heads bowed by the trials of the day. All simply placed one weary foot before the next.

They plodded on, for there was no other choice. They were legionaries.

Stiger nodded to himself as he considered them. He was their senior officer, at least until a new captain was appointed. The men of the Seventh were relying upon him to lead them through what was coming just a few short miles ahead. As he marched alongside his men, Stiger made another resolution. He almost felt called to do so.

"I will serve my men," Stiger said quietly to himself. It came out almost as a near whisper. Though most were older than himself, he would look out and care for them as a father might. If they survived the next few hours, he would work them to become the best soldiers possible. By becoming the best, better than those they would face, the men would be well-served. "Yes," he vowed, "I will do all that I can for them, and the empire."

Tiro joined Stiger after having checked on the rear of the column.

"They will recover, sir," Tiro said, breaking in on Stiger's thoughts. "They are tough boys. In some ways, losing so many friends and comrades always stays with you, but trust me, sir, they will recover. They always do."

Stiger realized the sergeant had seen him studying the men as they marched and misunderstood his thoughts. He glanced over at the sergeant. Dried blood coated Tiro's shield, which he held by his side. There was a large gash along the right side of the shield's facing that had not been there this morning. His helmet also had a fresh dent and would need to be pounded out.

Stiger abruptly felt a wave of depression wash over him. A week ago, he knew he would not have been so affected. These men were more than what he had thought them to be. They were more than simple beasts of burden. They were men, with their own thoughts, hopes, and dreams. How blind he had been.

"Of course they will," Stiger said gruffly. "We will rebuild the company."

"Yes, sir," Tiro said.

"We will do it together."

The sergeant eyed Stiger for a moment, before finally giving the lieutenant a nod and then looking away.

"Sir." Tiro suddenly pointed.

Stiger squinted. The light was beginning to dim, as the sun had begun to set over the horizon. A small bald ridge lay around a half mile to their front. It took Stiger a moment, but then he saw it. Atop the ridge, a long line of enemy infantry waited.

"Well, isn't that just shit," Geta said. Stiger had not heard the other sergeant approach. Had Geta overheard their exchange?

"We knew they would be waiting for us," Tiro said.

"That is a lot of men up there," Geta said. "You'd think the gods would send us some fortune after what we've just been through."

"Fortune?" Tiro barked out a harsh laugh. "We're the bloody infantry. We make our own fortune."

Stiger chuckled at that. It was an old, popular saying and also quite the lie. Legionaries were extremely superstitious, with many devoutly religious. Stiger had yet to meet an agnostic, even amongst the officer corps. By the simple nature of their profession, no one could afford to ignore the gods, nor would they willingly spurn them.

Stiger heard a distant crack, followed by another. He turned his ear to better hear over the constant chinking of armor and the steady tread of many sandaled feet. He strained to listen and even cupped a hand behind his left ear.

"It's the artillery, sir," Tiro exclaimed. Hours after setting out, they were nearing the enemy defenses. The line of infantry waiting for them only confirmed this. The long march was coming to an end, and hard fighting lay ahead.

The river was to their immediate left, perhaps ten feet away. Stiger looked along the river, hoping to see the legionary positions on the other side, or even just a look-out...something. Instead he saw nothing and after a few moments returned his gaze back to the long line of infantry atop the bald ridge. He glanced back the way they had come. There was no sign of the companies that were supposed to be following them. Stiger supposed they were coming. With any luck, reinforcement was just a few miles behind.

A nasty thought occurred to him. What if they had missed the crossing? What if the Seventh and Tenth were the only legionary formations across the river?

Surely they would have found the crossing.

The strung guide ropes laid across the river and the riverbanks torn up by many sandaled feet should have told them exactly where to cross. Stiger almost growled angrily as he forced himself to put such thinking aside. Speculation like this was maddening.

Ahead, Lepidus turned and signaled to him. Stiger jogged up to the captain, his legs protesting from the strain of the day. Lepidus's lieutenant, Sadeus, was by his superior's side. He gave Stiger a respectful nod, which was more than Stiger would have gotten just a few days before.

"Sir," Stiger said as he fell in alongside the captain. "That's a lot of men up there."

"Yes," Lepidus agreed. "I think, perhaps, as many as five to six hundred."

"We have fewer than three hundred," Stiger said, simply stating a fact. "This could get tricky."

Lepidus nodded and was silent a moment.

"What we are going to do is deploy in a line with three ranks," Lepidus said confidently. "Since you have so few, your side of the line will have to be just two ranks. We will anchor our line along the river. The water will protect our left flank. Our line will curve outward at the center,"

Lepidus waved his hand in the air to demonstrate the curve, "and bend around to the right, making it difficult, but not impossible, for them to flank us. That said, with so many up there... our right flank will be a problem, perhaps even the challenge we will have to overcome. Understand me?"

"Yes, sir." Stiger took a deep breath. "The enemy outnumber us and could easily swing around our right flank, rolling up our entire line."

"Good," Lepidus said with a grim look. "Since you fully comprehend the problem we face, you will take the right flank with the Seventh."

"Me, sir?" Stiger asked, surprised that the captain was giving him such a critical assignment and not his own lieutenant, whom he was bound to know far better.

"Yes, well," Lepidus said, seeming to understand Stiger's surprise, "your men stood with you against the Rivan Guard, and then again facing off the enemy cavalry. You have proven yourself steady and capable. I feel you are up to the challenge."

"Yes, sir."

"Stiger," Lepidus said. "You have the makings of a fine officer, and it is an honor to have you under my command."

"Thank you, sir," Stiger said, feeling somewhat embarrassed by the praise.

"You cannot let the enemy by under any circumstances," Lepidus said, turning back to the matter at hand. "If you do, they will roll up our flank like an old sock. I trust you will not allow that happen?"

"You may rely upon me to keep the flank secure," Stiger said, wondering how he was going to accomplish that.

Lepidus apparently could see Stiger's concern, for he continued. "I am betting the infantry up there on that ridge are not the enemy's best."

Stiger glanced back up to the ridge and wondered if the captain was correct. Could they be second rate? Could he dare to hope that they were? Thinking on the fight with the Rivan Guard and Tiro's words, Stiger wondered if it even mattered.

"Some just die harder than others," Stiger whispered to himself.

"I feel quite confident we will be facing second-rate soldiers," Lepidus said. "With the main bulk of the legion just over the river and poised to cross, well, the enemy general would be foolish to redeploy his best men."

"You think they are definitely second rate then?" Stiger asked. The argument was a compelling one. Though Stiger realized that, even if they were the enemy's best, Lepidus would resolutely lead them forward anyway. Stiger would follow. They had a job to do no matter how difficult and challenging the task.

"I hope." The captain shrugged. "If I am wrong, we may be swimming for it."

Stiger looked sharply at the captain and then realized he was jesting.

"A second plunge into the river might be pleasant," Lieutenant Sadeus said with a polite chuckle. "Though we may begin to spoil the men with such fun."

"It has been an exceptionally hot day," Stiger said.

"It has," Lepidus agreed, gaze returning to the ridge. He pointed, looked over at Stiger and Sadeus, and then raised his voice. "If you look closely, there is only one rank of the enemy. It makes them look like they've got more men on hand."

"I see," Stiger said, and he did.

"We are the legion," Lepidus said. The captain's voice was raised so that all of his men nearby could hear. Those who had been trudging along tiredly, mile after monotonous mile, picked up their heads. They had marched near twenty miles today and had waded across a river. All were exhausted, but they were trained to endure this and then give some more. Lepidus looked over at his men marching to his left. "That thin line won't stop us, will it?"

"NO," the men shouted back.

"Good," Lepidus called back, "because if it does, it means we don't train hard enough."

There was a moment of silence that was followed by quite a few chuckles that ran through the ranks as what the captain had said was repeated for those who had not heard. Stiger sensed a lightening of the mood.

"Sergeant Sacara," Lepidus said loudly.

"Yes, sar?" came the reply from a grizzled veteran farther back in the line of march.

"What happens if that line there stops us?" Lepidus asked loud enough for all to hear.

"More training, sar," the sergeant replied, with a surprising amount of relish. A groan went up from the men.

"Sergeant, do you think we will need more training?"

"We can always do with more training, sar," Sacara said. This was followed by even louder groans and exaggerated moans from the ranks. "But not today, sar."

"Why is that, sergeant?"

"We gonna whip them right good," the sergeant replied, "like a bastard that cheats at dice."

The men gave a hearty cheer.

"That's what I thought," Lepidus said. "That's what I expect from my boys."

The men gave yet another cheer, this one even louder.

Lepidus looked back to Stiger. "Now, lieutenant, kindly look to your men."

"Yes, sir," Stiger said. Sadeus gave Stiger a curt nod but said nothing. Stiger could read the strain in the other lieutenant's eyes.

Stiger stopped walking and watched the Tenth continue to march by. He waited until the Seventh came up and fell in alongside his sergeants.

"What did the good captain want?" Geta asked.

Stiger filled both Tiro and Geta in on what Lepidus expected.

"That's a lot of men up there," Geta said, eyes searching the ridge. For a moment, Stiger thought the sergeant looked a little uneasy.

"If you look carefully," Stiger said, "they only have one rank."

"What if they are holding more men in reserve on the other side of the ridge?"

"Then…" Stiger hesitated a moment. It was entirely possible the enemy had hidden reserves. If they did, Stiger realized, there was nothing he could do about it. Besides, such a suggestion was purely hypothetical, and there was no evidence to suggest the enemy had prepared in such a way. They certainly had an army on this side of the river, which meant they had the numbers. But it could be as Lepidus said, the enemy was saving their best to defend against the bulk of the legion. "Then we will adjust to whatever the enemy throws our way."

"Yes, sir," Geta said stiffly.

The march continued in silence, each step bringing them closer to the small bald ridge with the enemy line atop. The grade began to gradually increase as they started up the slope. When they approached to within six hundred yards from the enemy, Lepidus called a halt and began to deploy his men. Stiger did the same, positioning them to the extreme right of the Tenth, making sure that the left side of his line was firmly in contact with the end of their sister company. Once the line was set, Lepidus came over to consult with Stiger.

"Are your men ready, lieutenant?" the captain asked. The sun had fallen behind the tree line to their right. The light was beginning to die. Though Lepidus affected a calm and collected demeanor, Stiger could hear the strain in the captain's voice.

"They stand ready, sir," Stiger said, raising his voice. "Isn't that so?"

Stiger's men gave a cheer, which pleased him immensely.

"Very good," Lepidus said, "Then I think it is time to move ..."

The sound of hooves from behind caused them both to turn. Four horsemen were galloping up. Stiger recognized Colonel Aetius, who pulled his horse to a stop a few feet away. The other three were cavalry, likely serving as the colonel's escort. Sergeant Geta and Tiro came over, but stood at a respectful distance.

"A fine evening for a battle, gentlemen," Colonel Aetius said enthusiastically, gazing up the ridge at the waiting enemy. He then turned to the two officers. "You made good time."

"Thank you, sir," Lepidus said.

The colonel leaned forward in the saddle and gestured toward the ridge. "I presume you are going to push them off?"

"Yes, sir," Lepidus said with a natural confidence in his voice that Stiger wished he would one day be able to emulate. The strain seemed to have vanished. "I was about to give the order."

"Excellent," the colonel replied. "I have three companies of legionary infantry that will be here in twenty minutes.

Behind them, dogging their heels, are five additional auxiliary cohorts, say around twenty-eight hundred men and more still coming up."

Stiger exhaled a breath, feeling immense relief at the welcome news.

The colonel paused and surveyed the bald ridge, then gestured. "With the light failing, I don't feel we can afford to wait for them to come up before pushing forward. The enemy's second defensive line does not extend to that point there on the ridge. We cannot allow the enemy to remain up there overnight. They will surely dig in if we do so and in the morning it will be difficult forcing them off."

"Yes, sir," Lepidus said.

"I expect you to go in hard." Aetius gestured toward the hill. "Push them right off and back down the other side. You must take that ridge before nightfall."

"We will, sir," Lepidus said.

"Perfect," Aetius said, leaning back in the saddle and stretching out his back. "Gentlemen, we have a real opportunity here. Push those men off that hill. Just beyond it is the flank of the enemy's first defensive line." The colonel paused a moment and glanced back up toward the ridge. "We must break into their fortifications. We do that, and this fight here is over."

"Yes, sir," Lepidus said.

"Sir," Stiger spoke up. "What about the legion?"

"I have already signaled them," Aetius answered. "Their assault will begin shortly."

The colonel's horse sidestepped nervously. The colonel took firm hold on the reins and the horse stilled.

"Reinforcement will be here shortly," Aetius said. "I will hurry them along."

The colonel wheeled his horse around and galloped back the way he had come, his escort following, kicking up clods of dirt and grass in their wake.

"You heard the colonel," Lepidus said. "It is time."

"Yes, sir." Stiger glanced up the slope toward the enemy infantry lining the top of the ridge. They stood out against the darkening sky.

"There will be help … soon enough," Lepidus said. "We will push forward along the river and work our way up the ridge and shove them back."

Stiger looked to where Lepidus pointed.

"Very good, sir," Stiger said. "I will keep them from flanking us."

Satisfied, Lepidus strode off toward his company and the center of the line. Within a handful of minutes, the order was given to advance. The two companies began a steady climb up the small ridge, the slope increasing with each step. Stiger was already tired. His legs burned from the effort.

He glanced to the left and was satisfied that the men were staying properly aligned with the Tenth. Lepidus's extreme left hugged the water, and he extended his line there as the advance continued up the rise. Stiger snapped out a series of orders to ensure that the Seventh began bending the line back to make it more difficult for the enemy to flank him. The advance was slow and steady. The distance closed at an unhurried pace between the two forces. It went from fifty yards down to forty … a greater distance for the Seventh, which had bent their line around, forming a partially curved shape, from where it connected with the Tenth's line.

"Ready shields." The order ran its way down the line from the Tenth. "Shields up."

The entire line reacted like a wave from left to right, bringing their shields up and into position. Stiger's men still carried the long spears that they had acquired from the enemy. He had seen no need yet to discard the weapons, and Lepidus had given him no orders to do so, apparently trusting Stiger's judgment.

Studying the enemy line, Stiger saw that their opponents were light infantry, armed with a short sword, thick leather shirts studded with metal, and medium-sized rounded shields. At least, Stiger considered, the spears should give the enemy some pause for thought.

"Lower long spears," Stiger called up and down his line as, out of the corner of his eye, he saw Tenth Company toss their short spears at the enemy line. "Lower spears. Corporals... once the action begins and things get close, spears are to be dropped and swords drawn."

Stiger looked to the left, checking on the Tenth. As he did so, the two lines on that side met in a violent clash that seemed to make the air vibrate. Where Stiger was, with his line bent back, the distance to the enemy line closed to ten yards. Then the entire enemy line to his front suddenly shifted forward into movement, coming downhill to meet him, even as the legionaries worked their way up. The far end of the enemy line was moving as well, sweeping downhill to hit the flank of his line and come in at an angle. The enemy's move was almost like a door swinging closed. Stiger felt extremely exposed on the flank of the line. The danger of the enemy's maneuver was readily apparent to him.

He moved behind the ranks of men, found Varus, and tapped the corporal on the shoulder. "Get your second rank to form a ninety-degree angle at the end of the line. Once you do, bend it back around some more."

"There will be no second rank then, sir," Varus said. "No chance for a break for the first rank."

At that moment, the rank to the front of Stiger made contact with the enemy, long spears punching out, seeking purchase. Unwieldly weapons in unfamiliar hands, the legionaries mostly struck shields instead of flesh, spear points bouncing off.

"There will be no line at all if you don't hurry." Stiger then turned, looking for Tiro. He saw him and jogged over. "Sergeant, take the main line with Geta. I will take our flank."

A man screamed, then another. Stiger glanced around and saw that the spears were having some effect on the enemy light infantry, but not as much as he had hoped. A few of the enemy hesitated, shying away from the reaching spear points. The enemy's line became uneven, some closing with the legionaries and others holding back several yards.

"Drop spears and draw swords," Tiro shouted and drew his sword. There was a clatter as the spears were dropped. The steel-bladed swords seemed almost to spring into the hands of the legionaries. Stiger could almost sense the relief of the men, who were much more familiar with the gladius than the long spear.

Whether from fear or being caught up in the action, one legionary held tightly onto his spear for a moment too long. An enemy grabbed at the shaft of the spear and pulled. The man was yanked forward and out of the protection of the shield wall. Immediately dropping the long spear, the legionary drew his sword and made to step back. A sword battered against his shield and another on his shoulder. He staggered from the painful blow, which had clearly been communicated through his armor. Having sheathed his own sword, Sergeant Tiro reached forward, gripped the back of the man's armor harness, and bodily dragged him back into the line.

"By the gods, Merex," Tiro shouted in his ear. "I swear, if I had not promised your mother I would look after you, I would have left you out there to fend for yourself."

"Sorry, sergeant," came the reply from the legionary.

"Make it up to me by taking your place on the line," Tiro said.

The two legionaries on either side of where Merex had been pushed back with their shields at the enemy, covering long enough for the legionary to recover and take his place on the line, bringing his shield back up to lock with the others. The entire event had taken only a handful of seconds.

Stiger turned his attention to the oncoming enemy sweeping down the side of the ridge toward the end of his line. The door on his flank was swinging slowly, almost ponderously, closed, and it was being neatly done. Varus had the men in place, hinging on an almost perfect angle to the end of the line, ready to meet the oncoming wall of light infantry. The problem was that they were facing at least twice their number in a single line.

To Varus's left and behind, the fighting was intense, all the way from the line Tiro and Geta were managing down to the Tenth. This was the largest fight Stiger had been in. It was loud and shocking, though he found, with not a little surprise, he was not actually afraid. In fact, he almost felt comfortable and in control, as if this were what he had been born to do.

"Sir." Varus called his attention, and Stiger moved over to the corporal. "It's not gonna be enough. They will get behind us. What are your orders?"

Stiger found that he could not disagree, even though the enemy had yet to hit his flank. They had hit the entirety of the main line and the fighting there was desperate. He felt an icy dread in the pit of his stomach. Studying the oncoming attempt to outflank his line, Stiger was not sure what to do to keep the enemy from getting behind the two companies. If they did manage a successful turning movement, it would all be over. Both companies would collapse quicker than a poorly raised tent. Stiger understood this clearly. The enemy could not be permitted to get behind them.

He took another moment to look around and in a flash had an idea. Stiger left the corporal and hurried over to Tiro, who was working a stretch of the main line, calling out encouragements and criticism when he felt the need. Geta was farther to the left, where the end of the Seventh's line met with the Tenth, doing much the same thing.

"I want you to pull back a few feet, contracting the line," Stiger told him once he had gotten the sergeant's attention. "Pull every third man from the line."

Tiro simply nodded, eyes never straying from the action to his front. "Every third man?"

"Yes, send them to Varus," Stiger continued. "Quick as you can. We are in danger of being turned there."

"Yes, sir." Tiro began shouting orders to his line.

Stiger jogged back over to Varus.

"Tiro will be sending us additional men," Stiger said. "Extend the line as they come over."

"Yes, sir," Varus said, and there was palpable relief in his voice.

Stiger turned and once again studied the enemy to his front. The door was swinging steadily shut. He did a rough count in his head and quickly estimated that the men Tiro was sending over would not be enough to lengthen his line sufficiently. It would help, but the enemy just had too many men. Something else had to be done, and quick if he were to keep the enemy from wrapping around behind him and the line.

Several legionaries double-timed it over, and Varus efficiently slotted them into place, extending the line along the flank, stretching it out farther and farther. Stiger looked at the approaching enemy line and thought hard. His father had hired the very best to instruct his son in military history, tactics, and strategy. Stiger himself had purchased numerous histories and eagerly devoured each one. Yet, with all of his studying, he could think of nothing that would salvage the situation. He was facing disaster, and there seemed absolutely nothing that could be done to keep the enemy from wrapping around behind the legionary line.

Feeling helpless, Stiger became angered. It made him want to fight. He hefted his shield, and prepared to take his place on the shield wall. If this were to be it, no man would call him a coward. He would fight alongside the men and do what he could with shield and sword. It was the only thing he ... Stiger stopped as an idea began to take shape.

"That's it," Stiger said to himself, snapping his fingers.

"Sir?" Varus asked, looking over at his lieutenant.

"Flank only! The flank only! Prepare to advance," Stiger called. The fighting to his left was generating a lot of noise. Stiger raised his voice as loud as he could make it so that his entire flanking line could hear him. "We're gonna hit them hard, harder than we hit each other during drill. We are going to shove them back, cut them down, and break their line."

"HAAAH!" the men shouted in reply, momentarily drowning out the sound of the fighting. Stiger noticed that some of the enemy in the door swinging closed missed a step at the energetic shout from the legionaries. It almost made him want to smile at what he was about to do.

"Varus," Stiger hollered, "we will be pushing out and away from the protection of the main line to our left there. I want to be clear, we will be detaching from the main line. We hit those directly to our front, and hard. Once we break them, we will deal with any that make it around behind us on either side. Understood?"

"Yes, sir," Varus said with an uncertain glance at the enemy to his front only twenty yards away now.

"They won't be expecting us to advance," Stiger explained. "I am hoping to shock them with our attack. It should buy us some time to break those to our front."

Varus nodded his understanding and passed the word to the other corporals. The enemy was only ten yards distant now, and the far end of the enemy advance was lagging behind like a great tail as the door continued to slowly sweep closed. That actually helped what he was going to attempt. Stiger drew his sword. He would have only a few precious minutes before the tail caught up. He hoped that the shock and viciousness of the legionary attack would give those swinging around with the tail some pause.

"Ready shields," Stiger shouted harshly. "Shields up."

He looked to the left and then to the right. His men along the flank were as ready as could be.

"Kill!" Stiger shouted at them. "KILL!"

"KILL," the men took it up and shouted. "KILL, KILL, KILL!"

"Advance."

It seemed as if the entire enemy door swinging closed to his front skipped a step as the legionaries shoved forward, shields presented ahead, swords held at the ready behind.

An armored wall of heavy infantry, the main combat power and heart of the imperial legions, was moving toward the enemy in measured, steady steps. Stiger figured they had to make for an extremely intimidating sight.

"This is where we get our revenge!" Stiger shouted. "Kill!"

"KILL, KILL, KILL," came the shouted reply, and it seemed the legionaries put all of the frustration and rage of the day into the shout.

Then they were in contact. It began with a clatter of shield on shield. The air seemed to ring with the intensity of the meeting. The advance ground to a halt as the enemy stubbornly stood their ground. Stiger knew he had to keep the momentum going for his plan to work.

"Push," Stiger roared as loud as he could. The legionaries gave it a tremendous effort, putting their shoulders into the push, and took a half step forward before their shields parted and short swords darted out. Stiger heard a number of screams over the battering of shields and the clatter of swords striking metal and wood. "Again, push."

The men shoved forward, and the enemy line to their front gave a little and fell backward. The shield wall parted again and swords darted out, jabbing for soft flesh. There were several more screams. A legionary stumbled backward, dropping his sword and shield as he grabbed for his arm, which had been laid open to the bone and ruined. The man was roughly shoved aside by Varus, who took his place in the line.

"Push," Stiger roared, and the men pushed once again. Though it was difficult to see through the line, there appeared to be fewer of the enemy to the front. The legionaries were more heavily armored then those that they faced. It was a distinct advantage. A number of bodies lay haphazardly behind the legionary line, a testament to the effectiveness of the short sword and legionary tactics.

Stiger came across a wounded enemy struggling to sit up just behind the line, which literally had advanced right over him. The injured man was fumbling for a discarded sword a few feet away. Without any hesitation, Stiger struck downward with his sword and ended the man's life. He turned back to the action and called for another push.

Stiger glanced to his right. The tail of the enemy door was still swinging closed. He sensed he had only moments to decide the affair to his front. It was either that or give the order to fall back before the length of the enemy door slammed closed around and behind him.

"Hard push," Stiger called, effectively telling the legionaries to give this push their all. And they did, taking not the normal prescribed half step this time, but an entire step, slamming their shields as hard as they could against the enemy and immediately taking another full step. Then there seemed to be no resistance to their front as the enemy there backpedaled. The backward movement was so sudden and rapid that Stiger's legionaries were caught by surprise and broke ranks.

"Hold," Stiger shouted desperately. "Hold ranks."

The men responded, falling back into line. The surviving enemy to their front were running now, looking to put distance between the legionaries and themselves. They were falling back in the direction they had just come. The flanking line of the enemy was now broken, and the tail was isolated to his extreme right. Surprisingly, it was still closing on him from below and swinging around to come directly at him. He had only moments to reposition his men to face them.

"Wheel right," Stiger ordered, his voice breaking with the strain of continued shouting. "Wheel right."

Stiger's single line began to turn about, facing down the hill toward the enemy. He wanted the movement to be executed quicker, but knew he could not rush it and so he bit his tongue. Even before the wheeling movement was completed, the first men were in contact and the fight was on. Then his entire line was engaged.

Stiger's line was now facing downhill, in the direction they had just come minutes before as they climbed up the ridge. To his immediate rear, the main line continued to fight desperately, facing the enemy there uphill. Stiger took a deep breath. It was time to push this last threat to flank the two legionary companies down the hill and away. Stiger's men would have the downhill momentum on their side.

"Prepare to advance." Stiger waited a moment, giving the men a chance to prepare themselves. "Push."

The legionary line shoved forward a half step, then shields unlocked and short swords punched out. The legionaries were rewarded with a number of screams. Before Stiger could call for another push, the enemy's morale shattered. The line he was facing broke, turned, and ran down the hill.

"Hold your position," Stiger called, voice cracking again. Remembering what had happened to Cethegus and the rest of the Seventh, he did not want his men getting caught up in pursuit of the enemy. He had no idea where the enemy cavalry had gone. Though in the growing darkness, it was unlikely they would make a showing. Charging about on horseback at night was dangerous business.

The corporals took up his cry and kept the men in check, reforming them. Stiger's throat was dry. He longed to take a drink from his canteen, but there was no time. The fight behind him was still raging.

He looked backward and, in the dying light, studied the situation there. Since he had unhinged the flank, some of the enemy had gotten around Tiro's side and were causing the legionary line a bit of difficulty. Stiger turned to his own men, who were breathing heavily from their exertions and leaning upon their shields, which they had grounded.

"We're not done yet. Stand to. About face."

The line rapidly shifted, facing back up the hill.

"Wheel left," Stiger ordered and called a halt when he had the line properly aligned to where he wanted it. "Advance."

They advanced back up the hill toward the action. Stiger allowed the legionaries to step around him before falling in right behind them. His line hit the enemy flanking the main legionary line from behind. The first of their opponents were so absorbed in the fighting that they did not see the approaching danger until it was too late. So shocking was the legionnaires' appearance that they completely overwhelmed the few enemies who had gotten just behind the main line. The added weight on the extreme end of the line was telling. Without intentionally planning to, Stiger's side of the line began to roll up the enemy.

"Continue," Stiger shouted, intent on taking advantage of the situation he had inadvertently created. With each step, the momentum grew. "Continue. Keep going."

The enemy line began to collapse with surprising quickness on Stiger's side of the field. An enemy horn sounded close at hand, blasting out several notes. The effect it had on the battle was profound. The enemy infantry immediately began falling back—enemy officers, sergeants, and corporals working to keep good order. The legionary line pursued them a few yards and then was called to a halt by Captain Lepidus.

Stiger rested his shield on the ground, feeling a deep exhaustion take hold. He took out his canteen and downed a large gulp of warm water. At that moment, he was surprised to find the water tasted better than the finest of wines. He took another gulp, savoring the taste and the feeling, and then sealed the canteen before returning it to its place on his harness.

Stiger looked around. They were sitting securely on top of the ridge that the enemy had held just minutes before. In the failing light, he could see the enemy fortifications laid out below and before him, the river and the main body of the legion on the other side. The legion had yet to move forward, but it looked like they were readying to do so. He swung around and behind saw a large body of men approaching, the distinctively shaped legionary standards held high. These were the reinforcements Colonel Aetius had promised. They had started the climb up the ridge that the Seventh and Tenth companies had just won. Stiger's shoulders sagged with relief that those reinforcements were almost on hand, for he was thoroughly worn out.

"Sir," Varus said, drawing his attention. "I thought we were done for, but that... that was an incredible bit of maneuvering."

Stiger noticed the eyes of the men on him, and he once again felt uncomfortable. He was at first unsure how to reply, but then simply nodded. "The men deserve the real credit. They did the hard work."

A legionary horn to Stiger's left blew, and Stiger saw the Tenth's standard-bearer frantically waving the company standard for the main body of the legion to see on the other side of the river. A distant horn sounded in reply, and then blew another tune. It was the order to advance. Stiger saw the entire legion begin to move forward toward the crossing. The legion's artillery was still firing away, somewhat blindly attempting to soften up the enemy's defenses, as the crews were unable to see beyond the first rampart.

Stiger looked down upon the enemy fortifications and studied them critically. As he had seen before, there were two ramparts, but from his new position he could see them better. The first was the one along the river's edge. There were no side walls, just a single rampart facing the river. The second was along a ridgeline a hundred to two hundred yards behind the first, which was almost fish-hooked in shape, the end being what the men of the Seventh and Tenth were now standing upon. The enemy had surprisingly not extended the trench and rampart this far. Why? Stiger wondered. Why did they not fortify this position? He turned his attention back down below.

Much of the enemy's artillery was down behind the first rampart, in the bowl-shaped area before the second line. The enemy they had just forced off of the ridge were still moving in good order down the slope toward the artillery positions.

Stiger looked over to his right at the second enemy defensive line, which almost extended to their very position. He studied it carefully, noting the depth of the trench before the rampart, the wooden spikes driven into the soil, the height of the wall, and the wooden barricade topping it. He could just barely make out a large number of defenders lining the rampart, heads peeking out from behind the wooden barricade. These seemed to be looking at the legionaries who had just taken the end of the ridge that ran nearly to the water's edge. Stiger hoped fervently they remained behind those defenses and did not come out to fight.

Again, he asked himself why they had not fortified this portion of the ridge. There were no fixed defenses between the two legionary companies and the enemy artillery parked right behind the first defensive rampart. Stiger had no answer for why this was, but was not about to second guess fortune.

"What do you think?" Lepidus asked. Stiger turned to face the captain.

Stiger took a deep breath before replying. He was so exhausted that his legs were trembling with the effort of just standing still. Lepidus looked just as blown. The captain rubbed at an eye.

"I think we need to push down there." Stiger pointed toward the enemy's artillery positions. "If we get behind those manning the first rampart, we might create a general panic as the main body of the legion goes over to assault. With luck, we can rout the defenders there so that the legion can cross with minimum difficulty."

Lepidus nodded but then gestured toward the second defensive line, which was thick with infantry. "What about them?"

Stiger was silent a moment and then gestured back down the ridge that they had just fought up. "Let the companies just coming up deal with those bastards."

"That is what I was thinking." Lepidus nodded and turned to look at the colonel's reinforcements. "Sergeant Sacara."

"Sar," the sergeant said, moving over.

"Colonel Aetius is down there working his way up the ridge," the captain said, pointing. "Kindly send a runner to advise him that we are moving forward to attack the enemy's artillery and to get behind the first rampart. Tell him it is my recommendation that those companies just now coming up attack the second defensive line over there, hitting it from the side. Got that?"

"Yes, sar." The sergeant moved off to find a suitable runner.

Lepidus gave Stiger a nod and then moved back toward his own company.

"Form up," Stiger ordered, and it was immediately taken up by the sergeants and corporals. A number of men were so blown they had sat down when the action had ended. These painfully and slowly dragged themselves to their feet.

"Only a little ways farther," Stiger said, realizing his men were almost at the end of their rope. Though he was just as done in as they were, he had to be their strength. "We need to help our boys cross the river."

"We can do it, sir," a legionary said, and the men gave a rousing cheer. Stiger did not see who had said it, but it brought a smile to his face. These were good men.

"I know you will," Stiger said, looking around at the men as they fell into line. "But you won't have to do it alone. This is something we will do together."

A loud, deep thud behind him drew his attention back to the enemy artillery, which had begun to fire at the first legionary units starting to cross the river. From what he could see, the enemy commander was redeploying some of his men from the first defensive rampart along the river to confront the threat that the Seventh and Tenth now posed. Stiger looked over to where Lepidus stood. The captain called for the advance, and the two companies started down the hill at a slow and measured pace.

More enemy artillery fired across the river, while friendly bolts fired back at the enemy manning the barricade. Ballista balls screamed over the rampart, landing with deep thuds and great gouts of dirt and spray. Some landed close to the enemy machines, others fell short or went wide. Besides shredding the wooden barricade, Stiger concluded, the legionary artillery was not very effective. Only a few of the enemy catapults had been damaged and put out of action.

When they were halfway down the ridge, the friendly artillery fire ceased, and Stiger realized that someone on the other riverbank had seen them marching off the ridge and into action. He felt relieved that he would not be facing any friendly fire, and then he wondered why the enemy had not turned their own artillery on the Seventh and Tenth. Whatever the reason, Stiger was grateful for that small blessing and steeled himself for what was ahead.

As they neared the base of the ridge, a line of infantry waited for them. From the mismatched armor and shields, it looked to Stiger like a mixed bag pulled from a number of units and thrown hastily together. Stiger recognized many of them as the formation they had just faced on the ridge. Though these had clearly been reorganized, they could not be looking forward to facing the heavy infantry of the legions again in such a short space of time.

Stiger tried to see everything, committing it to memory as they marched closer to the scratch line of defenders. Along the inside of the defensive wall, a thin line of infantry crouched down behind the splintered and broken wooden barricade topping the earthen rampart, waiting for the moment they would be called upon to defend it. Archers interspersed amongst them fired down the other side, ducking back under cover to draw a fresh arrow and popping up once again. Occasionally one fell or dropped, rolling down the inside of the sloped rampart wall, pierced by an arrow from one of the imperial auxiliary units.

"Shields up," the call rang out. The shields were presented forward and locked together. "Draw swords."

Following just behind the shield wall, Stiger drew his own sword. His shield arm was shaking with the continued effort of holding the heavy thing. Stiger felt the fatigue of the day wearing down upon him, though with the approaching action, his aches and pains started to fade.

"Dress that line there," Tiro shouted at a legionary who had stumbled over a large fieldstone.

Then the two lines came together in a crash. Stiger had come to expect the jarring sound of the first impact. The enemy was arranged in two ranks. Stiger stood steady behind his second rank, calmly watching the fighting to his front. It did not seem like the time for a push. Tiro, Geta, and the corporals were working the front rank, keeping the men focused and under control. For the moment, things seemed fairly even. The men were tired, but they were also legionaries—the toughest, meanest, and most disciplined soldiers around. The empire's legions were notorious for wearing out their enemies.

Stiger wondered for a moment if he should do more. He glanced off to his left to see what Lepidus was doing. He was surprised to see the captain doing the exact same thing, standing back and simply watching for trouble or opportunities.

There was a loud thud that drew Stiger's attention. In the dying light, just behind the enemy infantry line, Stiger saw a catapult had released a stone ball. The round whistled through the air, heading toward the bulk of the legion on the other side of the rampart. With the passing of the ball, Stiger felt an urgency to break the line before him.

From what he could see, there were at least ten enemy catapults still in operation, each manned by a crew of eight to ten. He longed to be at them. A number of catapults stood quiet and still, with no crews to attend to them. Stiger glanced over at the captain and saw that Lepidus seemed to be thinking the same thing. Both men had turned at the same time and were looking at each other. It was almost comical. They were too far away from each other to be easily heard through the cacophony of the fight. Stiger mimed pushing forward, and Lepidus nodded deeply in agreement.

"Prepare to push," Stiger called, realizing that this final effort would likely render his men too blown for any further action. "Push."

The men hammered forward with their shields, taking the prescribed half step. The noise of the fighting increased as the shields scraped apart for a quick jab at the enemy. There was a great groan of effort from the Tenth as they shoved forward as well.

"Again," Stiger called loudly. "Push."

Stiger called for two more pushes, but the enemy did not break, nor did they yield much ground. The enemy had given a few yards and then stopped, standing firm. It became clear that the front rank needed a break. He called for the rotation of ranks. Sergeant Geta blew hard on a whistle he was carrying for this purpose. The swapping of ranks was efficiently done. The men from the first rank now became his second. They were breathing hard as they took up their position, ready to go back into action at a moment's notice should the man to their direct front fall or the sergeant's whistle call come again.

Glancing up and down the line, Stiger was becoming concerned. His men were tiring. Several legionaries were down, either dead or wounded, but there were also a number of enemy bodies behind the line from the push forward. Stiger was beginning to think it was desperation alone that held the enemy in place.

A legionary horn blared out behind him. It was the call to advance. He glanced backward, and his eyes widened. In the growing darkness, a thick wall of infantry was moving down the ridge to join the battle. Stiger could not believe his eyes. Those men should have assaulted the second enemy defensive line. Instead, they were marching to join the fight. Colonel Aetius had decided against their recommendation.

There was an abrupt lessening of noise, and Stiger's head snapped back around to the fight. The enemy to his front had seen the advancing reinforcements. They were falling back.

"Press them," Stiger called. "Advance. Let's break their will to fight. We end this now!"

Stiger's men and those of the Tenth advanced, giving one final effort. The two lines came back in contact, but it only lasted a few heartbeats before the enemy broke, turned, and ran into the gathering darkness.

Too blown for a pursuit, the legionaries allowed their shields to drop, bottoms resting on the ground. They leaned on them, breathing heavily from their exertions. Stiger did the same, watching the enemy disappear into the growing darkness.

The sound of a ballista ball whistling out into the darkness was followed with a thud and a crack.

Stiger's head came up. "Sergeant Tiro."

"Here, sir," Tiro said, exhaustion heavy in the veteran's voice.

"Our job's not done," Stiger said, loud enough for the men to hear. There was a groan at that. "We need to silence that artillery."

"Yes, sir," Tiro said, and then addressed himself to the men. "You heard the lieutenant. We still have some bastards to kill. Luckily for us, they come from the one branch of the military that's more hated than those weak-kneed bastards who prance about on horseback."

There was some chuckling at that. The men began to fall back into ranks. A few were too far gone and simply sat down on the ground, either unwilling or unable to go any farther. Tiro walked by one and simply patted the man fatherly on the shoulder, and continued past him without a word.

Stiger saw no reason to second guess the sergeant's decision to not make an issue of it. Instead, he hefted his own shield up. It seemed to be made of lead. He stepped up to the forming line. Looking left, he saw that the Tenth was doing the same.

"Advance," Stiger said, voice cracking, when he judged the men ready. The Seventh started forward toward the artillery.

CRACK! Another stone ball was fired, whistling off into the darkness.

Then, they were on the first machine. It had been abandoned. A small fire burned off to the side, which the crew had clearly used for cooking. Stiger thought about the enemy manning the second defensive line. If they came out from behind their defenses, everything that had been accomplished today could be for naught.

"Sergeant," Stiger said, calling over to Geta, whom he saw just feet away. "Set fire to that machine...burn it, if you would."

"Yes, sir." Geta immediately moved to burn the catapult.

The advance continued. They came upon another machine. This one was manned. The crew stopped reloading and picked up swords to fight. The legionaries charged the artillerymen, screaming as they came. The defenders were rapidly cut down and the deadly machine was theirs. Stiger followed behind them, keeping an eye on the action.

Stiger looked beyond the machine they had just captured. Less than twenty yards away was another catapult still in operation. Glancing in the direction of the rampart and the defenders struggling to hold the wall against a determined attack by the main body of the legion, Stiger took a deep breath and turned toward the other catapult. It was the last machine in operation.

"Onward," Stiger called, pointing his sword. "Take it from them! Come on now, just a little farther. Onward."

The men surged, or rather, in their exhausted state, staggered forward toward the next catapult. Stiger turned to follow and then stopped. He looked back on the machine they had just taken. It was his duty to render it inoperable in the event the assault failed.

"Corporal," Stiger said to Varus, who was moving by him and following the men. Stiger pointed with his sword at the catapult. "Burn that machine."

"Yes, sir." The corporal stepped off to a small fire pit that the artillery crew had maintained. He grabbed a piece of wood that was only partially burning. Varus turned and was prepared to carry it over to the catapult when he suddenly glanced back.

"Sir, watch out!" Varus called out the warning.

"Jumped up bastard," a voice hissed just behind him. "Treat me like dirt, will you?"

Stiger glanced around, saw motion behind him in the darkness, and dodged aside. A heavy blade punched painfully into his side, deflected by his armor. This was followed by a blow from a shield, which sent Stiger sprawling to the dirt. So violent was the blow that Stiger lost his own shield and sword. Rolling away, he barely avoided a sword strike from his attacker, which punched into the ground in front of his face. It had been meant for his neck.

Stiger recognized the weapon as a legionary short sword, a gladius.

"I will settle up with you, boy."

Stiger knew the voice. His attacker was none other than Sergeant Geta.

Drawing his dagger and recognizing he had only seconds to act, and recalling Tiro's advice, in desperation Stiger grabbed a handful of dirt and threw it at where he thought his attacker's head might be. He was rewarded with a cry of surprise. Stiger struggled to his feet and lunged at the man, who was trying to wipe the dirt out of his eyes. Stiger was on him in a moment, knocking his shield aside and stabbing with his dagger as his opponent punched his sword out toward Stiger's upper body. The sword tip scraped upward along Stiger's chest armor and dug under his cheek guard, into his cheek.

He cried out in pain, his cheek a hot agony, as he punched his own blade into the side of his attacker's neck. Geta stiffened, stepped backward, and gurgled a death rattle as he choked on his own blood. Stiger blinked in complete shock. He stood there, stunned, and staggered back a step.

The sergeant collapsed like a doll, legs kicking wildly as he died, jets of blood pumping from the wound to his neck.

Stiger felt blood running down his face and into his open mouth. He reached up and felt the wound. It did not seem as bad as it could have been. Had it reached his eye, he would have been blinded. Breathing heavily, he glanced around and saw Varus and Tiro looking on in shocked silence. There was no one else near enough to have witnessed what had just happened. Stiger's eyes traveled back down to Sergeant Geta, who no longer moved.

The sergeant had tried to murder him.

Stiger was exhausted, but the thought of one of his own men attempting such a heinous act outraged him terribly. Stiger felt his anger burn hot at Geta, and he kicked at the dead man's leg.

"Sir," Tiro said, stepping closer. Stiger almost flinched back from him. "It's over, sir. He tried to kill you, and you got him."

"You saw?" Stiger's hands had begun to shake, and he dropped his dagger.

"Aye," Tiro said. "We saw. It was why Varus stuck near you. We feared that he might try something like that."

"You knew, and said nothing?" Stiger asked, shaken.

"No evidence, sir," Varus apologized. "We thought he might try something, especially after you told him there would be a reckoning."

"Besides," Tiro said, "Geta manipulated the captain something good, but he couldn't do the same to you. Sergeants like him thrive under weak officers. You, sir, are not weak." Tiro paused to glance down at Geta's body. "With you dead, the company would have gotten, not just one, but two new officers, with a fresh opportunity to manipulate one of them to his advantage."

Stiger looked down at the body. Geta had only struck when there were few about.

"Had he been successful," Stiger said, thinking it out, "you would have said nothing, as the punishment for killing an officer is decimation. I would have been said to have died in battle with the enemy."

"The killing of every tenth man is a powerful incentive to keep mouths shut," Tiro admitted slowly and then shrugged. "Until he made his move, we could not do anything. We had hoped to intervene before he could hurt you."

Stiger took a deep, shuddering breath and then nodded in understanding. The sergeant was quite right. Tiro had acted honorably. Then what the sergeant said sank in. Tiro and the men had been looking out for him. Though he had felt it before, now he knew for certain. The men of the Seventh had accepted him.

"In the future, you will tell me when you feel my life is at risk from such filth," Stiger said, gesturing at Geta's body and looking from Varus to Tiro. "Is that understood?"

"It is," Tiro said. "I swear by the gods I will inform you myself."

Stiger looked over to Varus, who silently nodded his agreement.

"Let's get the men formed up," Stiger said wearily, looking around for his discarded sword and shield.

"No need, sir," Tiro said, pointing toward the rampart. Stiger looked over and saw legionaries pouring over the top of it and the defenders running for their lives. There were also fresh legionaries now moving around them, and no more sounds of the enemy artillery firing. Stiger realized that these men were those who had been making their way down the ridge to join the fight. He could see Lepidus thirty yards distant and his men gathered around their captain. Many had sat down or collapsed to the ground in exhaustion. The captain glanced in Stiger's direction and waved, a grim smile of satisfaction upon his face.

Stiger was too tired to wave back. He felt completely drained. He looked over at the catapult he was standing next to and sat down on one of the supporting crossbeams. He was grateful for the growing darkness, for his hands were shaking almost uncontrollably. He was so physically blown that his eyes started tearing and he blinked, trying to clear them. With some effort, he undid the ties and clasp on his helmet and removed it, dropping the heavy piece of kit to the ground. He ran a hand through his matted and sweaty hair. Stiger looked back up at Tiro, who had stepped closer.

"Have the men gather around." Stiger's voice shook from the strain. He cleared his throat. "In the darkness we don't want them mistaken for the enemy. And get that fire stoked up. I want some light."

"Yes, sir," Tiro said, offering Stiger a crisp salute. He turned and called out into the darkness. "Seventh! Seventh! Over here, boys. Fall out over here! Seventh over here."

The men drew near, set their shields down, and collapsed to the ground, exhausted. A number were so far gone they fell immediately asleep. Tiro and Varus built up the fire that the enemy artillery unit had set.

"Sometimes you just gotta love the enemy," Tiro said as he started a second fire a few feet away from the first, using firewood the enemy had neatly stacked for them. Exhausted men gathered around it in the darkness.

Stiger pulled out his canteen, unfastened the clasp, and drained it. He then leaned his head back against a beam that rose vertically from the crossbeam and closed his eyes. His legs and feet ached abominably. In fact, he decided his entire body was one big ache.

"Sir." Stiger opened his eyes to find Tiro with a torch in his hand. Stiger had not been asleep, but had been trying to calm his nerves and rest his tortured body. "Let me look at that. I want to see your wound, sir."

Stiger nodded, and the sergeant leaned forward and examined his cheek. He looked it over closely for a moment, and then probed the wound with his fingers. Stiger winced at the painful touch.

"It's a clean slice, sir. Something pretty to show off to the ladies. The surgeon will need to sew it up some, but that won't hurt half as bad as the vinegar he will use to clean it out first."

"You are just full of good news." Stiger chuckled and glanced around. Most of his men were asleep. A few sat by one of their two fires, staring exhaustedly and despondently into the depths of the flames. "Thank you, sergeant."

"No thanks needed, sir," Tiro said. "Some officers are worth the extra attention."

Stiger leaned his head back against the beam again and closed his eyes. He breathed deeply and fell asleep.

"Lieutenant."

Stiger blinked his eyes open. It was still dark out, though much cooler, so some time had passed. He blinked again and glanced around. His men were all asleep around him and the fires had burned low. Then he looked up and found Colonel Aetius standing before him, with Sergeant Tiro at his side. Stiger made to stand but, much to his relief, was waved back down by the colonel.

"How are you, son?" Aetius asked, glancing down at Stiger's bloodied cheek, chin, and chest armor. Stiger was sure he looked a sight.

"I will recover," Stiger said. "Sergeant Tiro suggested I see the surgeon."

"A wise recommendation," Aetius agreed solemnly.

"How is the battle going?" Stiger asked. "Have we assaulted the second line yet?"

The colonel kicked at the dirt before replying.

"The enemy pulled out before we could even attempt to turn it," Aetius said with a heavy sigh. "It seems much of their army withdrew this morning, leaving only a delaying force behind. I'm afraid the enemy has escaped yet again. But we did secure the river crossing so that the army as a whole can now move beyond it, which was our objective to begin with."

"I guess that will mean the pursuit will continue," Stiger said wearily.

"Not by us." Aetius sat down on the catapult next to Stiger. "Eighth Legion is moving up, and they are bringing along some bridging equipment. The Second and Fourteenth Legions will be along shortly, too. That means we will get a little rest before following."

Some rest sounded good, very good, to Stiger about now.

"I served under your father, you know, as a lieutenant like yourself."

"I did not know that, sir," Stiger said, suddenly on his guard.

"Your father made me the officer I am today," Aetius said, a distant quality to his voice, as if he were recalling fonder times. "I think you are very much like him."

Stiger said nothing. Speaking of his father could prove dangerous ground, though he realized that was not the colonel's intention.

"Well, I understand they found Cethegus's body," Aetius said, when Stiger said nothing. "It looks like you are in command of the Seventh, at least until a replacement can be found."

"There is not much left of the company," Stiger said, gesturing helplessly around at the sleeping men. There were precious few of them, perhaps as many as sixty, not counting those who had started the day on the sick list and not marched with the company. "The captain saw to that."

"Well... according to Lepidus, you managed to preserve them, so they are yours." The colonel sucked in a breath. "At least until a more experienced replacement becomes available, and I don't expect that to happen anytime soon. There is a shortage of good officers going around."

"Yes, sir," Stiger said, feeling both pleased and embarrassed by the praise.

The colonel stood, pausing to look down on Stiger. "In the morning, move back to the encampment and make sure you see the surgeon or Father Griggs. The paladin's priestly magic can heal. I don't want you dying from a festering wound."

"I will, sir," Stiger assured the colonel.

Aetius started to stride away, and then stopped. He turned back and studied Stiger for a moment. "Excellent work today, lieutenant. Your crossing saved a lot of lives."

"Thank you, sir."

Aetius turned and picked his way through the sleeping men, careful to not disturb anyone. He was quickly swallowed up by the darkness. A distant cheer sounded off in the direction of the second rampart.

"This was one tough day," Stiger said to himself.

"There will be others," Tiro said. Stiger looked over at the sergeant, who had sat down nearby on the ground and was leaning his back against the catapult. "With the legions, you can count on that, sir. Some will even be tougher."

"Truly?" Stiger asked in surprise. He had difficulty imagining a more difficult day.

"Yes," Tiro said. "This is only the beginning of this war."

"I will pray for easier days then," Stiger said.

"Yes, sir," Tiro said. "Make sure you include me in your prayers, for this was a bitch of a day."

"I will." Stiger leaned his head back and closed his eyes. His first thought was that he would live to see Livia again, and that brought on a smile. Then a wave of exhaustion rolled over him and he decided that whatever was in his future could wait, at least for a time. Now he simply desired some sleep.

EPILOGUE

Having climbed over the recently taken rampart, he took a moment to survey the battlefield beyond. His night vision was much better than a human's, and he could see quite some distance. A great feeling of sadness welled up in him at the sight of so many dead. Life was a precious gift from the creators, the gods. It should not be treated so casually, just thrown away. Though even the gods demanded such sacrifices, his nature rebelled against it. A solitary tear stung his cheek as he blew out a slow, sad breath.

"Sir?"

He glanced around at his escort, a legionary sergeant assigned to him directly by General Treim. The sergeant was to keep him from harm in the chaos of the aftermath of the battle. He recognized the wisdom of this. In the darkness, large numbers of legionaries were roaming about, looting the dead. Since he was not a legionary, he might be mistaken for the enemy. Despite that, he had little fear of anything befalling him. In the darkness, should he wish it, no one would see him.

"Sir," the sergeant called again. "Where are you?"

"Right here," he said, remembering that human night vision was poor.

"Ah," the sergeant said, pulling himself up and over the shattered wooden barricade that topped the rampart. "There you are, sir."

"Remain here," he said.

"I am sorry, sir," the sergeant protested. "My orders are to—"

"Serve my needs," he interrupted firmly. "I will not need you for a bit. You will remain here. I will be fine, I assure you."

The sergeant weighed the matter for a moment and then gave a nod of acceptance, clearly nervous.

"Thank you." He turned and left the sergeant, who remained behind as his charge walked down the reverse side of the earthen rampart.

There were a number of bodies about, mostly Rivan, though there were a few that were cloaked in scarlet amongst the dead. He sighed and wished once again he had not been assigned this mission. It had become a terrible burden and would surely prove to be more before everything was said and done.

Death was everywhere, it seemed. Around him, the dead littered the ground haphazardly. Off to his right, the dead had fallen in straight lines, clear evidence of an organized fight. He sighed sadly.

Despite the death that surrounded him, there was also life. Most of the looters had moved on from this area and gone up toward the second defensive line. The legionary companies that had seen the brunt of the fighting remained, and amongst them was the one he was looking for.

These exhausted souls were huddled around fires, most sleeping on their arms. He walked by one such company, studying those legionaries carefully. In the darkness he was nearly invisible and moved in such a way so that there was no sound at his passage. No one looked up or stirred. He moved on and shortly came to a smaller group sleeping around two fires and a captured catapult on which an officer was asleep, sitting on a support beam and leaning his head back against the wooden contraption for support.

He tilted his head slightly and examined the man. The lieutenant was young for a human. The officer's face was bloody from a vicious-looking cheek wound. He recalled the wound as the mark of the one he was looking for and smiled with satisfaction. He had surely found the one he had been hunting, Ben Stiger.

A few feet away, a sergeant sat against the same catapult. The sergeant's eyes suddenly fluttered and then opened with a start. He glanced around, saw no one, and closed his eyes again.

"Sleep, Tiro," Eli said gently to himself, recognizing the old veteran from days past, though the human had aged terribly since their last meeting. Such was the way with their race. "I will watch over your boys, at least until you wake. It will be just like old times, my friend, though you will never know that I was here."

The End

Author's Note:
Please Read!

Every story needs a beginning, and this one was Stiger's. Keep in mind this was only Part One of the Tales of the Seventh (TOS) series. It began life as a short novella and was first intended as a quick interlude between books three and four of the Chronicles of an Imperial Legionary Officer (CILO) series. Unfortunately, or fortunately, depending upon your point of view, it turns out... I can't write a novella! I know... no one was more surprised than me... well, perhaps my agents were. Telling this tale was just too much fun that I simply could not stop. So instead of a short novella, I've delivered a novel nearly the same size of my first book, *Stiger's Tigers*.

There are a number of important nuggets dropped into this book that directly reflect upon the CILO series, and also another series that I am working on... about which, at this point, I must unfortunately stay mum. You see, I planned these stories and tales out long before I settled down to tell them, and so I have plenty of material to draw from.

Please keep in mind, Eli and Stiger had a good number of adventures that occurred prior to the CILO series, and much of what occurred at this point is unknown. Many of these will be detailed in the TOS series. These tales will open up much of the backstory. They will also give you more of both characters' past, present, and—dare I say—future, along with a whole host of new characters, fantasy elements, political drama, intrigue, magical worlds, and, of course, both adventure and fighting. Stay tuned.

Additional Note from the Author

I hope you enjoyed *Stiger, Tales of the Seventh* and continue to read my books. Stiger and Eli's adventures will continue. On that, I promise!

A <u>positive review</u> would be awesome and greatly appreciated, as it affords me the opportunity to focus more time and energy on my writing and helps to persuade others to read my work. I read each and every review.

I would love to hear from you. There is a forum on my website. Feel free to register and share your thoughts!

Don't forget to sign up to my newsletter on the website to get the latest news.

Thank you ...
Marc Alan Edelheit

Coming Soon

Stiger and Eli's Adventures Continue in:

Chronicles of an Imperial Legionary Officer
Book 4
The Tiger's Time

Also Coming Soon
Tales of the Seventh
Part Three
Eli

Care to be notified when the next book is released
and receive updates from the author?
Join the newsletter mailing list at Marc's website:

http://www. MAEnovels. com
(Check out the forum)
Facebook: Marc Edelheit Author
Twitter: @MarcEdelheit

Also:
Listen to the author's free history podcast at

http://www.2centhistory. com/

Made in the USA
San Bernardino, CA
16 October 2018